Georgia,
you are a
lots of fun
Marlene
11/13/10

Silent Rain

Marlene P. Jones

All rights reserved. No part of this book shall be reproduced or transmitted in any form or by any means, electronic, mechanical, magnetic, photographic including photocopying, recording or by any information storage and retrieval system, without prior written permission of the publisher. No patent liability is assumed with respect to the use of the information contained herein. Although every precaution has been taken in the preparation of this book, the publisher and author assume no responsibility for errors or omissions. Neither is any liability assumed for damages resulting from the use of the information contained herein.

Copyright © 2010 by Marlene P. Jones

ISBN 0-7414-5892-6

Printed in the United States of America

This is a work of fiction. Names, characters, places, and incidents either are the product of the author's imagination or are used fictitiously. Any resemblance to actual events or locales or persons, living or dead, is entirely coincidental.

Published September 2010

INFINITY PUBLISHING
1094 New DeHaven Street, Suite 100
West Conshohocken, PA 19428-2713
Toll-free (877) BUY BOOK
Local Phone (610) 941-9999
Fax (610) 941-9959
Info@buybooksontheweb.com
www.buybooksontheweb.com

*Jerome, Jada, J'Niah – my inspiration
my mother and sister
thank you for the encouragement*

Prologue

Nyah believed a diluted version of love existed to devour women's souls and provide men with faceless, nameless orgasms. She heard firsthand how destructive and consuming love could be, after spending countless hours with girlfriends who had been seduced by lyrical men citing promises of 'happily ever after' only to realize too late that their prince charming was anything but.

She lay motionless on the bed, staring at the ceiling, acutely aware of the mystery man's arm across her stomach, feeling his warm breath on the side of her face, waiting for him to fall asleep and release her from his hold. She closed her eyes and smiled, replaying the last two delightful hours spent with the handsome stranger. Every inch of her body had responded without reservations to his feathery kisses, probing caresses and she could still feel the tantalizing effects all over.

The warm fuzzy feeling dissipated quickly and reality crept in. What was she thinking? Lying next to a man, she had known for only four hours, daydreaming about sex. She needed to get out of his bed and out of his cabin. Holding her breath, she gently lifted his hand and slowly inched her body away from him. He moaned and she froze. She did not want to wake him and have to endure painful after sex small talk. To her delight, he rolled onto his back and turned his face away from her. She slid from the bed and tiptoed around the room gathering her personal belongings then she got dressed and left his cabin without looking back.

The warm night breeze stroked her skin like a million tiny fingers through the long form-fitting beige summer dress she wore as she hurried along the corridor towards her cabin, but the tranquil sounds of soft Jazz lured her to the lounge. She entered the dimly lit room and sat at a round table in front of the stage where the four-piece band played *'Round Midnight'*. The pianist, a silver haired man, acknowledged his audience of one with a slight nod and she smiled. They played two more songs before deciding to call it a night and she had to abandon her moment of bliss.

Feeling rejuvenated and wide-awake, Nyah walked towards the bow of the ship. She leaned against the rail and stared at the string of lights along the horizon. She knew being alone on the deck was not a safe place to be at three in the morning, but she was not going to allow fear to cripple her and prevent her from enjoying the last night of her vacation by forcing her to retreat to her cabin before she was ready.

When her friend Sheila suggested they take a cruise together, Nyah was skeptical at first; being fearful of water. But when she found out that Leah Blaque would be one of the musicians performing, she agreed, and offered to pay for both of them. Sheila canceled at the last minute; citing something about a broken heart, so Nyah decided to travel by herself. She needed the rest and welcomed the opportunity to enjoy some good music.

She closed her eyes and inhaled deeply; relishing the fragrance of the ocean, the peaceful hum of the deep; listening to the whirring sound of the ship as it parted the water and forged ahead towards the next port.

"You didn't say goodbye."

Startled, she turned her head and stared up at the stranger she left sleeping in his cabin. He stood a couple of feet away from her, his back leaning against the rail. The moonlight hugged his shaved head and his olive colored face looked even more handsome than it did earlier in the evening when he approached her table as she ate supper in the dining hall. His light brown eyes sparkled with mischief. Seeing him again sent all her senses into overdrive and certain parts of her body began to tingle. For a brief moment, she knew she would not oppose any suggestion he made, especially if it involved a reprise of their past recent activity.

"You fell asleep so quickly, even if I said goodbye, you wouldn't have heard me." Nyah looked at him through her lashes and smiled.

"I'm ready again, if you are," he moved closer to her but he did not touch her.

"You must be a glutton for punishment, don't you need some time to catch your breath?" she said, and he chuckled.

"My power nap did the trick," he said, turning to face her.

"What's my name?" Nyah met his gaze squarely.

"Is that a test question?"

She smiled, and shook her head.

"I didn't expect you to remember." She turned and started walking away from him. "Goodnight."

"Can I call you sometime?"

"What for?" She snickered softly and continued walking.

He had to spoil great banter with such a ridiculous request. Sure, he was good, no, amazing in bed, but she knew that when she left the cruise ship later that day, he, along with all her other experiences aboard the ship would be left behind.

In three steps, he was close enough to touch her arm. She turned around, and looked up at him. She could not tell if he genuinely wanted her number or if he simply wanted another romp and frankly, either way, she did not care.

"I had a great time tonight, but tomorrow we'll go back to our own separate lives and everything will continue being right with the world."

"I guess that depends on your view of the world. So, is that a no?"

Nyah pressed her hand against his hard chest, reached up on her toes and kissed him lightly on the cheek.

"Thanks for a memorable time, goodnight."

As she walked along the corridor towards her cabin, she was relieved, yet slightly disappointed that he did not follow her.

"Sweet dreams, Tracie," he remembered her name after all; well at least the name she gave him. She glanced over her shoulder for one final look at the handsome stranger, but he was already gone.

One

The doorbell rang.

Nyah heard it but hoped whoever it was, would go away.

No such luck.

The bell rang again and its high-pitched resonance grated her nerves. She sighed heavily and sat up, grudgingly swung her legs over the edge of the bed and groped for her slippers. Hovering between sleep and wake, her body was exhausted, having just completed the move into her new house. Last July, when she returned to Wisconsin from her vacation, she received a call to interview for a full time teaching position in Riverdale, a small town six hours drive away from the Big House and her Grandmother. The decision to leave her hometown was not an easy one, but something she felt she had to do to preserve her sanity; and it was closer to her best friend Sheila who lived forty minutes away in Michigan.

Weaving her way through the myriad of boxes, misplaced furniture, and pictures, she walked through the foyer to the front door.

"Who is it?" she asked, securing her unruly hair on top of her head with a scrunchie.

"My name is Brian; I'm with the phone company ma'am." She wrapped her robe around her body, tightened the band at her waist and opened the front door. A stout black man stood on her porch, an oversized grin on his face, with a tool belt hanging from his shoulder. "Morning," he said and handed her a sheet of paper. "I'm here to install the four jacks you ordered."

Nyah took the paper and glanced at it quickly, then handed it back to him. He was four days late and impatient as hell, she thought.

She motioned for him to come inside, "leave your shoes at the door." She led him through the house and was very specific about where she wanted the jacks placed.

"How long will it take you to finish the work?"

"Shouldn't be more than an hour," he said and set out to complete his task.

Two and a half hours later, she left the house at the same time as the telephone man; annoyed that she was running late for her appointment with the principal at the new school. She checked the map before leaving her driveway but still had to stop and ask for directions twice before she walked through the salmon colored doors and into the school office.

"Hello, may I help you?" The secretary was a serious looking older woman with cropped silver hair and wire glasses perched on the tip of her nose.

"My name is Nyah Parsons; I have an appointment with Mrs. Brown at 11:00." The secretary looked at her watch, "I'm sorry I'm late." She hated being late for anything and even though to some people ten minutes was not really late, she was not pleased with her tardiness.

The woman picked up the receiver and began to dial, "have a seat, I'll let her know you're here."
Five minutes later, Natalie Brown a petit white woman emerged from a back office.

"Nyah, it's good to see you again and thanks for coming on such short notice." She shook Nyah's hand firmly. "Let's take a walk." Nyah listened as Natalie talked about the history of the middle school and commented on the student achievement awards displayed on the walls, and the team trophies locked inside glass cases.

Natalie knocked on a classroom door.

"Is it okay to come in?"

They walked into the room, without waiting for an answer.

"Gabby, this is Nyah Parsons, your new teaching partner."

The young woman extended her hand to Nyah.

"Good to meet you, welcome aboard."

"Thank you."

"I've heard some wonderful things about you." Gabby said with a sideways glance at Natalie who smiled and nodded her head.

"I mentioned the work you've done with women victims of violent crimes in our staff meeting," said Natalie. "A few months ago, I had the pleasure of reading your article, *Remove the Chains* in the *Women for Change* magazine, it was thought provoking, to say the least." Nyah remembered that article well, and the backlash she received because of her portrayal of men and their insatiable need to dominate.

Nyah met a few more teachers before following Natalie back to her office to sign the six-month contract and receive the keys to her classroom.

"We'll have this signed by the Superintendent and a copy ready for you to pick up within a week. If your probationary six-month period is successful, we will have a two-year contract ready for you at that time. Do you have any questions?"

"Not right now," she said, "but I will call if anything comes to mind." She knew that she had her work cut out for her, beginning a new teaching job so close to the end of the school year.

"We are excited to have you here, the principal at Ridgewood Elementary had nothing but great things to say about you," Natalie stood up and extended her hand, "Welcome to Canbury Middle School Nyah, we'll see you next Monday."

****

Nyah left the office feeling pleased with her new job offer. To celebrate, she decided to treat herself to lunch at a Greek restaurant in the mall before going shopping to pick up sundry items for her new house. The echoing sounds of children's laughter, screams and non-stop chatter filled the schoolyard as she walked to her car at the back of the parking lot. The chill from the March breeze was not enough to penetrate her jacket and she was grateful for that.

She put on a CD, fast-forwarded to one of her favorite songs, Bessie Smith's *Backwater Blues*, and hummed along as she drove down Jefferson Road.

"Crap," she muttered when she realized at the last minute that she missed the right turn on Kenwood Avenue, she quickly moved into the right lane to try to exit at the next street. A horn blew followed by the piercing sound of metal colliding. Nyah gripped the steering wheel tightly as the force of the impact pushed her car sideways across the left lane, bringing her car to a stop on the opposite side of the road facing a speeding pickup truck. She held her breath and braced for a hit but miraculously, the truck screeched to a halt a couple of feet away from her car. Nyah sat immobilized, her heart racing, grateful that she was still alive.

The events happened quickly, but in the back of her mind, she knew it began with her. She did not check her blind spot and failed to see the black Durango driving beside her.

"Are you hurt?" A man stood next to her car window wearing sunglasses and a knit hat pulled over his ears.

"I don't know," she said hesitantly, "I think so."

Her hands trembled as she tried to open the car door. He reached down and opened it for her then stepped back, giving her room to get out. Her legs were shaky and she stumbled. In one quick movement, he grabbed her elbow to prevent her from falling.

"Thanks." She managed to steady herself and pulled her arm away from him. "Were you driving the truck that hit me?"

"You changed lanes without signaling, by the time I saw what you were doing, it was too late."

She walked around to the passenger's side to look at the damage caused in that one moment of poor judgment on her part. The impact crushed the front right side of her car; the bumper had fallen off and was lying in the middle of the road.

The stench of oil mixed with gasoline leaking from the front of her car was so strong; she could almost taste it in the back of her throat.

"I didn't see you," she said, "you appeared out of nowhere."

"Hardly, look at the size of my truck; you'd have to be blind not to see me."

"You must know it's not very bright to drive in someone's blind spot." She looked at him for the first time and in the dark recesses of her mind believed there was something vaguely familiar about him, but dismissed it as déjà vu.

"Maybe what you need is a driving lesson or two on road etiquette and how to signal before changing lanes." His tone was condescending. Arrogant son of a bitch, she thought. On any other day, she wouldn't hesitate to put him in his place but her will, was momentarily weakened and all she wanted to do was get away from him and retreat to the security of her home. The sound of sirens pulled her attention away from him. A police car followed by an ambulance, blazed towards the scene and stopped a few feet away from her mangled car. Traffic had started to back up and small groups of bystanders gathered on the sidewalk on both sides of the road, whispering among themselves, pointing at her car.

"Is there someone you want me to call for you?" He asked.

"No, I'm fine," Nyah hoped she did not sound as hopeless as she felt. She was completely alone in a strange new town, but he did not have to know that.

The police asked her to move her car to the shoulder and questioned her and the driver of the truck separately, along with bystanders who claimed to have witnessed the accident. They remained at the corner of Jefferson and Rosewood, were the accident occurred for an hour after the police and ambulance arrived. The paramedic checked her over and left after she insisted that there was no need for them to take her to the hospital because she was coherent and unharmed. Finally, she got a ticket for 'careless driving' with a warning.

Regaining her composure, Nyah rummaged through her handbag and took out an old business card that she used for her small tutoring service in Wisconsin, crossed out the old phone number and wrote her new cell number. She walked over to the truck just as the driver was about to leave the scene. He stopped and looked at her, but did not get out of his truck.

"I'm sorry for the inconvenience, here's my card," she handed him the card and cleared her throat. "Please let me know the cost of repairing any damage to your vehicle." There was a small dent on his front bumper, hardly noticeable but she felt she had to go through the motions of taking responsibility for putting the dent there.

"Nyah Tracie Parsons," it surprised her that he pronounced her name correctly. She usually had to correct most people. He took out his cell phone, began dialing and her cell phone began to ring. "Just checking," he said and for a split second, she noticed how attractive he was. She still had the gnawing feeling in the pit of her stomach that she had met him before, but could not remember where. He laid the card on the passenger seat.

"Don't worry about it, I have insurance. You might want to be more careful on the roads Nyah Tracie Parsons," he said before turning up the volume on his already loud rap music and driving away. His arrogance irked her and she was sorry that his truck only got a dent.

Nyah endured the ten-minute drive to the Honda dealership sitting in the passenger seat of the tow truck trying not to gag on the driver's body odor. There were pieces of dirty paper and half eaten food scraps everywhere. The clerk at the front desk assured her that an adjuster from her insurance company would come out the next morning to assess the cost of repairing the damage to her car. The dealership also provided her with a rental car.

* * * * * * **

Nyah breathed a sigh of relief when she walked through the front door of her house. She stood under the hot water for a long time and watched the suds carry away the sweat and dirt that had attached itself to her body while she stood at the accident scene. Putting on her favorite cashmere robe, she went to the kitchen to make a cup of tea. Realizing she had not eaten all day, she decided to cook spaghetti with sauce. Holding the piping hot tea in both hands, she took several small sips and breathed deeply before walking into the living room. She turned on the CD player and music streamed through the speakers, filling the room with smooth Jazz. She looked around at all the sealed boxes and began to feel overwhelmed by the move, the job and now the accident. Sinking her body into the sofa with her feet curled under her, she closed her eyes and focused on the music. The serene moment did not last very long. Her cell phone buzzed.

"Are you alright?" She recognized the voice instantly.

"I'm fine," she was surprised that he called.

"Good."

The doorbell rang.

"Why are you calling?"

The doorbell rang again. Nyah did not wait for him to answer; she hung up and walked to the front door.

"Sheila!"

"Hey woman, what took you so long to answer the door?" Happy to see a familiar face, Nyah threw her arms around her friend. "Where on God's green earth did you move to? Shit, I must have gotten lost about ten times trying to find this place."

"I'm glad you're here." Nyah said pulling her friend inside the door.

"Well, what do you think?" Sheila asked, sporting a huge grin on her face.

"About what?" Nyah was oblivious to the fact that Sheila was modeling for her.

"Do you notice anything different about me?"

Nyah looked at her friend, "no, not really," she answered truthfully. Sheila always looked the same to her. Weave down her back, long polished nails, flawless makeup covering her russet colored face.

"Bitch, I lost 5 pounds."

"A whole five pounds. I see it now." Nyah rolled her eyes and left her friend standing in the foyer.

Sheila threw her overnight bag on the floor and looked around the foyer, nodding her head in approval. "This is nice Trace. What's cooking, somethin' smells good," she followed Nyah into the kitchen, opened the pot and inhaled the aroma of the spaghetti sauce. "I hope there's meat in this sauce, vegetarianism is your thing, not mine."

"There's no meat in there you carnivore," Nyah joked.

"And guess what, I will be until the day I die." Sheila said with impact. "I'm not going to eat beans and tofu when I can have steak and fried chicken. Where's the phone, I'll just get me some real food." She ordered pizza with everything on it.

"Hey, did you get a new car?"

"I wish. Some guy hit my car today, that's just a rental."

"Are you okay?" Sheila was concerned.

"I'm fine, just a little shaken."

"Too bad you're not hurt; you could sue the bastard and get some money to pay off this house." Sheila opened the fridge, took out a can of pop and sat with Nyah at the table. "What we need is a vacation. Let's book another cruise. This time, we'll go someplace exotic, like the Mediterranean."

"Another vacation? You stood me up the last time."

"With good reason. I..." Sheila began.

"Oh my God," Nyah jumped to her feet.

"What?"

"That's where we met. I knew there was something familiar about him."

"Who?"

"The person who hit my car earlier today. He's the guy from the cruise; remember the one I told you about?"

"What guy? You mean mister, tall, handsome, buff, one night only."

"One and the same."

The doorbell rang.

"I can't be sure, I mean I saw him once, seven months ago, that and he had on a hat and sunglasses. I'm almost positive it was him."

"What are the odds?" Sheila asked, holding out her hand. "Is this your treat?" Nyah gave her twenty dollars. She went to the door and returned with a small flat box in her hand.

"Think he recognized you?" Sheila asked stuffing pizza in her mouth.

"I don't think so, if he did, he didn't let on."

They spent the rest of the evening, talking about the accident, Nyah's new job and Sheila's desire to meet a man who was not broke or ugly. At around midnight, the sound of horns blowing got Sheila's attention.

"I'm gonna hang out with some friends for a bit," she said grabbing her purse and heading for the front door.

"Have your key?" By the time Nyah reached the living room, Sheila was halfway out the door.

"Yep, I'll see you later, maybe."

That night, after she settled in bed, Nyah revisited the night she spent with the handsome stranger while on the cruise seven months earlier. His touch, his smell, the way he made her feel was deliberately buried in her casket of forgettable life experiences, until now.

Two

Most of the next two weeks were spent unpacking boxes filled with stuff Nyah should have thrown away a long time ago, but she had a sentimental side and liked to hold on to things. While organizing her bedroom, she opened a box marked 'personal crap' and found old diaries, books and a photo album of her life in college. Sitting on the bed, she began flipping through the pictures, smiling, remembering faces and places.

Nyah's smile quickly faded and feelings of anger stirred in the pit of her stomach. The picture her brother took of her at their sister's wedding seven years earlier, standing beside the groom, his arm around her shoulders, had no place among her belongings or in her memories. She ripped the whole page from the album and tore the picture into small pieces, went into the bathroom and watched as the water spun them out of sight. She resealed the box but not before removing the wooden butterfly necklace that her grandmother gave her the day before she left for college and hung it over the framed picture of her grandmother on the nightstand beside her bed.

Nyah started her teaching job at the school a week after her accident and was grateful to have Sheila around for company. Within a month, the house was beginning to feel more like home.

Sheila returned from one of her overnight trips late on Saturday afternoon and announced that they were going to a breakout party that night. She protested because she was tired but Sheila insisted. Nyah had gone to enough breakout parties with Sheila to know they were just glorified house parties hosted at overpriced hotels, attended by wannabe rich black men dipped in cheap cologne, weighed down by heavy gold plated chains, hitting on anything with two legs.

Nyah stood in front of the full-length mirror, wearing the Christmas gift Sheila gave her two years ago, with a displeased look on her face when Sheila walked into her bedroom.

"You look hot!"

"I look like a prostitute." The short black dress had holes across the chest; exposing too much cleavage, slits down the side and silver tassels lining the bottom. "Can't we do something else? I really don't feel like going to a meat fest tonight." Nyah knew that it was pointless trying to talk her friend out of doing something once she made up her mind to do it.

"Do something else like what exactly? Trace, you have moved to this little town in the middle of nowhere with old white people, one mall, and absolutely no black men. Where is the fun?"

"Riverdale is a great little town; I enjoy living here. Besides, your life is exciting enough for both of us. We can't all spend our time pursuing mindless men and money." As Sheila walked towards her, Nyah wondered how she managed to fit her size 12 body into a size 8 dress.

"With an attitude like that, you are going to remain one cold bitch at nights." Nyah shivered as Sheila brushed pass her carrying a makeup bag and disappeared in the bathroom.

"I've heard there'll be some fine chocolate men with money at this little shindig. We need to look the part so we can catch some of that good fortune." Sheila enjoyed the company of men, and she was not shy about it. Nyah knew she only used them to get what she wanted and when their usefulness had worn out, she would trade them in for another model, much like an old car.

It had been that way since they met in Junior High when they were twelve. Sheila lived with her mother, a younger brother and two older sisters. "That girl is nothing but trouble," Gran always said. She hated authority, was always fighting with her mother, teachers and sometimes with the law. She was a free spirit but she lacked direction.

As their friendship grew, Sheila would convince Nyah to steal candy from the store and skip school to hang out with older boys. They continued their juvenile delinquency stunts for about 3 months until a mall security officer caught them trying to leave a store with two pairs of jeans and a sweatshirt in her backpack. The day Gran heard about what she was doing, Nyah got a beating that scared her straight. It was the first and last time Gran laid a hand on her. Sheila and Nyah managed to remain friends for fourteen years but after that day, skipping school and stealing were no longer a part of that friendship. Nyah believed that lack of strong paternal role modeling created an opening for her friend to see men as nothing more than a nice ride and an expensive plate of food. However, who was she to judge, she has never met her own father.

* * * * * * * **

Forty-five minutes later, they pulled up to the entrance of the Hampton Hotel in downtown Detroit. The chilly night air pricked Nyah's face and sent a chill through her body as she stepped out of the car. She tightened the red scarf around her neck and fastened the last two buttons at the bottom of her coat, happy with her decision to wear the dark brown slacks and beige turtleneck instead of the tiny black dress with the holes Sheila wanted her to wear.

She always believed her hips were too narrow and her breasts too big to wear form-fitting clothes so she wore clothes that diverted attention from her amplified body parts. The valet took the keys and drove the car away.

"Look at these cars, someone's definitely gonna get lucky tonight." Sheila was excited.

"You know what they say about men who drive big, flashy cars." Nyah nudged her friend, "they are over compensating to make up for what they lack in other areas."

"That's not always true," Sheila defended, "I once dated a guy who had both." The two friends laughed.

"Man, this guy really knows how to throw a party in style," Sheila beamed linking her arm with Nyah as they entered the hotel lobby and seeing the glittering cascade of mirrors and chandeliers. The combined scent of flowers and spice infused the open space and the shiny marble floors echoed the clicking of their heels as they walked towards the booming sound of rap music.

"I love that tune," Sheila said as she bobbed her head to the song and rapped along with the lyrics *'We got to fight the powers that be, lemme hear you say, fight the power'*. A little too militant for my taste, more your shit. The beat is kicking though."

Nyah did not respond. The rich green and pastel colored Victorian furniture placed as accent pieces throughout the large open space mesmerized her.

They entered a dimly lit, ultra modern, multi-level hall. The dance area was elevated and the bar was circular with clear bar stools. The air in the room had a stale mix of body heat, sweat and cologne. The atmosphere pulsated with sounds of muffled conversations, laughter and gyrating bodies. Nyah felt the bass vibrating deep in her chest.

"Find us a table, I'll be right back." Sheila walked in the direction of the bar, leaving Nyah alone at the entrance of the room. She looked around for an empty table and spotted one in a corner close to an exit sign. Clutching her purse, she darted towards it and in her haste; she bumped into a man, spilling his drink all over the front of his shirt.

"I'm sorry," she apologized picking up a napkin from the table beside them and blotted the front of his shirt.

He brushed her hand away," are you blind, watch where you're going."

"I'm sorry," she said again, "please let me buy you another drink."

His tone softened when he looked at her.

"No harm done pretty lady." Nyah conjured up a smile, and after one last apology, she continued walking to her destination and sat down on a steel armchair. She removed her sweater, put it behind her and leaned against it.

The music was infectious and Nyah began to move her head to the rhythm.

"Would you like to dance?" The same man stood by her table, grinning at her, flashing a gold tooth.

"No, I think I'll sit this one out," she said and hoped that was enough to make him leave.

"Come on, it's the least you could do after spilling my drink, just one dance." He stretched out his hand waiting for her to take it. Nyah opened her purse and took out ten dollars.

"No, thank you," she said putting the money in his outstretched hand, "your next drink is on me."

She was relieved when a waiter approached the table. The man pocketed the money and walked away, mumbling under his breath.

"Would you like a drink?"

"Cranberry ginger ale please."

Nyah paid the waiter and the girl left, returning a few moments later with her drink.

She scanned the crowd and saw Sheila sitting on a stool at the bar talking to a tall man in a stylish jean outfit. He leaned in close and said something to her and she pushed him playfully. Nyah smiled at her friend's flirting abilities. True to her word, she knew Sheila would not leave the party empty-handed. The DJ started playing a *Soul* tune and she could no longer resist the urge to dance, so she got up and weaved her way through the crowd to the dance floor. She found a spot at the back and began to move her body to the music.

"You do that so well."

She recognized the voice behind her instantly, it was impossible to mistake the deep rumble. She continued moving to the music and he stepped closer to her and matched her rhythm. When the song was over, Nyah turned around, and stared into the light brown eyes of the man she slept with on the cruise and who she believed might be the arrogant ass who hit her car.

"I see you are fully recovered." The faint cedar scent of his cologne teased her nose and she saw his muscles flex through the light blue shirt he wore as he bent to talk in her ear.

"Are you stalking me?"

He pulled her against his hard body, resting his hands on her hips and continued swaying to the music.

"Would you like me to stalk you? You are just as beautiful with your clothes on." She tried to pull away but he tightened his hold.

"I guess I'm at a disadvantage, I've met you twice…"

"Three times actually," he said smiling at her. "This is our third meeting."

"And I don't even know your name," she continued.

"You've never asked my name, you just wanted my body." Nyah used more force but was unable to free herself.

"Take your hands off me." He released her and she turned to leave, he was infuriating and she did not want to have anything to do with him.

"Mark Allen," he said just before she walked away. Good for you, she thought.

Her heart was racing and she could not understand why she kept bumping into Mark, maybe he really was stalking her. It had cost her close to three thousand dollars to fix her car, luckily for her, she only paid the five hundred dollar deductible and when she did not hear from him again, she tossed him, like rotting garbage, from her mind. She never thought that she would see him again.

"Hey Nyah," she stared at Gabby's reflection in the mirror as she appeared from one of the stalls, "what are you doing here?"

"I'm here with a friend."

"Wow, it's great to see you outside school; I love your outfit." Gabby washed her hands. "Maybe you can join us for a drink later."

"Thanks, but perhaps another time." She said.

After Gabby left, Nyah stared at her reflection in the mirror and smiled reassuringly. When she returned to the hall, she looked around for her nemesis and spotted him sitting on a lounge chair with his arm around a half-naked young woman who had her hands all over his chest. He whispered something in her ear, and she stood up, took his hand, and led him to the dance floor. What a

Jerk! Nyah was disgusted. Typical male behavior, she thought, hitting on her with a girlfriend in tow, maybe even a wife.

Nyah walked back to the table and sat down. She watched him dance and was captivated by the way he moved his muscular body. Her mind recalled with disturbing detail, the night they spent together on the cruise ship and the memory stirred a longing within her. Annoyed with herself for being smitten with such a self-absorbed, egomaniac, Nyah shook her head to release all thoughts of him from her conscious mind and left the room to get some fresh air. It was obvious he was a ladies' man and she was certain he knew the effect he had on desperate, weak-willed women.

She searched her purse for a mirror and discreetly checked her hair and face. Her makeup was still intact but the humidity in the room made her hair curlier.

"Did you enjoy the show?"

"You really need to stop following me around. What show?" He smiled, and she knew that he must have seen her watching him dance. She handed the clerk her ticket, took her coat and started to put it on when Mark took the coat from her, held it up and she slipped her arms inside.

She turned to face him.

"I don't like being stalked Mr. Allen."

"Com'on, do I look like a stalker to you?" His intense gaze emitted an energy she found difficult to resist. He was intoxicating and the sooner she could get away from him, the better. Turning, to make a quick exit, she bumped into Sheila.

"I've been looking all over for you." Sheila looked at Mark and gave her an approving wink, then she touched the man standing behind her and introduced him as Trent Martin.

"I'm ready to go Sheila," she said through clenched teeth.

"Trent, this is the friend I was telling you about, Tracie and her friend…," she pointed to Mark.

"He's not my friend," she said quietly.

"Mark," he said extending his hand, first shaking Sheila's hand and then the man beside her. Sheila pushed her arm through Nyah's.

"Would you two excuse us for a minute?" Without waiting for a response, she pulled Nyah towards the wishing fountain. "Trace, I think I'm in love."

"With who?" Nyah was puzzled and hoped her friend was not referring to the tall, skinny man she just introduced. He was at least twenty years older than she was and his face was long with highly pronounced cheekbones that made him look like a walking skeleton. His skin looked rough under a sparse graying beard. What Nyah thought was Denim was actually blue faux suede and he wore matching shoes.

"Isn't he fine?" Nyah wondered if they were talking about the same person.

"Sheila, you can't be serious, you just met this man…" Sheila cut her off mid-sentence.

"I know, but he's looking right and it's feeling right." Her voice was excited and she was smiling from ear to ear. Nyah followed her gaze to see Trent walking towards them.

"You mean he's got money," Nyah said under her breath.

"Ready babe this party is getting old," he spoke with a lisp.

Sheila touched her arm, "Trace, do you think you can get a ride home, there's another party that Trent wants to go to, and his car is in the shop so I have to be the designated driver. Don't wait up."

Before Nyah could respond, Sheila gave her a quick hug, Trent saluted her, and they walked away. Although not completely surprised, she was disappointed that

Sheila brought her to the party, against her will and left her to fend for herself all evening.

Nyah walked towards the entrance of the hotel and realized she had forgotten her sweater at the table. The mood in the room had changed from high energy to mellow. The DJ played slow jams and couples slow danced everywhere in the room. She inched her way through the sweating bodies and grabbed her sweater from the back of the chair. She spotted Mark in a corner dancing intimately with the same girl that she had seen him with earlier. She smiled and shook her head; he was just a ladies' man, probably on the prowl for his next victim. She knew for certain, it would not be her. Having had enough, she quickly left the hotel, walked into the crisp night air, hailed a cab and within forty minutes, she was at home.

Three

"Class we only have a few minutes before the bell rings. I want everyone to stop talking in five, four, three, two, and one." The room was silent. "I am still waiting for book reports from groups one, three and seven. I have already extended the deadline people, I need the reports by Friday or you are all looking at a big, fat F. The bell rang and the room buzzed with screeching chairs and banging desks as the classroom quickly went from thirty bodies to one.

"Bye Miss P."

"Take care Brendan, see you tomorrow." Nyah hoped to leave the school at 3:45 to reach the train station to pick up her mother by 5:00. Pearline called last Sunday to announce her visit to Riverdale and she was not looking forward to seeing her mother again.

"Hey Nyah, do you have a minute," her teaching partner entered the classroom.

"Sure," Nyah stopped preparing her lessons, stood up and smiled. Gabby was about four inches taller than Nyah and her shoulder length black hair, which Nyah saw only once in the staff washroom was always wrapped with a colorful scarf. In the two months since she had been teaching at the school, Gabby was one of the few who welcomed her and insisted she attend staff functions, maybe because they were among the three black teachers on staff. Regardless, Gabby was the first one to extend the hand of friendship. The thought of socializing with her outside work was not appealing especially because in one of their conversations, Nyah found out that Gabby and Brenda, an old acquaintance of her's from high school, were good friends. Gabby seemed like a nice person but trying to stay true to her promise of not mixing business with pleasure, Nyah tried to keep her relationship with Gabby strictly professional.

"So, did you enjoy the party the other night?" Gabby asked.

"It was okay, that's not really my scene," she said simply and waited for her to continue.

"What are you doing next Saturday night?"

"I'm not sure yet, why?"

"Well, I'm having a surprise birthday party for a friend and I was hoping if you don't have other plans, maybe you'd like to come. It would be nice to get together outside school." Gabby seemed genuine. Her spirit was gentle and even though Nyah felt a strong connection to her, she did not want to be burned as she was with Brenda. Not wanting to turn her down nor commit, Nyah told her she would let her know by Friday evening.

"Good, that's a start," she said smiling, "I hope you can make it. I'm sure you'll have a good time."

Nyah left fifteen minutes later to pick up her mother. She did not want to see her mother. In fact, they could not stand each other and it was evident whenever they were alone together. The train station was sparse, with just a few people standing around. Some were reading and some listened to music but all were waiting, as she was. The train finally pulled in at 5:10 and the passengers began exiting through the last two doors. Nyah spotted her mother immediately she was hard to miss. She wore designer glasses and pulled her black hair back in a tight bun. They noticed each other and waved. Her tanned complexion was flawless and she looked younger than her 47 years. She was impeccably dressed in a tailored pantsuit with matching shoes and handbag. Her mother was proud of her multicultural heritage even though Nyah believed she embraced one side more than she embraced the other.

Nyah's great grandfather was a black minister and jazz pianist from Louisiana and her great grandmother was quarter Cherokee Indian from Houston, Texas. They moved to Europe from New Orleans in 1927 to join a big band orchestra and to start a church congregation when Gran was 13 years old. Born and raised in Brussels, Belgium, her grandfather was fluent in French and Italian. His family moved to the same neighborhood as Gran where they met in church when Gran was 15. They fell in love almost instantly and two years later amid protest from his family, they got married. His family disowned him so he quit school and worked as a carpenter to support his new wife. They tried for years to start a family but Gran was never able to carry a fetus to term. Finally, in 1942 at the age of 28, she gave birth to a girl, Nyah's mother. The pregnancy was very difficult and during the delivery, her blood pressure dropped significantly and both she and the baby almost died. Pearline was two years old when they moved to Wisconsin in 1944.

"Hello Nyah," Pearline said but did not embrace her daughter. "Your hair has grown and you look like you've put on some weight."

"Hi mother how was your trip?" she asked ignoring her mother's comments.

"Too long, my back is killing me; the five-hour ride from Toronto was torture." Pearline was on her way back to Boston after attending a fashion conference, and visiting Nyah was just an inconvenient stopover. They collected the bags and walked to the car.

"Would you mind if we got something to eat? The food they served on the train was horrid. I'm starving."

The two women had very little to say to each other as Nyah drove to the mall. Pearline commented on some of the picturesque buildings and asked about the town's history. Nyah told her what she knew, which was very little, having been there only 3 months. She had been living in Riverdale since the middle of February and only knew the directions to work, home and the coffee shop on the corner of Liverpool and Nelson.

They arrived at Macy's, a family restaurant inside the mall, ate, made more small talk and at the end of the meal, Pearline offered to pay the bill.

As they walked through the front door, Nyah's cell phone rang. It was Sheila and she chose not to answer it, knowing their conversation would go on forever.

"This is a cute little house, the foyer is nice. Is this table a Brookside? And the floor, it's unique having it inlaid like that." Not waiting for Nyah to respond to any of her comments, Pearline continued gushing about the curving staircase. "Everything looks nice. I am surprised though, this is not characteristic of your taste. Did someone help you with the décor?"

You do not know anything about my taste or me, Nyah thought.

"No, I managed to come up with it all on my own." Nyah knew her tone was sarcastic but her mother was getting on her nerves.

Born in Birmingham County, a small town just outside Sacramento Nyah lived in a small apartment with Pearline, Graydon, Pamela and Charles, a man she later found out was not her biological father. At age 7, without explanation Pearline brought her to visit her grandparents in Wisconsin in one of the biggest houses she had ever seen and never returned for her. Pearline reinserted herself into Nyah's life a year and a half ago and she resented it.

Pearline asked for a tour of the rest of the house and Nyah was not surprised that most of her comments were negative. The tour ended at the bedroom next to hers.

"This is your room." Nyah rested the bags on the bed.

"My room? Oh no, I wouldn't want to impose, I've already made reservations at the Holiday Inn."

"I thought you were staying here, I have the space," she said.

"That's fine, but I've already paid for the suite. No need to bother yourself."

Nyah shrugged. "My mistake. I'm going to make a cup of tea, would you like one?" She was not willing to try to convince her mother to stay with her for the night.

"Not tea, vodka, if you have it," Pearline said, "I'll be down shortly. If you don't mind, I'd like to freshen up."

Nyah waited half hour for her mother to come downstairs. When she finally showed up, she wore a different outfit.

She sat on the chair across from Nyah.

"As you know, this August mom will turn seventy-five and I am planning another surprise party for her." She took a drink and continued. "Trying to get the family together to do anything is like pulling teeth and frankly, I don't need the stress. I have secured a caterer and a band to provide the entertainment, that's where my job ends."

"Why are you telling me all this?" Nyah asked.

"Well, I'm getting to that. Every year for the past four years, I have gone out of my way and spent my money to do something nice for mom around her birthday and every year around the same time, she takes off. What I would like you to do is call her and without giving away the surprise ask her to stay home until after

August. You know that she won't listen to me, but we all know she'll listen to you."

"Mom, what if she just doesn't want a party, why force her to have one?"

Pearline stood up abruptly.

"I'm not here to seek your permission to have a party for my mother, I simply need you to call your grandmother and tell her to stay home until after her birthday. Is that too much to ask? Because if it is, tell me now and I'll ask Graydon to do it."

"Do whatever you want to do mom." Nyah shrugged her shoulders and stood up.

"You know, this was such a mistake, I'm not sure why I bothered to come here and ask for your help. You are so disagreeable." She picked up her handbag and started walking towards the foyer.

"Mom, I'm not saying I won't do it, all I'm saying is, if you want to have a party for Gran, maybe it shouldn't be a surprise." Nyah tried to conceal her frustration.

"That's my choice. Can I count on you to call your grandmother for me?"

"Sure," Nyah said flatly.

"Good, thanks. Now, could you call me a cab, I am tired and I have an early flight in the morning."

Nyah did as Pearline asked. She did not offer to drive her to the hotel or try to change her mind about staying. The cab came, they said goodbye and her mother was gone.

****

The night air was balmy but not enough for Nyah considering it was almost the middle of May. She hated feeling cold so she tightened the thin scarf that she wore around her neck while she waited for someone to answer the door.

"Hey, come in," Nyah smiled and stepped past the stocky dark-skinned man who greeted her, he extended his hand, "I'm David, Gabby's husband."

"Nyah," she said and shook his hand before giving him her spring jacket. He led the way; she followed him into a large open room filled with laughter, chatter and the smell of food. She glanced around, admiring the dark wooden furniture pieces accented with red and burnt orange pillows and throws, the African pictures hanging from the wall and the wooden sculptures displayed on the fireplace mantle. She liked Gabby's home; it was warm, cozy, and colorful. Gabby emerged from another room wearing a beige sari, carrying a vegetable tray.

She smiled when she saw Nyah and after putting the tray in the middle of the table, she greeted her with a hug.

"Nyah, I'm so glad you could make it, come meet everyone." She clapped her hands to get the attention of the people in the room. "This is Nyah, a friend of mine from school, Nyah, this is everyone," Nyah circled the room with her eyes and waved once to acknowledge each person, noting their reaction to seeing a new face among them, "make yourself at home dinner is almost ready, we're just waiting for the birthday girl to show up."

"Hey, come join us." A woman with caramel complexion, long auburn hair and eyes that looked like a cat, light brown with a tinge of green, patted a space on the love seat beside her. "I'm Sage, that's Julie, Trey, Rick," Sage pointed to each person as she said their names. "You know Gabby of course and the football player who opened the door is her husband David." Gabby placed another tray on the table and interjected.

"We're not married yet," she walked to the window, pulled back the drapes, and peeked out into the darkness.

"Give me a break Gab, I think you guys are already married by default," Sage said, and looking at Nyah she added, "They've been dating since high school."

"Married by default, that's a good one," Rick teased, "Sage, baby you're beautiful, and that's why you don't ever have to make any sense whatsoever." Sage threw a pillow at him.

Nyah shifted uncomfortably in her seat when Brenda came into the room holding a wine cooler, sat beside Trey and joined the conversation.

"I'm just saying, I don't know if I could sleep with a man for eight years and have nothing to show for it." She held up her left hand and waved her fingers around.

"Bren, that's none of your business," Sage commented.

"Hey Ny, funny seeing you here," Brenda addressed Nyah.

"You two know each other?" Gabby asked excitedly.

"Yeah, Miss Parsons and I go way back. It is still Parsons isn't it? You didn't get married or nothing like that did you?"

"Hi Brenda," she was caught off guard by Brenda's presence, "nope, not married." Nyah said, knowing exactly where Brenda was going to try to take the conversation.

"Are you still spewing that women's liberation, man bashing shit? Guys, Nyah was our resident 'social advocate' in high school. If ever there was a *cause*, she was in it, on it or *under* it." Brenda laughed half-heartedly, and judging by the quizzical brows around the room, Nyah knew she was the only person in the room who realized that Brenda had just tried to insult her. "I remember you saying you wouldn't change your name for any man, I guess nothing's changed?"

"If you got married, you wouldn't take your husband's last name?" Sage asked Nyah.

"Marriage is not on my list of things 'to do', so probably not, no," she answered simply.

"Ah, "Trey said as though a light went off in his head, "you are one of them independent feminist chicks who hate men."

"I swear Trey; you're the man version of Sage." Rick laughed.

"Hey," Sage protested.

"Yes I am independent, and I hold strong views on feminist issues but I don't hate men; they excel at hating themselves and each other." The room fell silent and everyone stared at her curiously, as if her words were blasphemous but she was used to being scoffed at by insecure women and weak-minded men because of her outspoken views on the institutionalized nature of marriage.

"Well I would take his name because I'd want all the *single* women to know he was my man and I was his property." Brenda's little speech made Nyah cringe.

"Why spoil a good relationship with marriage." Rick said, cutting through the silence, "you know what they say; *if it ain't broke…*"

"Men are useful for at least two things I can think of inside or outside nuptials, don't you think so Ny?" Nyah knew Brenda was trying to elicit a reaction from her but she was not going to respond. It was not the place and certainly not the time.

Gabby ran from the window whispering loudly. "They're here, they're here."

There was a flurry of activity as each person quickly abandoned the conversation and scurried around to find a place to hide. Sage pulled Nyah behind the sofa with her and David turned off the lights. Gabby walked to the door and waited for the bell to ring before she opened it.

"Surprise!" They all jumped from their hiding spot and the excitement quickly turned to grumbling.

"False alarm, it's only Mark and his *shadow*, Dwight," Gabby said jokingly, hugging them both. "You two are fashionably late as usual."

Nyah's heart began to race and her groin began to quiver when she saw him standing at the door dressed casually in a black shirt that exposed well-defined muscles and jeans. If she were naturally suspicious, she would believe that their meetings were orchestrated but she was not, so she settled for it being a small world, the fact that he knew Gabby. The new revelation did nothing to nullify her opinion of him as a womanizer, that was already set in stone but she had to admit, he was a ruggedly *beautiful* man.

"You know how we roll," Dwight said beating his chest. When they stepped inside and Mark saw her, he did a subtle double take but he did not acknowledge her.

"Surprise!" Sage yelled over their shoulders. Standing behind them was a bewildered interracial couple. Gabby's friend was a slim white woman with streaked blonde hair and an attractive face. Gabby hugged her affectionately and said, "Surprise."

With the element of surprise ruined, the house was once again jumping with party buzz.

The dinner was buffet-style. There was a lot of food but Nyah had no appetite, she could not finish the few pieces of cauliflower on her plate. She felt out of place, like an outsider. The twenty-something crowd talked about music videos, movies and the latest fashion trends, subjects that made her painfully aware how out of touch she was with the latest fads. None of the conversations engaged her intellect so she remained silent and listened.

She attempted to stay away from Brenda but not with much success. Brenda was a staple there and everyone liked having her around, she made them laugh. As the evening crept on, she began to understand the dynamics of their relationships. Mark, Dwight and David were best friends, since elementary school. Julie liked Rick but Rick and Dwight liked Sage. Brenda spent most of the evening, trying to get close to Mark who spent most of his time joking around with David and Rick.

Mark hardly spoke to her and when he did, it was brief and superficial. However, she was aware of his every move, and felt her body getting warmer as she watched him interact with his friends. It seemed like all the women in the room wanted to get close to him and the men wanted him to laugh at their jokes. He captivated her with his confidence and the sound of his voice when he laughed, which he did easily and often.

"Mark, let me ask you this," Brenda said at the top of her voice and the people sitting close by stopped talking. "If *we*, hypothetically speaking, got married tomorrow, wouldn't you want me to take your last name?"

"Oh no; not this again." Rick said and turned up the volume on the television. Brenda wrestled the remote from him, hit him with it and turned the volume down. "I agree with Nyah, why should a woman *have* to take my last name if we got married?"

Brenda looked at Rick and snickered. "Yeah, that's great; if I were talking to you, but I'm not. You'd be lucky if you got a woman to marry your black ass."

Mark repeated the question slowly and said, "If you take me, I'd want you to take my name."

"Do you disagree?" He looked at Nyah and her belly did a somersault.

"Not all women need that kind of validation," she said curtly. "But I guess like most men, you need to flaunt your acquired property."

"I wouldn't mind being flaunted. You can flaunt me anytime Mark." Brenda said unreservedly.

"Flaunt Brenda, not flogged, there's a subtle difference." Rick teased and she hit him in the arm.

"I believe marriage is a binding commitment between two people who agree to share everything for the rest of their lives," he said, keeping his eyes on her.

"Sounds more like prison to me," Nyah said, matching his gaze.

Gabby sat down beside David and put her arm around him.

"Isn't taking a man's last name traditional and symbolic? It's almost like saying you wouldn't wear the engagement or wedding ring."

"Does either of those things prevent infidelity?" Nyah asked hoping that someone would change the conversation.

"Nyah, you sound like a woman scorned," Sage said.

"Yeah, you sound so bitter," Brenda added.

"Hardly, I find it more useful to spend my energy fighting for equity and justice, than to worry about what name defines me or the size of my diamond."

"I wouldn't want to be the man to spar with you in a dark alley. He would definitely need a helmet," Trey's comment evoked laughter around the room.

"You're a jerk Trey." Gabby got up and disappeared into the kitchen. Nyah excused herself and joined her.

"Can I help?" Nyah asked, no longer interested in being part of a dead-end conversation.

"Sure, grab a towel. I'll wash, you dry," Gabby pointed to the folded towels on the counter.

"Thanks for inviting me, great party."

"I'm glad you came. Listen, ignore those guys, they are just fooling around. The night's not done yet, we're either going to stay in and watch a couple of movies or go dancing, we can't decide." They talked about Gabby's plans for the summer and how wild and crazy her family gatherings would get when all eight of her siblings got together.

"So how do you know Brenda?" Nyah asked trying not to seem too interested.

"We met at a fundraiser about two years ago; she had just moved to Detroit from Texas, we hit it off right away."

"Hey, where do you want me to put these?" Mark entered the kitchen carrying four empty beer bottles. He walked up to Gabby and kissed her on the cheek and she blushed. "Where do you want me to put these?"

"By the back door," she said, "why don't you make yourself useful, you can wash, Nyah can rinse and I will get the rest of the dirty dishes from the table." She left the kitchen.

Nyah suddenly felt a fluttering inside her stomach. She used her wrist to brush back a lock of curly hair that had fallen over her right eye and looked up at him.

"You know," he said, picking up a plate, "we must stop meeting like this."

"Did you know I would be here?" She asked pointedly.

"No, but it was a nice treat to see all of you again." His arm brushed against hers and she felt a current pass through her body.

"All of me?" She asked and watched his eyes shift to her ample breasts and then back to her face. She groaned in disgust at his uninhibited display of lust. "You've hardly said two words to me since you've been here," she said, glancing up at him.

"Not true, we just had our first fight." He smiled and handed her the plate he had been washing for the last minute.

"Travelling solo tonight?"

"Solo?"

"I mean, without a woman," she said.

"A woman?" He asked, feigning shock in his voice.

"I'm sure a good-looking, virile man like you, must have at least one woman on every arm?"

"Ouch. How many arms do I have?" He put his hand over his heart as though her words wounded him. "You think I'm a player, don't you?"

She smiled, "what I think is irrelevant. When I saw you at the party, you were… quite the entertainer."

"Oh, the party. I was doing a favor for a friend," he said grinning. "So you think I'm good-looking?"

Nyah did not answer.

"You think I'm beautiful," she said and when he laughed, her heart skipped a beat.

"Don't you?" Before she could respond, Dwight stuck his head inside the door.

"Yo, we should go man; we have an early flight tomorrow."

"Hey, you go, I'll be alright," he said without taking his eyes off her.

"Suit yourself," Dwight said and left the kitchen.

"Are you traveling somewhere?" She asked, knowing he was within his rights not to answer.

"Business, for a few days," he said. She wondered what type of work he did but did not ask.

Mark held up a towel, dried her hands and led her through the door to the side of the house. The chill she felt quickly disappeared when he wrapped his arms around her, lowered his head and covered her lips with his own. He pried her lips apart and touched the tip of her tongue before closing his mouth over hers again. She pressed her body against him, threw her arms around his neck and returned his kiss, matching his intensity. When their lips parted, he raised his head a few inches to stare at her. They were both breathing hard.

"I've wanted to do that since the day you nearly ran me off the road." His voice was throaty and very deep.

"I think your memory is faulty, as I recall, you hit me. I wasn't sure you remembered who I was." Her voice was just above a whisper.

"You're not that easy to forget." He brushed his lips against hers, "can I get a ride home?"

"Where do you live?" Her words were lost in his mouth.

"Detroit."

She nodded, not trusting her voice to speak. Every fiber in her body was on fire.

"Now?"

"Whenever you're ready," he said.

She tore herself away from him, went into the living room and picked up her purse from the coffee table, relieved that everyone was engrossed in the movie.

"Are you leaving already?" Gabby stopped her at the front door.

"Yes, great party thanks, for the invite. Please say goodbye to everyone for me."

"I'm glad you came, see you at school on Monday," Nyah hugged her and left.

She walked briskly to her car to find Mark leaning against it, waiting for her. Then she glanced around to see if anyone was looking before she got in the car, reached across the seat to let him in and drove to her house.

She opened the front door and walked into the foyer with Mark right behind her. After putting down her purse, she turned to face him, never having experienced such wanton desire for any man. From the moment he walked through the door at Gabby's house, her body betrayed her. She took his hand and led him into the living room.

"Can I get you anything?" she asked.

"What do you think?"

She reached up on her toes to meet his lips half way, they were soft and his breath was minty. As their kiss deepened, she moaned and pressed closer to him.

He pulled away for a brief moment to remove his shirt and she ran her fingertips across the vast expanse that was his chest, followed a trail down his stomach and unzipped his jeans. He sat down on the sofa and she straddled him. He raised her arms above her head and pulled off her sweater.

Starting at her neck, he slowly raked his fingers down her chest and cupped her breasts. He lowered his head and wrapped his lips around one nipple, then the other, teasing them with his teeth through her lace bra before he removed it and repeated the same gesture on her bare flesh. She closed her eyes and threw her head back savoring the feeling. In her haze, she felt him shift her body slightly to put on a condom and heard the rubber snap. Her body quivered with anticipation.

She moaned as he used his hand to move aside the only barrier that remained between them and when he entered her, he filled every inch of her right down to the soles of her feet. He kissed her fervently and she wrapped her arms around his neck and took from him all that he was willing to give her, matching his sweet, slow rhythm and when her body exploded, she saw stars. Shortly after, she heard a low rumble and his body shook with delight. Breathing heavily, he buried his face in her hair and she clung to him until their breathing slowed and their heart rate returned to normal.

Nyah stood up, adjusted her underwear and put on her blouse.

"Does your girlfriend know you're cheating on her?"
"Is that your way of asking if I have one?"
"Do you?"

"It depends on what day you ask me." He fixed his boxers and zipped up his jeans. "You could just ask me to leave."

"I could," she said running her fingers through her hair, "but I'm certain you have your own moral compass." Nyah watched him intently as he stood up and pulled his shirt over his head. Leading the way through the foyer, she handed him the keys to her car.

"It's okay, I'll grab a cab," he refused.

"Why? Just let me know where you're going to leave it and I will get a ride to pick it up." She stepped past him and opened the front door; a gush of wind blew across her cheeks.

He paused and turned to face her, "it's been a pleasure."

"I second that," she smiled.

Closing the door, she pressed her back against it and listened until he drove away. She bolted the door and put the chain on before going upstairs to take a shower. She stood unmoving while the hot water washed away his touch, his scent, the sex she had with a man she trusted to take her car but not to sleep in her bed.

Before she fell asleep, Nyah pressed the play button on her answering machine; there was one message.

'Hey girl, guess what, I AM GETTING MARRIED!' She deleted the message, turned off the light, and slept like a baby.

Four

Nyah called a taxi to take her to the airport to catch her 6:45 flight. It had been four days since she lent her car to Mark, and no phone call. She did not know if he was dead or alive or where her car was. She had no way of reaching him, except through Gabby's boyfriend David, and she was not willing to involve them in her personal affairs.

It was her plan to drive to Chicago to attend three workshops, one of which was facilitated by her favorite African American author, and sometime during the weekend, she hoped to visit a friend from college who lived in the windy city. When she heard the doorbell, she hurried to answer it, hoping it was him, ready with her few choice words but they would have to wait for another time.

"Nyah Parsons?" A lanky black man was standing at the door with his hands in his jacket pocket. Believing it to be the cab driver, she signaled for him to wait, picked up her overnight bag and the flask with her tea off the table. He held up a set of keys and dangled them in front of her. "Here you go."

"What's this for?" She asked puzzled.

"I was told to give you the keys to that car." Nyah glanced behind him and was stunned to see a red Mercedes sitting in her driveway."

"There must be some mistake, that's not my car."

"That's not my problem, some guy asked me to drop it off at this address and he told me to give you this." Nyah took the business card and read the name.

"That arrogant son of a bitch."

"Whatever lady, my work here is done. That's a nice ride, if you don't want it, I can take it off your hands." The young man got into a waiting car and drove off.

Nyah was fuming. She stormed through her foyer and into the living room, picked up the phone and began dialing the number on the card when she heard a horn blow.

"Shit," she put the phone down, stuffed the card in her pocket, vowing to let the owner of the car know exactly what she thought of him and his red Mercedes when she got to her hotel in Chicago.

The plane ride seemed longer than two hours and for the entire trip, she could not stop thinking about the red car sitting on her driveway. Perhaps it was payment for services rendered. Egotistical bastard. Served her right for sleeping with a man she knew very little about. She was not impressed and she would make that very clear to him the next time they spoke.

She parked her rental car and went to her room to take a shower and get some rest before going to her first workshop early in the morning. After she settled in, she removed the card from her pocket and stared at it. Counting backwards from ten, she dialed the number, he answered on the third ring.

"Where's my car?" She could not conceal her anger.

"Didn't you get it? I sent it by messenger this afternoon."

"I think you sent your payment to the wrong woman, my sex was free." Even with the phone away from her ear, she still heard him laughing. "I'm glad I amuse you."

"I think red's your color, it goes well with your sense of humor."

"You don't know anything about me, or my sense of humor. Where's my car Mark?"

"Can we talk about your car over dinner?"

Nyah sighed heavily, "No thank you, besides, I'll be out of town until tomorrow night." She bit her lip, regretting that she shared her personal information with him.

"I can join you, wherever you are."

"There's something you need to understand about me," her tone was harsh, "I'm immune to bullshit and I don't play games. You clearly do. You have insulted me with your extravagant, hoochie gift which, by the way, you will find taking up space in my driveway waiting for you to pick it up at your earliest convenience, preferably before I get home tomorrow." Nyah slammed down the receiver, closed her eyes and breathed deeply trying to hold off the headache that was creeping from the back of her neck to her temples. She gritted her teeth and picked up the receiver to call him and apologize, but changed her mind. She knew her behavior was rude and uncalled for, but there was something so smug and self-assured about him, it drove her crazy. What made him think he could *buy* her with such an expensive gift?

The conversation, hearing his voice made her restless. She wanted to get a good night's sleep so she would be alert in the morning but her mind was unsettled. She took a tiny pill from a bottle, placed it on her tongue and waited for it to dissolve. She hated taking medication to calm her nerves. After all, she was not weak, she had full control of her life but one pill occasionally, she convinced herself, was harmless.

Nyah arrived at the hall early, sat in the center of the second row, and browsed through the handout she received from the clerk at the door.

She sipped her tea hoping it would help to lift the haze that had settled around her head. The room was filled to capacity and buzzing expectantly as the occupants waited for the facilitator to begin the presentation. After the meeting, Nyah approached the author with her curriculum vitae two articles she had written and asked for permission to start a Sister Round Table Chapter in Riverdale. She got the green light.

****

When the cab pulled into her driveway, Nyah noticed that the red car was still there. She was certain she had made herself clear to Mark about having the car removed but he disregarded her wishes and she knew she had to get it removed herself.

'Hey Sis, I have been trying to reach you for a couple of days, call me when you get a chance' was the first message left on Nyah's answering machine. Graydon's voice sounded anxious, which was unusual for him. The next message was from Sheila "Hey girl, I'm trying to reach you, CALL ME BACK!' She was practically shouting through the phone. 'Nyah, it's your mother, please call me ASAP.'

'Hi Nyah, it's Gabby, Sage and I are going to see Leah Blaque in concert in Detroit, wondering if you want to come let me know.'

Nyah spent her Saturday night returning phone calls. She did not call Pearline; she already knew what she wanted. She felt bad that she had not spoken to her grandmother since she moved to Riverdale.

"Hi Gran," Nyah said shamefacedly.

"Who's this?"

"It's me Gran."

Tracie, honey, is that you?" Her voice was shaky but cheery as always. "Where have you been and why are you just now calling me? I could have been dead, in my grave and you wouldn't know." Gran stopped to catch her breath. Nyah dismissed the thought of Gran dying; convinced her grandmother would probably outlive her.

"I'm sorry Gran, I know I should have called sooner, but I have been really busy here, with school and trying to settle in."

"The only thing you're busy doing is running away from your life child." Gran was never one to mince words; she said exactly what was on her mind. After living with her for 17 years, Nyah had gotten used to her sharp tongue but it did not lessen the stabbing effect.

"Gran, I'm coming to visit you."

"You are, when, tomorrow?"

"No, I can't leave my students right now, but maybe sometime in August."

"August? Your mother told you to call me didn't she?" Nyah smiled secretly. "I know she's trying to plan some silly birthday party for me even after I said I didn't want one."

"Who told you that?" Nyah tried to sound innocent.

"I'm old, not stupid. She try to do one every year, and every year, I leave just around that time." Gran started to laugh.

"Gran, you know that's mean," Nyah scolded jokingly, "mom really wants to do this for you."

"I don't know why, she don't even like me all that much," she said, her voice sounded like she was talking through a hollow tube. "No matter, maybe if I give her this one, she'll leave me alone."

"She thinks you don't know about it," Nyah said.

"That's not too bright on her part, if I knew all the other times, why wouldn't I know now. Don't worry, I can act surprised if I have to." Gran got serious. "I hope when you come back here, you'll be ready to deal with some of them issues that's stunting your growth."

"I'm growing just fine." Nyah said, dismissing her grandmother's concern.

"You know what I'm talking about."

"I love you Gran and I promise I'll call you more often, just make sure you pick up the phone," she hung up before her grandmother could say anything else and called Gabby to confirm Sunday night.

* * * * * * * **

Nyah swung her purse across her chest and hurried through the front door after hearing the horn blow for a second time. Gabby arrived at her house after five o'clock to pick her up for the Leah Blaque concert and as she passed the car sitting in the driveway she tried not to look at it, or think about the man who gave it to her, a task that proved difficult. She had not driven it yet even though she wanted to, but she was determined to stick to her guns and resist falling prey to the materialistic connotation that such a gift represented. She made a mental note to call a tow truck and have it removed first thing in the morning.

"You bought a new car?" Gabby asked as she slipped in the back seat of the Volvo, "and a pricey one at that."

"It's not mine, I'm just keeping it for a friend until tomorrow," she lied, well not technically, the car did not belong to her but she was not willing to share the fact that Mark had given it to her as payment for being his whore. The thought made her cringe.

Forty minutes later, they drove into the parking lot of a Hakka restaurant just outside Detroit.

"I hope you don't mind, Dave invited a couple of his friends to join us for dinner, I think they are going to the after party."

"Hey, I'm good with whatever, I am just happy to see my girl Leah in concert." Nyah could not contain her excitement. They decided to have drinks on the patio and wait for the others to arrive. Nyah was deep in conversation so she was not aware of David and Dwight's presence until Gabby stood up to greet them. David suggested that they get a bigger table because he invited Mark and he had a date with him.

Nyah felt uneasy, the last time she spoke to Mark she was very rude and even though she thought he deserved it, she decided to apologize before the night was over. As they approached the table, she recognized the girl from the breakout party that she attended with Sheila. He greeted his friends and introduced his date, whose name was Simone. Maybe the Mercedes was for her Nyah thought. For a split second, their eyes locked and she felt butterflies in her stomach. She forced a smile and after they sat down, across from her, she had a sinking feeling that it was not going to be a good evening. Simone could not keep her hands off him and he did not seem to mind. She got up and headed for the washroom.

"Do you want me to order something for you?" She stopped and turned to face Gabby.

"Anything without meat is fine." Nyah could not get away from the table fast enough. Shit, why was he there? She did not feel like spending her whole evening, watching him fondle his girlfriend. She stared at her face in the mirror and conjured a smile. She was strong, beautiful and smart. She knew better than to allow another human being, especially a man, to take an ounce of power away from her. Armed with a new resolve, she walked confidently back to the table and sat down. The first thing that she noticed was Mark's arm resting on the back of the chair behind Simone as she nestled her body against him and her resolve flew out the window.

Nyah felt trapped for the rest of the evening. He talked and joked with his friends as if she was not there, he ignored her and she wondered why that bothered her. He disappeared before the concert began but when Leah began singing, she forgot all about him, losing herself in the music. She did not know that they planned to attend the private after party hosted by Leah until she overheard Dwight giving Gabby directions to the hotel. The beautiful feeling quickly ended when Nyah realized that she could not go home right away, since she was at the mercy of another driver and her frustration began to mount.

After about an hour, Nyah had reached her limit and decided she was going to take a cab home. It was great while it lasted; the dinner and the concert but the after party was overkill. The penthouse was bursting at the seams with people and everyone, including her traveling companions, was caught up in the excitement so she used the opportunity to sneak out, certain that no one would miss her.

When she reached the lobby, she sank her tense body in the suede chair and decided to call Sheila hoping she was at her sister's house in Dearborn a few miles away.

"Hey Sheila, can you come get me?"

"Where are you?" Sheila sounded distracted.

"I'm at the Bristol," Nyah said.

"I can, if you're willing to wait 2 hours.

"Two hours?"

"Yeah, I'm kinda busy right now." She lowered her voice almost to a whisper. "He took some Yohimbine and I have a small window of opportunity here."

"What's that?"

"Trent's been having some trouble lately in the performance department."

"That's too much information, forget it, I'll take a cab."

"You sure, I'll come, if you're really desperate."

"Don't worry about it, have a good time." Nyah hung up the phone and shook her head.

"How's the car running?" She jumped at the sound of his voice.

"I wouldn't know," she said dryly as he sat down beside her. "I'm not the sort of woman you can buy with *things*." Her voice was even and cool.

"Do you think I'm trying to buy you?"

"What do you want Mark?"

"Why did you leave the party?" She was not aware that he was even there.

"That's none of your business, but if you must know, I'm waiting for a cab."

"There are cabs waiting outside."

"Okay, I needed some air."

He leaned back in the chair, folded his arms across his chest and stared at her intently.

"Do you need a ride?"

"No, thank you," she said almost too quickly.

"I would love to see your lighter side and maybe even a smile. I don't bite, unless you want me to," he teased.

"Is sex all you see when you look at me?"

"Is that a trick question?"

"Isn't your *girlfriend* missing you by now?"

"So that's what this is about."

Nyah laughed. "You think I want to leave because you are here with another woman?"

"You tell me."

Nyah stood up to leave annoyed that he was trying to delve into her private thoughts.

"As much as I'm enjoying this stimulating conversation, I'm afraid it's time to go." She started to walk away, in two strides he reached her and touched her arm.

"Have dinner with me tomorrow night."

"Threesomes are not my thing. Where's my car Mark?" She grew tired of playing his game and was prepared to walk away from him and her car.

"It's on your driveway, I'll pick you up at eight," he walked into the elevator and pushed the button. She released an exasperated sigh, "Are you sure you don't need a ride?" He asked.

"I'm sure," she said before the elevator door closed.

She decided to wait for Gabby in the lobby who showed up shortly after Mark left. Nyah had a feeling that he told Gabby that she was ready to leave. On the way home, she listened as the two women talked about Mark and his new girlfriend, the concert, and the possibility of everyone repeating the fun together once a month.

Five

It took Nyah a long time to decide what she should wear on her date with Mark. By the time the doorbell rang, she had changed into her seventh outfit and he was half hour late. She settled for straight-leg black slacks, a thin blue turtleneck top and a stylish dark brown biker jacket.

When she opened the door, instead of seeing his face she saw a bunch of pink roses. He spoke from behind them.

"Sorry I'm late." He handed her the roses and smiled. She took them and invited him in. As she walked into the kitchen to get a vase, he said, "You look great."

"Thank you, can I get you something to drink?"

"Raincheck?" he asked from the living room. "I made reservations for nine and we have a forty-five minute drive." Nyah arranged the flowers and placed the vase in the center of her dining room table.

"We should go then," she said, "thanks for the flowers."

He held the passenger door open for her, held her hand and practically lifted her into the truck after she tried to get in on her own and realized the step was high for her. He walked around to the driver's side and slid into the seat beside her; she thought he smelled like the forest just after a rainfall.

"Comfy?" He smiled at her and adjusted his rear-view mirror from which dangled a gold tiger pendant. When he started the engine, the music was blazing and he apologized quickly turning down the volume. Nyah recognized the rapper's voice but she could not remember the name of the song.

"I hope you like Italian food," he said.

"I'm not picky." She did not feel the need to let him know that her grandfather was half-Italian and it was the food of choice when she lived with her grandparents.

"So, tell me something about you that I don't already know."

"What do you think you know about me?"

"You're beautiful, guarded, and you want everyone to believe you hate men."

"You're wrong on two counts. If you must know, I love Jazz."

"Jazz, I wouldn't figure you for a Jazz girl," he said, "I see you as more the quiet storm R&B type."

"I like R&B," she said, "I just love Jazz more, the music is soothing and it speaks to the soul."

"That's deep," he said, looking at his phone. Nyah noticed it was the third time since they had been driving that his phone buzzed. "It's alright, a little too laid back for my taste." He pressed a button and turned his attention back to her. "But you love Leah Blaque; she's not a Jazz artist."

"She's the exception. There's something about her voice and I love the lyrics to some of her songs." Nyah realized she was gushing and stopped talking, convinced she sounded like a star-struck groupie.

"Wanna meet her?" She looked at him wide-eyed.

"Who, Leah? No, I think I'll just admire her from a distance," she said timidly, "you know her?"

"Let me know if you change your mind," he grinned and her heart melted.

Thirty minutes later, they pulled into the parking lot of *Amore Italia* an Italian restaurant she had heard about but never visited. Inside, the host seated them by a crackling electric fireplace. The pot lights glowed softly and classical music chimed through tiny round speakers in the ceiling. He held the chair for her and she sat down on the soft velvet seat. Shortly after settling, a waiter approached the table and took their drink and dinner orders.

His phone vibrated again, he looked at it and this time decided to answer it. He excused himself and walked towards a corner of the room. Nyah heard the distinct sound of his voice but his words were inaudible over the drone of low chatter in the room.

She watched his tall, well-built body swagger towards the table and looked away when their eyes met. He wore dark pants with an off-white v-neck sweater and every step he took told her he was confident and self-assured. He apologized when he sat down and promised her he would not answer any more calls.

The fog that had temporarily clouded her mind, that caused her to forget the reason for the dinner in the first place, lifted. She looked around and thought the restaurant was too intimate - dim lighting, fireplace and couples fawning over one another at tables designed for two, made her question his true motives for asking her out and for taking her to this particular restaurant.

"This is nice, but what are you doing?"

"I'm enjoying dinner with a beautiful woman."

"Look, I'll save you a lot of time and energy. I have no desire to assume the role of mother, whore or therapist for any man. Frankly, I found your little *payment* insulting and demeaning."

"Payment?" He looked at her questioningly.

"Yes payment; what else could it be? How many men do you know who would buy a Mercedes for a total stranger?"

"You are not technically a *total* stranger," he teased.

"You know what I mean," Nyah shifted in her seat.

"Someone stole your car. I merely replaced it."

Nyah did not expect that response.

"Someone stole my car, you're joking right?" She was speechless. "Why didn't you just tell me that to begin with?"

"It was more fun having you believe it was for services rendered," he said chewing on a piece of bread. "And for the record, your body is worth more than ten Mercedes." His words caught her completely off guard and she stared at him defiantly.

"You're objectifying me?"

"I'm not; I meant it as a compliment."

"Comparing my body to a car is not a compliment in my book," she said.

"I'm sorry if I offended you." His apology and his smile disarmed her and she relented, which was something she did not do too often.

"Look, maybe I shouldn't have jumped to such a conclusion, but it's always best to be clear about your motives. It prevents misunderstandings. I still can't keep it, it's too excessive."

"Okay, let's make a deal. Keep it for six months and if you still don't want it, I'll take it back."

"What kind of a deal is that?" When she realized he was not going to back down she finally said, "four months, and not a day longer."

"Deal," he reached his hand across the table and they shook on it. His hand swallowed hers and he used his thumb to caress the back of her hand. She smiled and withdrew her hand slowly.

His voice kept her captive every time he uttered a sound. She found everything about him appealing but he would never hear that from her lips. They talked about politics, the economy and other current issues, and to her delight, he was more informed than she thought he would be.

He pulled into her driveway alongside the car at around 12:30 and turned off the engine.

She turned her head to look at him.

"That was nice dinner and conversation, thank you," she said, breaking the silence. He got out and walked around to open her door. She held his hand and jumped from the truck closing the door behind her. He pinned her gently against the side with his body, lowered his head and kissed her slowly. His hands caressed the sides of her face as he continued to deepen his kiss. Her legs grew weak, threatening to fold underneath her when he parted her lips and searched for her tongue with his own.

She turned her head away and whispered, "We shouldn't do this here, I have nosy neighbors."

"It's just a kiss."

Pushing lightly against his chest, he stepped back but he held her hand, brushing her open palm against his lips. The bottom of her stomach fell into her groin and she had no doubt in her mind that she wanted him to follow her inside and devour her, even if it was only for two hours. His cell phone rang, and he reluctantly looked to see who was calling but he did not answer it. She looked at his phone, smiled and slipped past him to get to her front door. She did not feel like being the 'good time girl' tonight. Her grandmother's words echoed in her ear, *'a man will eat whatever you set before him, even if he's not hungry'*. Moreover, she was certain he had other options judging by the number of times his phone rang all evening. She opened the front door, stepped inside and turned to face him, standing just outside the door.

"Thanks again for dinner," she said.

"It doesn't have to end." His voice was husky.

"I have to get up early tomorrow. Goodnight."

"I'll call you," he said and she closed the door. She knew most men used those words, to placate a desperate woman. She was far from desperate and she knew better than to sit by the phone with her heart in her throat waiting for the illusive phone call.

****

"Are you and Mark seeing each other?"

Nyah was puzzled by the randomness of Gabby's question. They had been browsing in the mall for an hour and up to that point, their conversation had been about school and fashion.

"What! Where did that come from?"

"Don't you think he's smoking hot?" Gabby asked, fanning her face. Nyah became flustered when an image of him naked flashed across her mind. "I thought you guys hit it off at the party, but since then, nothing; not one word from either of you. I was hoping for some good news by now."

"No news here, at least where Mark is concerned," Nyah said, "I'm not his type."

"How do you know what his type is?"

"I don't really, I'm just going by that girl I saw him with at the restaurant."

"Who, Simone? Yeah, she's most definitely his type; the sluttier the better," she claimed. "But I also saw the way he looked at you."

"What way was that?" Nyah asked curiously. When she did not answer, Nyah realized that a dress in the store window had distracted her.

"*That* is a gorgeous dress." Gabby pointed to the sleeveless, black and red dress displayed on a mannequin. "It has my name written all over it. Come on," she led the way inside the store and held it up to admire the detailing around the hem. "Prada knock off; nice. *Five hundred dollars*! Who can afford that?" She put the dress back on the rack after goggling it one last time and started browsing through the other racks. "I think David wants to do something crazy for the fourth of July, I just can't figure out what, he's always trying to surprise me." She turned to Nyah, "what about you and Mark, do you two have any plans."

"Gabby, you need to stop. There is nothing going on between Mark and I, doesn't he have a girlfriend?" Gabby picked up another dress to look at it.

"With Mark, it's hard to tell, everything is a big secret with him." She held a short, blue pinstripe wrap dress up against Nyah's body, "this would look nice on you; I think you should try it on." Gabby began sifting through the rack to find a size small enough to fit Nyah. "What size do you wear, zero?"

"Zero? No, I wear size two and I don't do wrap dresses; they make my breasts look way too big."

"Mark's a breast man," Gabby said nonchalantly, "the bigger the better. I'm sure he'd love to see you in this little number." Nyah did not comment but she wondered how Gabby would know something so personal about him.

"Let's get something to eat, all this browsing has made me hungry," Nyah said, and led the way out of the store towards the food court. She was uncomfortable with how easily Gabby divulged Mark's personal business.

"Gabby Bryant, is that you?" They heard the voice behind them and turned around to face a tall man with chocolate complexion in his early thirties. His black hair was cut low and neat to a fault and he wore a dark suit with a navy blue shirt and matching tie.

"Edward Blake," she beamed, "long time no see." He put his briefcase down and they embraced for a few seconds. "My God, how are you," she continued.

"I'm holding it together," he said.

"You look great," she said. His eyes shifted to Nyah. "I'm sorry, this is my friend Nyah Parsons, Edward is a friend of mine from high school. Well he was a senior when I entered grade nine."

He shook Nyah's hand, "call me Eddy, it's a pleasure to meet you," and held it a little longer than she liked but let it go when she cleared her throat softly.

"Hi," she said.

"Eddy," Gabby said, "we were just going to get something to eat, would you care to join us?" She glanced at Nyah to get her approval.

"Why not," he said, glancing at his watch, "I've got a few minutes and it will give us a chance to catch up."

They reminisced and laughed about the fun they used to have in high school for half hour. He had recently separated from his wife of four years, they had two boys and she took the children with her when she moved to Chicago. He has been living in Riverdale County for three months after moving from Houston, to join a small medical practice as the third doctor on staff.

Underneath all the laughter and bravado, Nyah thought he seemed sad, considering what he was going through, she thought he had a good reason to be. He kept glancing at her, asking her questions she felt were intrusive for someone he just met. After all, he was Gabby's friend, not hers. Not wanting to appear rude, she smiled and supplied him with short, courteous answers, Gabby on the other hand volunteered that she was new in town, what she did for a living and her current marital status adding that she was available. Nyah strained to conceal her disapproval with Gabby for divulging her business to a total stranger and vowed silently to reprimand her when they were alone.

Finally, after about an hour, he looked at his watch and stood up.

"Ladies, it's been wonderful, but I'm afraid I must say farewell, give me your number Gab," he took out his phone book and wrote her number in it. "Let's get together again soon."

He reached inside his jacket pocket, pulled out a card and handed it to Nyah. "It was a pleasure Miss Parsons; give me a call sometime. If you ever need a tour guide, I'm your man." He placed his hand across his chest and bowed.

"Don't be a stranger." Gabby said, hugging him.

"He's a bit much," Nyah commented casually as they walked to the parking lot.

"He's a rare commodity; I guess he can afford to be." Gabby said.

"Why, because he's a doctor?"

"That *and* he's available. Are you interested?"

"Not today and I don't appreciate you sharing my personal business like that," she said and walked away.

* * * * * * * **

When Nyah walked through the front door, her house reeked of fried chicken.

"I didn't know you lived with someone else."

"I don't." They walked to the kitchen and Nyah put her bag and keys on the counter.

"Hey Sheila."

"Where have you been? I have been trying to reach you for over an hour. I let myself in, and used your vegetarian pot to cook some chicken, I know you don't mind." Sheila turned around and noticed Gabby standing by the counter. "I'm sorry; I didn't know we had company."

Gabby walked over to the stove where Sheila stood manning her pot and extended her hand.

"Hello, I'm Gabby." Sheila had flour all over her hands and when Gabby saw them, she quickly withdrew hers.

"Can I get you anything Gab?" Nyah asked as she opened the sliding doors to let the chicken smell escape.

"No thanks, I'm fine."

"Are you mad at me?" Sheila asked.

"Why would I be mad at you?"

"I'm sorry about the other night. I was trying to be the dutiful fiancé but, his shit wouldn't stay up" she said, laughing.

"Don't worry about it Sheila and that's not stuff you tell somebody," she said and put on the kettle to make tea.

"Nyah, I have to go and do some marking." Nyah thought Gabby seemed edgy.

She looked around the kitchen, rolled her eyes, and sighed. "You're gonna clean this mess up right?"

"Don't insult me Nyah. When have I ever not cleaned up after myself?"

"Good," she said and walked Gabby to the front door.

"Your friend Sheila is quite a character."

"What do you mean?" Nyah was surprised that Gabby voiced an opinion about her friend so quickly.

"It's nothing," she said lightly, "I'll see you at school tomorrow."

"Sure, good night." Nyah realized she was still annoyed at Gabby for what happened earlier in the evening.

She closed the door, went back to the kitchen and made her tea.

"Who was that crabcake?" Sheila was wiping the counter.

"Crabcake Sheila?" Nyah chuckled.

"I didn't like her vibe."

"She's alright." Nyah walked through the sliding doors and stretched out on the lounge chair. Sheila followed her and sat down on the chair next to her.

"I am going nuts trying to plan for this wedding."

"Are you really going through with it?' Nyah asked staring at her friend in disbelief.

"Don't hate, he's really a good guy, he treats me good and when the parts are working, the sex is off the chain."

"Sheila, you can't be serious, you just met this man, and at a party no less, what do you really know about him?"

"You hypocrite, miss 'one night stand on a cruise ship'."

"That's different and you know it. *You* bailed on me, remember, I was feeling a little frisky; he was available, end of story. I'm not going to marry the man."

"Trace, don't lecture me, I get enough of that from my mother, can't you just be happy for me?" She seemed disappointed that Nyah would not share her enthusiasm. Nyah sighed, reached over and touched her arm.

"I'm happy, if you're happy," she said, rubbing her friend's arm playfully.

"So does that mean you will be my maid of honor?"

"Only if you pay me," Nyah said jokingly. She was used to her friend being impulsive and she knew she could not get Sheila to change her mind after she set it on doing something.

They spent the evening browsing through bridal magazines; Sheila wanted a big wedding with all the trimmings, which Nyah thought was such a waste of time and money.

"Have you set a wedding date?" Nyah asked.

"July 14th," she said sheepishly.

"Well at least we have a little over a year."

"A year," she laughed, "this July, 14th."

"What? That's in 3 weeks."

"Then we have a lot to do in 3 weeks."

Nyah stood up and stretched.

"All this wedding talk is making me antsy; I'm going for a run. Do you want to come?"

Sheila shook her head and continued flipping through the magazine.

"I don't need to run, I get enough exercise," she smiled brazenly.

"Suit yourself; I'll see you in about an hour."

"Maybe not, I might have to meet Trent's kids and grandkids for a family meeting later; I'm just waiting for him to call."

"Wow that's major, good luck with that gramma," Nyah teased and went inside to change before her evening run.

Six

Nyah walked through the sliding doors from the backyard to get a glass of iced tea, and heard the doorbell. She laid her gardening gloves on the kitchen counter and hurried to answer the front door. She lunged at her brother almost knocking him over and held him tight.

"I am so happy to see you. I've missed you."

He held her at arm's length and stared at her.

"Did you get shorter?" He laughed and she playfully punched him in the chest.

"Let me help you with your bags." He handed her the smallest one and she led the way into the living room. "Why didn't you call me to tell me you were coming today, I would have started cooking or something?"

"I've been trying to reach you for weeks, but you don't answer your phone."

"I was going to call you back," she said, "I haven't been very good at returning phone calls lately."

"Tell me about it."

He looked at her clothes and she followed his eyes back up to her hair, they burned a hole right through her.

"You look like shit," he said ruffling her hair. She had spent the morning in the backyard pulling weeds from the flower garden.

"So do you," she shot back, referring to his wavy brown afro, spiked at the ends; that he refused to trim. He has worn it that way since he cut off his dreads; he said for a job, but she believed it was for a woman. He also sported patches of hair growing out of his face that he called a faded beard.

"This is my signature look, what's your excuse?" He laughed and followed her into the backyard where she put him to work helping her to pull weeds from the flower patch around the fishpond. She put on her broad hat to shade her eyes from the unforgiving rays of the hot June sun.

While they worked, they talked about his new career as an artist. Graydon was two years older than she was and at twenty-eight, she had hoped he would be more focused and settled in his life, but she knew he had a nomadic spirit that defined who he was. He started studying to be a chef in college but dropped out in his third year to pursue his painting full time.

"Are you still playing in that band?"

"Yeah, the extra money comes in handy."

Nyah stared at him and smiled, her heart felt good, whenever he was around, she always felt safe.

"What have you got to eat? I'm starved," Graydon said after about an hour.

"Do you want to go out? I know a great restaurant on Broadview I think you would love; my treat."

"That's what I like to hear," he said removing the gloves and putting them on the patio table. They took his bags to the guest room after giving him a tour of the house, showered, changed and half-hour later they walked out the front door.

"You're driving in style Sis; what happened to the simple life?"

"This car is not mine, it's just a loaner."

"That's an expensive car to borrow; I think that I'll take it for a spin later?" He said rubbing his hands together.

"Why not now?" she said and threw him the keys.

Within twenty minutes, they sat across the table from each other at Milo's Bistro, a place Nyah thought of as a home away from home. She loved sitting on the front patio watching people walk by, and the food was not bad either. They were enjoying their meal when, Sage approached their table.

"Hey Nyah, fancy meeting you here." Sage wore a green floral sundress and piled her hair loosely on her head.

"Sage, nice to see you," she said and introduced Graydon. Evidently, he was smitten with her. He asked her to join them but she declined because she had a lunch meeting but she asked for a rain check and he agreed.

"Who's that?" he asked after she walked away.

"Her name is Sage Livingston." Nyah smiled at her brother's uninhibited display of lust. He turned his head to watch her walk away.

"She's hot, does she belong to anyone?"

"I don't know, why don't you ask her?"

"That doesn't matter," he said, popping his collar. "One ride on this black stallion and she'll be hooked."

"Gray, you're borderline narcissistic," Nyah said grimacing.

After lunch, she took him to visit the art gallery and to buy paint supplies at the craft store.

"What do you think about a portrait of Gran for her birthday?" He showed her a picture of their grandmother when she was about thirty-five. She still had not selected a gift for Gran and a portrait seemed like a perfect idea.

"I was thinking we could drive down to Wisconsin together."

"Sure we can. If I pay for the supplies, would you say the portrait's from both of us?" she asked.

He laughed.

"You know I'm not gonna pass up such a great offer."

* * * * * * **

The next three weeks were crazy. Nyah was so caught up in Sheila's life that she hardly spent any quality time with Graydon. Not that he noticed. He spent his time painting the landscapes and selling them at a kiosk he managed to set up in the mall. He also visited art galleries in Ohio, and Detroit and tried to sell them there. Her house was starting to look like an art swap shop, with painted canvases everywhere.

"How are the wedding plans coming along?" He teased, knowing she was not having a fun time helping Sheila plan her wedding. Nyah sat at the kitchen table surrounded by flowers, glue and crystal vases trying to put together centerpieces for the reception tables. Trent had a family situation, as Sheila put it, and she left to support her man. Graydon pulled up a chair beside her and began eating an apple.

"Shoot me now," she said jokingly. He laughed.

"So do you have big plans for your birthday?" She had been so busy she did not even remember that her birthday was coming up. "The big two-six, you're getting old Sis."

"I'll always be younger than you," she teased.

The doorbell rang.

"Could you get that, it's probably 'Miss Thang' coming to tell me I have forgotten to do something important for her 'big day' tomorrow," Nyah said, imitating Sheila's voice.

Graydon came back into the kitchen.

"Hey Ny, there's some guy named Mike here to see you."

"Mike? I don't know any ..." She walked past him towards the door, "Mark?" she was surprised to see him standing at the front door. Her heart skipped a beat when he smiled at her.

"Is this a bad time?"

"What are you doing here?" she asked. She had not heard from him since their 'date' and after a couple of days went by, she knew she had served her purpose.

"Let's go for a ride," he said. Graydon was leaning against the wall at the entrance of the kitchen listening to their conversation.

"Did you come to pick up your car?"

"It hasn't been four months yet."

"That car in the driveway is yours man?" Graydon asked.

"No." Mark looked at Graydon, "you won't mind if I borrow her for a while?"

Graydon looked at Nyah, shrugged his shoulders, "she's all yours," he said and went into the den.

"Who's he?" Mark asked as they walked down the driveway.

She glanced over at him and smiled coyly.

"Jealous?"

"Yes," he said, holding her hand as she stepped up into the truck. They pulled out onto the street and he turned his stereo on.

"He's my brother," she said but he did not seem fazed by the revelation, and something told her he already knew that.

They were on the road for more than an hour before Nyah asked him where he was taking her.

"Relax and enjoy the ride."

She rested her head on the back of the seat with her face away from him gazing at the water as they drove along the coast into Ohio.

Within twenty minutes, they pulled up into the huge parking lot of Cedar Point amusement park.

"What's this?" she asked, rubbing her hands together. She had not been to an amusement park since she was fifteen and she was having a hard time containing her excitement.

He took her hand and led her through the crowd towards the entrance. After going on the first few rides, Nyah could not get enough and gladly accepted his challenge to ride the Magnum XL-200; a new rollercoaster ride recently added to the park. She had seen the ads for the ride on television but to see it this close was impressive. They endured the 45-minute wait to get on, sat in the second to last row from the back and she instinctively looped her arm through his. The ascent was slow, and from two hundred feet in the air, the roller coaster plummeted on a steep angle, turned sharply, and went through a tunnel. Nyah enjoyed every second of the 2-minute ride. She loved the exhilarating feeling in the pit of her stomach. When the ride came to a halt, her head was spinning and she almost lost her balance, but she held Mark's arm to avoid falling.

After that, Nyah could only stomach the Carousel, the Giant wheel and the Calypso. Mark won a big bear for her, and she got him a large dinosaur that he carried on his shoulders as they left the park at around 10:30. It had been a while since Nyah laughed so hard that her heart hurt.

"We have one more stop, I want to show you something," he said and after a short drive, pulled his truck into a warehouse parking lot filled with expensive cars. Nyah could hear the rap music coming from the ajared door, where a large intimidating black man stood, with his arms folded. When they approached the door, Mark greeted the man warmly and he allowed them to pass. Inside, cameras were everywhere.

"Is this a movie set?"

"Naw, they're shooting a music video." He held her hand and guided her towards a man sitting on a chair behind a camera. Nyah did not recognize the song that was playing but she thought it had a smooth groove. There were five young women, scantily clad, gyrating their bodies in front of the camera running their hands all over a rapper she did not recognize who was lip-synching to the music.

The man behind the camera yelled, "cut, cue the dancers," as they approached him, he acknowledged Mark and both men embraced each other playfully.

The man looked at Nyah.

"Is this a new one for the video?"

"Naw man, she's with me." Nyah gave them a piercing look but they were too engrossed in their male bonding to notice.

Mark took her hand, "let me show you around."

When they walked off Nyah said, "This one? What am I a piece of meat?"

"Come on, you know what he meant," he said smiling.

"Actually, no I don't. He does not see the dancers as women with souls, they are just objects."

He led her down a narrow hallway into a recording studio. There were plaques and awards of recognition covering a whole wall.

Then he took her into a room that had a small one-way mirror overlooking three other rooms each with a piano, drums and other instruments.

"Welcome to my office." He closed the door and she could no longer hear the music from the other room. He sat behind a glass desk and turned on a computer. "Make yourself at home."

"Is this your recording studio?" she asked.

"It is. Well, I have a partner so it's half mine." He busied himself on his computer and within minutes, music streamed into the room.

"You don't look like a musician," she said, realizing they had never talked about what he did for a living. "What do you play?"

"I'm a producer," his voice was casual. "But I play keys, and drums."

"And the guy back there?"

"That's Vince, our music video director."

It occurred to Nyah, that Mark did not introduce her. She guessed with good reason, considering he had a girlfriend.

"He's doing a video for Tony, one of the artists I write for. Maybe you've seen one of his rap videos."

"I don't watch rap videos. In fact, I cannot stand most of them. I do not approve of their demeaning portrayal of blacks and women in particular. I guess I shouldn't be surprised that you would choose this type of work."

He chuckled, leaned back in his chair and stared at her. "What's wrong with the work I do?"

"I'm sure you don't need me to spell it out."

"Please, enlighten me," he smiled.

Nyah got up and stood directly in front of him. "Some music videos depict unrealistic, unattainable, sexually charged messages that promise impressionable young minds fame and fortune which realistically can only be achieved when they close their eyes at night."

"Or through talent, hard work and dedication," he interjected.

"True, but that's not how the videos are represented. Fast money, fast cars, fast women, *these* messages are communicated and I'm sure the video makers, like your friend there, know that. You may not have the big round chains hanging from your neck, but the way you dress, walk and sometimes talk reflects the music videos you produce." She knew that she sounded preachy but she saw the negative effects of rap videos on the students in her classroom.

"What about freedom of expression and freedom of choice. Shouldn't people have a right to do what they want?"

"I fully support individual and collective freedoms but, to put it plainly, how can you eat vegetables, when all you get, all the time on your plate, is steak?"

"Interesting analogy." He laughed, walked to a small fridge, took out a bottle of water and opened it before offering it to her. He took another one for himself.

"You are extravagant. Why didn't you replace my car with another Honda Civic?"

"I thought you'd look better in a Mercedes." The corners of his lips curled slightly as he leaned back in his chair, folded his arms and stared at her. His gaze aroused her. "I'm sure I don't have to tell you about this industry. Power, money and sex sells; plain and simple."

"So you live the lie just to sell music." She lost her train of thought when a Jazz song began to play. "That's a beautiful song," she said, "who's singing, she's got a great voice?"

"Jasmine." He stood up, moved from behind the desk and held out his hand. "She's an R&B singer but wanted to try something different so I wrote this crossover song for her. Would you like to dance?" She hesitated, then took his hand and moved closer to him. Standing at least a foot taller than her 5'2 frame, he rested his chin on the top of her head and hummed softly, as their bodies moved in sync to the slow groove. They continued to dance even after the song ended and another one began.

Without saying a word, he tilted her head upward and she held her breath as his lips pressed softly against hers. She parted her lips and he pressed harder, intensifying his kiss. Her lips took on a life of their own as his tongue probed the inside of her mouth and he moaned. Her cell phone rang and she reluctantly pulled away from his embrace to answer it.

"Happy birthday baby," Gran was almost shouting through the phone.

"Thanks Gran," Nyah said. She was glad to hear her grandmother's voice.

"See, sugar, I remembered, I'm not that old after all."

"Who told you you were old?" Nyah smiled and looked at Mark who was watching her intently. "Gran, I can't talk right now, I'll call you tomorrow, and thank you for remembering."

"Be good; if you can't be good, be careful," she said and hung up.

A knock on the door interrupted her thoughts.

Mark yelled for the person on the other side of the door to come in and a man stuck his head inside. Nyah was unnerved that the door was unlocked; if Gran had not called, she would probably be half-naked.

"A bunch of us are going to get something to eat, I thought you two might like to join us."

"Naw man, we're good."

"Okay, suit yourself." With that, he shut the door.

"Don't you have a lock on the door?" Mark walked to the door, bolted it, and then back to where she was standing beside the sofa. He removed the cushions and pulled out a sofa bed.

"It's your birthday?"

"You heard that? Tomorrow is my birthday."

"Happy birthday tomorrow."

He began to kiss her as he unbuttoned her blouse and let it fall from her shoulders. In one swift motion, he pulled off his t-shirt, let it drop to the floor, and gently lowered her onto the bed. She watched as he removed his pants and his boxers and her eyes devoured him.

Using his arms to support his weight, he bent over her and covered her waiting lips with his own. He left her lips tingling and planted feathery kisses down her neck and along her shoulders. She held her breath and waited for him to take her nipple into his mouth when he did, she was sure she had a mini orgasm. He wrapped his tongue around one and then the other. He moaned deep in his throat as he bit, sucked and licked them.

He removed her jeans and kissed her hips, her thighs, down to her toes before coming back up and settling at her pleasure center. Her breathing became staggered, he was taunting her and she loved it. When he finally entered her, Nyah was no longer aware of her actions. She was unable to contain her mounting passion until every nerve ending in her body exploded. When she ascended from the clouds, she did not want to move or speak.

"Happy birthday," he whispered and for her, it was a happy birthday indeed.

Seven

Nyah woke up with a headache. She tried to move but could not. She was lying on her side, her knees bent, nestled in Mark's body with her face turned away from him. Her head rested on his outstretched arm, her back pressed against his chest and his other arm swung across her like a paperweight just below her breasts, pinning her in place. She felt the rhythmic rise and fall of his chest as he snored softly. She loved feeling his skin against hers but knew that being in his arms created a false sense of security that could not last beyond the moment.

She pushed against him gently and he groaned but did not wake up. Her cell phone started ringing, growing louder with each ring and in her effort to free herself, she woke him. She jumped to her feet and stood next to the sofa bed.

"Good morning," his voice was husky. He stretched and every muscle in his body flexed.

"Good morning," she smiled and reached for her blouse to cover her naked body.

"Should I close my eyes?" he teased, then reached across the bed and playfully wrestled the top away from her. The phone stopped ringing briefly and then it started again. She ran to her purse and scrambled to find the phone.

"Hello," Nyah cleared her throat and said it again.

"Girl, don't make me kill you on my wedding day."

"Sheila, what time is it?" Nyah walked back to the sofa bed and used his t-shirt to cover her breasts.

"What do you mean 'what time is it?' where the hell are you? It's almost 11:30 and I've been trying to reach you since last night."

"I'm sorry," she said playing tug of war with him for the t-shirt, which he let go and chuckled when she stumbled backward.

"Is that all you can say." Sheila sounded very annoyed. "We've been waiting for you all morning."

"Sheila, I'm sorry. I'll be there as soon as I can."

"My wedding is at four, and I'm not even close to being ready. I need you here, now Tracie! Where are you anyway, and who is that I hear in the background?"

"I'll be there soon." Nyah said and hung up. "Do you have a bathroom I can use?" He motioned to a door in the corner of the room. When she entered, she wondered why he had a full bathroom in his office. He followed her into the shower and within fifteen minutes, she was in a state of euphoria screaming his name again.

* * * * * * **

By the time they climbed into the truck to make the two hour drive to Dearborn for the wedding, it was already passed 12:30 o'clock. Luckily, Sheila's mother insisted that the clothes for the bridal party should be kept at Sheila's sister Diane's house, a five-minute drive from the hotel. When they pulled into the driveway, a frantic Sheila came running out of the house with her weave in rollers. Mark walked around to the passenger door and opened it. She searched his eyes trying to read his thoughts but couldn't.

"The wedding starts at four at the Wyndham Hotel. I know it's short notice but you can come if you'd like."

"Tracie, I don't even want to know what kept you, because it's not about you right now, it's about me."

"Calm down Sheila, I'm here." Sheila ignored Mark as she reached around him, grabbed Nyah's arm and pulled her towards the entrance of the house. Nyah was disappointed that she did not have the chance to say goodbye before he backed out of the driveway and drove off.

Nyah spent the next two hours in a daze. She had a pounding headache as she went through the motions of helping Sheila get dressed and to the hotel by 5:00. They were an hour late but Sheila was walking down the aisle by 5:30. To Nyah's surprise, there were at least three hundred people in the church. When they sent out the invitations two weeks earlier, she did not expect that everyone would be able to attend on such short notice but by the looks of it, most of them showed up.

The procession was long; there were eight bridesmaids and two flower girls. The dresses were green and gold and each girl carried a bouquet of baby's breath with four yellow roses. Nyah's dress was all gold with a green sash and she pulled her hair back and held it in place with a gold band. She carried an artificial bouquet made of green and gold roses. Sheila's friend sang Luther's *Here and Now* as she walked down the aisle to her husband in waiting.

Nyah got through the ceremony, the signing and the picture taking with a headache and a smile. She wanted to make sure there were no details overlooked. By the time the reception started, she was mentally and physically exhausted. The couple chose the song *Midas Touch* for their first dance. They danced slowly and kissed all the way through the song. Nyah found their open display of affection slightly embarrassing and thought they should have gotten a room. She stood at the edge of the bridal party's table nibbling on a piece of bread when she spotted Brenda dancing with one of the ushers. She had seen her earlier in the day but had no occasion to deal with her because she was so busy with the wedding.

They met at a party Nyah's last year of high school. Brenda still had one more year to go; Sheila introduced them. Brenda's father had transferred from Houston, Texas to manage an electrical plant in Wisconsin.

For a while, the three of them hung out together and were inseparable, everyone called them 'the three musketeers'.

All the girls, including Nyah noticed when Trevor Johnson came to Fairfield High. He was the cutest and the coolest boy any of them had ever seen and he knew it. He flirted openly with all the popular girls and rumor had it, it was more than just flirting. Brenda would often fantasize about him and planned that he would be the one to take her virginity. He lived close to Gran's house and Nyah would sometimes walk home with him from school. She soon found out that he was very different from the image he portrayed at school and they became friends. Before long, a rumor started to spread around the school they were sleeping together. Brenda confronted Nyah and accused her of stealing her man. It was pointless trying to convince her that the rumors were not true. Nyah suspected that she might have started it.

"Hey Ny," Nyah hated being called that, especially by Brenda, but she kept quiet about it; she was too tired to let Brenda upset her.

"Hi Brenda, I didn't see your name on the invitation list."

"I couldn't miss my home girl's wedding," she smiled but Nyah knew there was no substance behind it. She looked around the room, "No date?"

"No, I'm here by myself."

"Isn't this like old times? The three of us together again. I see you still haven't done much with that hair."

Nyah grew tired of her, "at least it's all mine," she said and walked away. She hated being so petty, but Brenda brought out the child in her.

As the night wore on, she could not stop thinking about Mark. She hoped he would have come to the wedding but was not surprised that he did not. After all, she meant nothing more to him than a good lay every once in a while.

A few men asked her to dance and she refused them all. She was too tired and they'd had too much to drink.

"Who the hell do you think you are?" Nyah glanced in the direction of the shouting voices. The groom's sister was shouting at Bernadette, Sheila's aunt.

"You don't know shit," Bernadette retorted, "you best mind what you say about my niece or it's on."

"Bring it on bitch, come with it." The two women began to push each other and before long, they were rolling on the floor, screaming at each other. Some bystanders cheered, some jeered and finally, three men pulled them apart but not before getting some blows and a few choice words themselves. Nyah soon learned that Bernadette was defending Sheila's honor after the other woman accused her of marrying Trent to get her claws into his money.

The wedding guests had dwindled to about 20 people and the bride and groom were nowhere to be found.

"Have you had enough?" His voice penetrated her thoughts.

"You read my mind. How long have you been here?" she asked.

"Long enough. I'm sorry I could not make it sooner. How was it?"

"Long and tiring, my head is killing me."

"Let's go." She took his outstretched arm and snuggled against him.

Nyah floated in and out of sleep most of the drive to her house. When she opened her eyes, Mark was standing by the passenger door staring at her. She smiled at him and held his hand as she jumped down from the truck.

"Do you want to come in?" she asked.

"I do, but I won't. I can see you need to get some rest, besides, your 'father' may not approve that I've kept you out past curfew," he said through a half smile.

"I had a great time at the park."

"You can smile after all." He followed her to the porch and waited for her to open the front door. She turned to face him and he kissed her. "Sweet dreams and happy birthday."

She closed the door and leaned her face against it.

"That was a very long two hours," Graydon startled her.

"Hey dad, you shouldn't have waited up." She stopped to lean her head against his arm before heading upstairs to her bed. "Good night, I'll see you in the morning."

Eight

Nyah hated packing and coupled with the unpredictable weather in Milwaukee, it was difficult to know what clothes to take with her to the Big House.

"Not done packing yet?" he asked, walking into her room.

"This is such a waste of time, deciding what to wear shouldn't be such a challenge," she stared at five different outfits spread across the bed.

"It's only for the weekend, how many times do you plan on changing?"

"You're right," she said randomly picking three outfits and tossing them into the suitcase.

"We'd better get going if we want to beat the morning traffic," he grabbed her suitcase and left the room.

She called Mark when she was certain Graydon was downstairs, there was no answer on his cell phone but she left a message telling him she would be gone for the weekend.

They had been driving for three hours when he finally returned her call. She did not prolong the conversation because she knew Graydon was listening. He told her to call him when she got to Wisconsin; she agreed and closed the phone, knowing she did not intend to call him.

"Was that Mike?" Graydon asked.

"Mark!" She looked at him sharply, "his name is *Mark*." Her brother smiled and immediately she knew he was saying the wrong name on purpose.

"You're such a brute."

"Is it serious?"

She hesitated before answering.

"No, we just sleep together," she said, "no strings; that's just the way I like it."

He looked at her as though she was from another planet.

"That doesn't sound like you."

"Then I guess you don't know me." She rested her head on the back of the seat and gazed out the window. Truth is, he knew her too well, but she was not going to let any man, not even Mark, dethrone her because of sex.

* * * * * * * **

The Big House looked the same with the brown roof and the red bricks but Nyah had not expected it to change much in the seven months since she moved to Riverdale. Gran's party was on Saturday and she decided to come a little earlier to spend time with her grandmother alone before the others arrived and to help Pearline with last minute preparations if she needed it.

As she walked through the front door, she felt a wave of calm cover her like a blanket and realized the energy in the house was still the same. The house smelled of cinnamon and apples and she knew Gran was baking apple crumble.

"Hello, is anybody here? Gran?"

"Who's that? Nyah, is that you sugar we're in here." She walked briskly in the direction of Gran's voice who she found sitting at the kitchen table, stirring a cup of hot chocolate. The décor in the kitchen had not changed either. It still had the wooden paneling in the ceiling and the green velvet wallpaper remained untouched since granddad bought the house back in 1953.

"Gran," she hugged her grandmother's shoulders as tight as she could.

"Baby, not so hard, my bones are brittle, these tired eyes are glad to see you. Where Gray at?" Nyah continued to hug her grandmother, not wanting to let go and sensing this, Gran patted her back and she let go.

"He's getting the bags from the car. Hey Miss Marjorie," Nyah hugged the heavy-set, middle-aged woman who was in the kitchen with Gran.

"Let me look at you," she tapped Nyah's bottom. "You hungry? You're so skinny."

'I'll get something later." Nyah smiled at the woman who has lived with Gran as a nurse and housekeeper for the last ten years since granddad died. She never got married and she had no children, so she thought nothing of it when Gran asked her to move into the Big House.

"I'm a little tired from the trip. I think I'll take a nap before I eat but maybe Gray might want a plate," Nyah said as he walked into the kitchen.

"Nap?" Her grandmother laughed. "Honey, you're too young to be taking naps in the middle of the afternoon, leave that up to the old folks, like me and Marjorie."

"If you're talking about food, you don't have to ask me twice, I'm starving." Graydon walked over to Gran, gave her a hug, and a loud kiss on her cheek.

"How's my favorite grandson?" she asked, "and listen, you need to save them big wet kisses for your young lady."

Graydon laughed.

"Hey Miss M," he hugged Marjorie. "Did you change your hair?" He asked.

Marjorie patted her short black hair and blushed, clearly flattered by Graydon and his flirting.

"I got my ends trimmed yesterday," she said shyly, "you like it?" She handed him a plate of food.

"I'm feeling it," he smiled as he took the plate, "you look gorgeous."

"Graydon," Gran scolded, "stop flirtin' with the woman, you're fitting to give her heart failure." He laughed and sat down. "Tracie, your room is upstairs waiting for you."

Nyah left the kitchen anxious to see her old room. Everything was as she remembered it. She ran her fingers along the edge of the antique dresser and smiled as she thought back to the day her grandfather brought it home and how excited she was. She sat on the bed and bounced up and down, happy that the spring was still working.

It was five o'clock when she woke up, she had been sleeping for over an hour. She went downstairs and inhaled the pungent oily smell of fried fish coming from the kitchen where Marjorie was preparing dinner.

"Hey Marjorie, where's Gran?"

"I believe she's resting in her room, she says she'll be down for supper about six."

Nyah strolled over to the stove and opened every pot.

"Everything smells so yummy well, except for the fish," she said looking at Marjorie and thinking how content she seemed being the housekeeper, putting Gran's needs well ahead of her own.

"Don't worry; I'll rustle up some bean stew for you."

"You're the best," Nyah smiled. "So do you know who's coming to Gran's party tomorrow?"

Marjorie wiped her hand on her apron, opened the fridge and took out some vegetables.

"Everyone, the whole family I believe. Miss Pearline told me to make provisions for everybody."

"You can't prepare for the whole party by yourself." Nyah said, not at all surprised that her mother would give Marjorie so much work to do.

"Heavens no honey, I'm only cooking the meals for the house guests. The birthday party don't have nothing to do with me. Miss Pearline is taking care of all that." Her voice sounded relieved.

* * * * * * **

Gran's friends from her church congregation and family members started pouring into the Big House. Almost everyone who came into the kitchen brought a dish with food in it and Nyah was busy helping to arrange the food on the table. She was glad to be a part of the festivities it kept her mind occupied.

Her uncle Floyd, Gran's adopted son and his three friends were sitting around a small table playing dominoes. He has lived in the Big House with his second wife Patsy and their two young children Britney and Moses for the last three years. He picked up odd jobs here and there but mostly he just lived off Gran's generosity.

She stopped at the table; he stood up and kissed her on the cheek. His breath smelled like beer and peanuts.

"Nyah, when did you get here?" He did not wait for an answer he just pointed to the men around the table and introduced them. "Leon, Biggs, Sunny, you remember my niece Nyah." She skimmed the table with her eyes and greeted them.

"Aren't you a pretty little thing?" Biggs name was synonymous with his size. He was a clean-shaven dark skinned man with a round face and close-set eyes that he fixed on her chest. He was new; she had not seen him before.

She ignored his comment and turned her attention back to Floyd, "where's Aunt Patsy?"

He sat back down, "she won't be here this weekend; she's gone to visit her folks in Florida. Her mother is not doing too well."

That was the end of the conversation because he slammed a domino down and yelled loudly at the other players. She was on her way to the family room when she heard him say.

"Good to see you, big niece."

Graydon walked through the front door, carrying a large white box.

"Hey Sis, give me a hand," she removed the vase from the coffee table and he put it down.

"What's this?" she asked.

"No clue, mom asked me to pick it up from the caterer. Who's all here?" She told him Floyd and his friends were in the living room playing dominoes. "Count me in next game guys," he shouted.

It was about six fifteen and Gran had not come down so Nyah went upstairs to see if she was alright. Tapping softly on her door did not get a response so she called out.

"Gran, can I come in?" Without waiting for an answer, she cracked her door and stuck her head inside. Gran was sitting in a chair with her eyes closed. She tried to close the door quietly and leave.

"It's all right baby, come in."

"Sorry, I didn't mean to wake you," she said as she walked in and sat down on the floor beside Gran's chair.

"I wasn't sleeping, just resting the old eyes," she smiled and ran her fingers through the back of Nyah's hair. "Child, your hair looks like a bird's nest." She laughed and patted Nyah's shoulder. "Are you all right? You've been quiet since you got here, how is life treating you?"

"Everything is fine Gran, I really like living in Riverdale."

"I'll make your home the next stop on my tour." She shifted on the chair and motioned for Nyah to sit beside her. "I can't do as much travelling as I used to, the spirit is willing but the flesh, that's another story. I want to stay close to home so I can keep an eye on the restaurant; things just ain't going right around here these days."

"What things?" Nyah asked when she noticed that Gran had a faraway look in her eyes.

She took Nyah's hand and held on to it tightly.

"Just some things I got to take care of, you don't worry your pretty little head about it. I serve a mighty powerful God." Gran loved church. Nyah could not remember a time when her grandmother was too tired or too sick to stay away from church services, and until she turned fourteen, she *had* to go with her every week.

"Honey, when are you gettin' married? I'm not gonna live forever you know, and I'd like to see you walk down the aisle and give me some great gran babies before I move on."

"Married, don't you need a man first?"

"You mean to tell me there are no men down there in Riverdale?"

Nyah smiled and rested her head on Gran's shoulder. She wanted to tell her about Mark but she did not know where to begin, what could she say? *'Gran, I know this hot guy, we'll never get married but the sex is great.'*

"Don't you worry, God has a plan for you and the right one will come along soon enough. Listen, could you go downstairs and get Marjorie for me. I smell like an old woman, I need to take a bath."

"Gran, you haven't changed a bit." Nyah laughed and kissed her on the cheek.

"Change is overrated my love, the only thing that changes in this world, is time."

Nyah hugged her grandmother trying not to squeeze her too hard.

"I love you Gran."
"Me too baby, me too."

* * * * * * * **

Gran made her appearance at around eight and when she entered the room, the whole place lit up with her smile. Nyah could not remember the last time she saw her grandmother unhappy, not even at her grandfather's funeral.

There was enough food to feed an army and after everyone ate, some of the women were filling plastic containers with leftovers to take with them.

That night, Nyah could not sleep. Although most of her memories of the Big House were good ones, being there also stirred up feelings from the past that she wanted to remain buried. She kept thinking about having to see her mother and her sister in the morning. She was worried about her grandmother, who did not have as much spunk as she used to, even though she tried to hide it.

After lying awake and staring at the ceiling for what seemed like hours, she decided the only way she was going to get some sleep, to be fresh for the party the next day was to take a pill to help her relax, it worked and she fell asleep counting backwards from one hundred.

Nine

"Nyah, we have to get going, I need your help to put some finishing touches on the hall," Pearline spoke from the behind the closed door.

"What time is it?" she asked, having a hard time keeping her eyes open.

"It's almost 9:30 and I don't think it's prudent for you to sleep the day away knowing the party starts at 7 o'clock. Her mother always made everything seem so urgent, a trait Nyah found very irritating.

She dragged her body out of the bed, took a shower and got dressed. On her way downstairs, she stuck her head inside Gran's room to say 'happy birthday' but she was still asleep. By the time Nyah got downstairs Pearline had already gone to the hall, and left instructions for Graydon to take Nyah there as soon as possible.

"It's about time you got here, we still have a lot of work to do," was how she greeted Nyah when she walked into the hall. She did not say a word she just listened while Pearline spewed out orders. "The helium tanks are over there," she said pointing to two rusty green tanks on the other side of the room. "You can start by blowing up the silver balloons." Nyah got right to work and by one o'clock, they had most of the balloons tied to the back of chairs.

"Wow, this place looks great."

Pamela breezed into the room looking like a fashion model right down to the Gucci bag hanging from her arm. Her half sister was never a part of the execution committee at family events; she preferred not to get her manicured nails dirty. She worked as a Marketing executive for one of the largest ad agencies in New York and was opposed to hard work. She had her first daughter at sixteen, fourteen years ago, for a boy in her calculus class. His parents conveniently moved away when they found out she was pregnant. She married Sean, the father of her three boys Byron, Shane and Sean Jr seven years ago. They were not close and the gap between them widened when Nyah was shipped off to live with Gran. Until she showed up, Nyah wondered if she was going to make an appearance at Gran's party.

Not far behind, was her daughter Nikki dressed in jeans and a t-shirt; talking on the cell phone. She greeted Nyah before Pamela did.

"Auntie Nyah," she rushed over to Nyah and gave her a big hug.

"Hey Nikki,"

"Auntie, I haven't seen you in forever, where have you been? I've missed you."

"Hello Nyah, how are you?" Pamela finally acknowledged her. "It's nice to see you."

"Hi Pam, nice to see you too." They exchanged an awkward hug and Pamela announced she had to go to the Big House to unpack and settle in. They continued decorating the hall until around two-thirty when Pearline announced that she had to go to the hairdresser.

"Do you want to come with me? Sasha works wonders with my hair. She could probably do something with yours." Pearline never approved of the way Nyah wore her hair. She thought it looked frizzy and unkempt. Pearline took some of Nyah's hair and rolled it between her fingers. "You have such soft hair, why don't you straighten it instead of wearing it so curly all the time."

"I like my curls," Nyah defended. "They reflect who I am as a black woman."

Her mother laughed.

"You are hardly black, my dear," she said. "I'm merely suggesting that you change your hair style, you look like a child."

"And I guess that's not a good memory for you?" Nyah said sarcastically. Her mother stared at her and sighed heavily.

"Know what, just forget I said anything. Do you need a ride back to the house?" she asked.

"I think Gray is coming to get me soon. I'll meet you there." Nyah said and continued working.

"As you wish." Pearline's tone was void of emotion.

Nyah tried to stay focused on the one good reason she had for being in Wisconsin and hoped that it was enough to help her tolerate being around her mother and sister for the next twenty-four hours. She called Gray to pick her up and by the time, they got back to the Big House she was way past irritated.

"You're not saying much," Graydon commented.

"I'm tired, that's all." She did not want to tell him about the conversation with their mother. He had gone through the same scrutiny before he cut off his dreads. She was certain that it would seem trivial to him anyway.

There was a big purple banner across the entrance of the dining room that read 'Happy 75th Birthday Gran'. The house was full of family and Pearline's friends whom she invited to Gran's party. Most of them were from out of town and she invited them to stay at Gran's house that night after the party. Marjorie was busy trying to keep up with all the lunch demands that Pearline placed on her.

There were family members there that Nyah had not seen since the family reunion three Christmases ago. Uncle Junior had everyone in stitches. He was not her 'real' uncle but he deemed himself the family comedian and he kept everyone entertained. Being around her aunts, uncles and cousins reminded her how important family was to her and she knew she would miss them when the weekend was over.

Gran limped down the stairs and her smile turn to a frown when she saw all the people in her house. Pearline was standing by the fireplace talking and laughing with Pamela and Uncle Floyd. Nyah thought her hair looked the same as it did before she went to the hairdresser, pulled back in a bun.

"Pearl, you know I don't want all these people staying in my house. I appreciate the party but I appreciate my peace and quiet more." The room got quiet.

"Mom, it's only for one night."

"One night's too long; you should've arranged a hotel room for them."

Pearline ignored Gran and continued talking to Pamela. The 4300 square feet house was big enough to fit everyone but Gran was not concerned about the space.

"You hearing me Pearl?"

"Mom, we'll talk about this later. I'm not going to have this discussion with you now." Pearline was agitated.

"I don't care what you have to say, the discussion is over. I don't want these people sitting up in my house eating up all my food and using off the soft toilet paper." Her last few words trailed off as she disappeared into the kitchen. Nyah followed her and put on the kettle to make a cup of tea.

Pearline pushed the door so hard when she entered the kitchen it banged against the wall. Pamela was right behind her.

"What the hell is your problem mom?" Gran turned around and glared at her.

"Since when is it all right to cuss out your mother? You told me you were having a birthday party for me, you didn't say nothing about having my house full of strangers."

Pamela defended Pearline.

"Grandma, these people are family and friends of the family, you've known them for years. They have come all this way to celebrate your birthday with you. The least you can do is let them stay here for one night."

"Are you gonna clean up after them? I didn't think so. Marjorie ain't nobody's slave. They ain't staying here and that's final. The only two people I want here is my grandbabies Gray and Nyah."

"What about Nikki and me?" Pamela sounded hurt.

"What, you don't have enough money to book a hotel room?" she asked Pamela. "You know you don't like staying in this old house." Gran waved her hand to dismiss the conversation. "You can stay if you ain't got no place else to go." Gran started to leave the kitchen but turned around and smiled. "Now, it's my birthday and I got a party to get ready for. Nyah, come give me a hand baby."

As they left the kitchen, Nyah heard her mother say, "That woman can be so infuriating."

"Don't worry about her mom, she's old." Nyah knew if Gran heard Pamela comment, she would have retorted.

As they walked up the stairs, Gran started chuckling. When they closed her bedroom door, she laughed.

"Share the joke Gran."

"I bet those two think I'm old and senile, well I've got a few surprises waiting for them."

Marjorie came into the room.

"Miss Matty, I can help you get dressed. Miss Nyah needs to go get herself together. It's four thirty."

****

By the time Nyah arrived at the hall it was just past 7:30. They left the house late because Gran made a big fuss about not wanting to ride in the limousine. She thought the seats were too small and full of germs.

The hall looked wonderful; the caterers enhanced what they had done earlier in the day. Blue and silver balloons hung everywhere and the crystal chandeliers softened the lighting in the room. There were seven tables each with ten chairs and each table had a clear, round vase that was half-filled with water and tiny candles floating on water lilies.

Gran sat at a table with her three children and their spouses. Pearline sat beside an older man whom Nyah had not seen before, the younger cousins sat at a table close to the front of the room and the older cousins were at the back.

Nyah sat a table with Graydon, his date Cecelia, Pamela, Debbie and Derrick who were friends of Pamela, along with two more couples who were mom's friends. Gran's friends from her church occupied the other three tables.

Uncle Richard, Gran's adopted son, an ordained minister, began with an opening prayer and his wife Gail sang a beautiful song while their son Deon accompanied her on the piano. Pearline planned a seven-course meal and while everyone ate, people paid tribute to Gran. In one corner of the room, presents piled high on two tables. Nyah wondered how they were going to get them back to the Big House.

Mom gave a short speech along with Gran's two sons, she did not include Nyah's name on the list of family speakers but when it was time to open the floor Nyah took the opportunity to say something.

"Happy birthday Gran, you may be older but I believe you are the wisest and most striking woman I know. I hope to embody your sense of self-appreciation and agency when I get to be your age. You are my inspiration and I love you."

Uncle Junior knocked his glass first.

"Here, here, whatever you said, I second it." A few others joined by raising their glasses to toast Gran.

After the formalities were over the dancing began and Nyah danced with Graydon first. When the song ended, she walked out into the foyer to get away from the heat that was starting to build up in the room.

"You've always had a way with words." The voice behind her halted her and the hair on the back of her arms stood up.

"What are you doing here Sean?"

"My wife's inside, and I came to wish your precious grandmother happy birthday, who knew she'd live so long," he sneered.

"You're such an asshole, don't let me stop you." Nyah turned to walk away but he reached out, grabbed her arm, and began caressing it with his thumb.

"Get your hands off me," she said between clenched teeth. He raised both his hands in the air and took a step back. "Don't you ever touch me again or so help me God." Nyah's pulse raced as she walked towards the entrance of the building.

"You still feel good, as sexy as ever," she picked up her pace. When she reached the parking lot, she tried to open Graydon's car but all the doors were locked. She needed to get the keys but did not want to go back inside and risk running into Sean again. She paced frantically up and down, trying to shake off his touch and his words that were still ringing in her ear. Her stomach began to churn and without warning, she threw up everything she ate. She crouched down beside the car; her body was shaking uncontrollably. Until now, all thoughts of him were dead and buried. Sean was the last person she wanted to see or expected to see at her grandmother's party, and it was clear by her reaction that she could not stand being in the same place with him. She closed her eyes and began to breathe deeply; she needed to calm her nerves before going back to the hall.

"What's going on, are you all right?" She recognized Graydon's voice but she did not look up at him.

"Nothing," she said drying her eyes with the back of her hand, "I'm good, go back inside." She did not have to see his face to know he was not convinced that she was okay. "Gray, I'm good," she looked up at him and tried to smile.

"Mark's here."

"What?" Nyah leapt to her feet and dusted off the back of her dress, "what's he doing here?"

"He's inside, why don't you ask him. He came looking for you and when we couldn't find you, Sean said you ran out here."

Seeing the vomit on the ground behind her, Graydon opened his car and gave her a hand towel. Nyah wiped her mouth and handed it back to him.

"Are you sure, you're okay?" he asked rubbing her back.

"Gray, you worry too much, my stomach is just upset, probably from something I ate." She smiled at him one last time to reassure him and spotted Mark standing at the door dressed in a suit without the tie. She straightened her blue, pinstripe wrap-dress and ran her fingers through her curls, trying to regain her composure. She approached him, still feeling shaky from her encounter with Sean and managed a smile.

"Mark, this is a surprise, what are you doing here?" Her heart melted in her chest when she got close enough to see how handsome he looked.

"Listen, I'll catch up with you later man," Graydon said and left them alone.

"Thanks man," he said to Graydon and turned his attention back to Nyah. "You didn't call me."

"I know, and I'm sorry about that. It's just been..." He did not allow her to finish her sentence.

"I missed you," he said.

"You did?" She found that hard to believe, but was happy to see him anyway, "I've only been gone a couple of days."

"You look beautiful," he said and his eyes left hers, trailed down her body, lingered at her breasts and settled on her lips, "nice dress," he opened his arms and she stepped into his embrace, his body was hard and strong, she did not want him to let her go.

"Oh I'm sorry," Nikki, cleared her throat, "I didn't mean to interrupt. Auntie, they're waiting for you inside."

"What for?" she asked and took a step back from Mark.

"I think it's time to cut the cake and Gran doesn't want to cut the cake without you, but if you're busy, I'll tell them to go ahead." Nikki glanced at Mark when she said that.

"Mark, this is my niece, Nikki." They shook hands.

"I'll be right there." Nyah told her and motioned for her to leave. "Do you want to go inside?"

"That's your call."

"My whole family is in there."

"Sounds scary," he said light-heartedly burying his hands in his pocket.

"Not really," she scratched her forehead, "I just don't want them to get the wrong impression about you, about us..." Nyah could not hide how nervous she was.

He raised her chin so she could look into his eyes instead of on the ground and was grateful that he did not try to kiss her, she still had the taste of puke in her mouth.

"Relax, I'm cool with whatever they want to think, but if you're not, I can wait for you here."

Nyah stared absentmindedly towards the hall; searching her thoughts for a solution. She knew she meant nothing to him and was not comfortable deceiving her family into thinking otherwise.

"Let's go," she said, pulling him by the arm. "You came all this way..." She took a deep breath, "I'm sure it'll be fine." They stopped just outside the door.

"Your grandmother is waiting for you to cut the cake." He smiled, opened the door for her and held her hand as they walked towards the front of the room. She tried to pull away, but he would not let her.

"Come help me cut the cake baby." Nyah joined the other seven family members who were waiting for her to cut the cake. "On three, one, two, three," there was a noisy cheer and everyone cut a part of the four-layer cake, "now get your spoons ready." It was a tradition in the family, at birthdays, weddings, and anniversaries, to feed the person to the right with cake. Nyah fed her aunt Gail at the same time she got her piece from Nikki, who completely missed her mouth. Laughter erupted because of the mess everyone made trying to feed each other without looking, one of the silly family traditions that Nyah loved.

Ten

The caterers stopped serving dinner at 10:30, shortly after Mark arrived and the band began to play *One O'clock Jump,* one of Gran's favorite songs since she was a young girl growing up in Belgium. Most of her friends got up and started to dance, throwing their hands in the air and moving their hips from side to side. Their energy was infectious and a few of the younger cousins joined in on the fun. The band continued to play Count Basie music for the next half hour. Then they switched to Michael Jacksons' *'Rock with you'* and Chaka Khan's *'Ain't Nobody'* for the younger crowd that had replaced Gran and her friends on the dance floor. Graydon walked Mark through the room introducing him as her boyfriend to everyone. Although he took it in stride, it made Nyah very uncomfortable.

"I'm sorry about all that," she said when he joined her at the punch table. "I hope it wasn't too weird for you."

"You need to relax, let's dance." The song ended before they had a chance to reach the dance floor and Gran motioned for them to come to her table. He rested his palm on the small of her back as they strolled over to the table, and Gran smiled, as they got closer.

"Who is this handsome young man hugging on my granbaby?"

"Gran, this is Mark," Nyah said.

"Pleased to meet you, Mark," she opened her arms for a hug, "Nyah didn't tell us you were coming." Mark reached down and hugged her tenderly. "Hmmm, you got some strong arms there to wrap around my granbaby," she said and squeezed his bicep. He chuckled, flexed it for her and she cheered.

Embarrassed, Nyah whispered, "Gran, Mark and I are just friends."

"Friends, I see. I hope he don't look at all his *friends* the way he look at you," she said loud enough for those close by to hear accompanied by a hearty laugh.

"I'm Pamela, Nyah's older sister and this is my husband Sean." Nyah kept her head straight to avoid looking at Sean, who she could feel staring at her intently.

"What's up," Mark shook Sean's hand and put his arm around Nyah's waist. She ran her fingers through her hair and began to chew on her bottom lip. The room was getting hot and she knew if she did not move away from him, she would be sick again. Pamela waved to a couple across the room and she breathed a sigh of relief when she dragged Sean with her to greet them.

"Mark, could you get an old lady some punch dear?" He was barely out of earshot when Gran looked at Nyah, "what was that about?"

"What Gran?" Nyah knew exactly what she meant but she did not want to get into it.

"I saw your reaction when Pam and Sean were standing here; you looked like you had peppers in your drawers."

"Gran, it was nothing, there was nothing to see." Nyah said hoping Gran would leave the subject alone.

"Nothing?" Gran didn't believe her, "don't insult me by lying to me like that, I know somethin' happened between you and that devil Sean, and you need to come clean about that or you'll always be running and never finding any peace." Nyah could feel the life energy flowing from her body. She had spent the last seven years steeling her heart from the pain and in one night, her foundation was starting to crack. She could feel the tears welling up in the back of her eyes and a lump growing in her throat.

"Gran…" she began.

"Thanks Mark." Gran looked away from her, took the drink from Mark and sipped it thoughtfully. "You two young people should go dance."

"I second that," Mark said. Nyah shifted her eyes from her grandmother to look at Mark. She smiled sweetly and took his hands and as they walked towards the dance floor for the second time that night, this time, Pearline stopped her.

"Nyah, I would like you to meet Spencer, a good friend of mine. This is my youngest daughter Nyah." They shook hands but he squeezed it so hard she flinched. Mark must have seen what transpired because he extended his hand to Spencer, introduced himself then gently reached for her hand and massaged it. She knew that even if he was pretending, she welcomed his attentiveness. Pearline waited for her to introduce Mark and when she did not, he introduced himself.

"So Mark, what kind of work do you do?" Pearline took a step closer to him.

"I'm a producer," he said.

"Oh, that must be very interesting work." Pearline's voice was softer than normal and Nyah wondered what she was up to.

"I think I'm going to get some fruit punch," Nyah said.

"I'll get it," Mark offered but she stopped him.

"No, it's fine, I'll go." As she walked to the punch table, Nyah rubbed her temple with the tip of her fingers. She wanted to take a pill but she knew it would make her groggy.

"Where ever did you find him, he's looks yummy, I love the muscles," Pamela beamed.

"The last time I checked, you were a married woman and your husband is standing right over there." Nyah said annoyed at the way her sister stared at Mark. She knew Mark was not officially hers, but Pamela did not know that.

"I'm married, I'm not dead. Is it serious between you guys?"

"That's none of your business," Nyah said.

"I guess it's not," she said and went to join Pearline and Spencer to get a closer look at Mark.

Nyah decided to forego the punch and headed towards Gran's table and as she approached it, Graydon jumped ahead of her.

"Hey Gran, wanna dance?" Graydon asked, grinning.

"I will, if you hold me up," he took her hand and led her to the dance floor.

The DJ started playing one of Nyah's favorite songs and she looked around to see if Mark was still talking to her mother but he was not there. She searched the room trying to find him.

"Looking for me?" Mark was standing behind her.

"I thought maybe you'd had enough," she turned to face him.

"It's not so bad." He took her hand, "may I have this dance?" She hesitated, waiting for someone else to come along.

"You may."

He drew her close and they began dancing in the spot where they were standing.

"What were you and my mother talking about for so long?" she asked, trying to keep her voice light.

He pulled her closer to him.

"Nothing."

She pushed her arms through his and caressed his back under his jacket, rested her head on his chest, inhaled the musky sent of his cologne and listened to the melodic rhythm of his heart.

He wrapped both arms around her in a tight embrace and she smiled when he began to sing the lyrics to the song as they danced. *'Play another slow jam, this time make it sweet, a slow jam for my baby and for me, ooooh'.*

The moment was magical and even though she knew it was not real, she closed her eyes and pretended that it was.

Gran was ready to go home at around eleven thirty; she was determined not to ride in the limousine, so she left with Uncle Richard. Floyd had to use his friend Biggs's courier truck to take all her presents home. Nyah, Graydon and Mark helped to clean up the hall and by 12:30, they were on their way back to the Big House.

Most of the out of town family members were there playing dominoes, socializing; trying to keep the party alive. Gran changed out of her party clothes into slacks, a sweater and the signature purple headband she used to keep her wig from falling off. She was sitting in her favorite chair chatting with some of her friends about the condition of the world and the good old days when Nyah and Mark entered the house.

"Do you want anything to drink?" Nyah asked him.

"Naw, I'm good," he said.

"Mark, come in, make yourself at home." Gran graciously extended an invitation to him and he accepted. "Nyah baby, make us old ladies a cup of tea. I don't know where Marjorie has got to." Nyah put a big pot of water on to fill three large teapots then she went upstairs to wash off her makeup and brush her teeth before serving the tea to Gran and her friends. Mark was playing cards with three of her cousins and she watched them play for a while before taking her tea into the den for some peace and quiet. She lowered the back of the futon, promising to take a short rest.

When Nyah opened her eyes, the house was quiet and the only light in the room came from the street. Mark was stretched out on his back next to her snoring softly. He had removed his shirt but he still had his pants on. She inched her body closer to him and buried her face in his side. She gently rubbed the fine hairs on his chest and brushed her fingers against is exposed nipple.

He moaned softly, covered her hand with his own and began playing with her fingers. She held her breath when he pulled her to lie flat on top of him. She wiggled seductively and rubbed the tiny hairs growing on his head. His hands followed a trail down her back, inched up her dress and cupped her bottom, pressing her against his mounting desire. He kissed the corners of her mouth before covering her lips with his. He rolled her onto her back; took his time pulling the strings that were holding her dress together and removed her bra. She arched her body to meet his lips as they closed over her bare nipple and moaned when his palm gently rubbed the other one. Still feasting on her breasts with his tongue, his hand travelled down her body and parted her legs. He caressed her thighs, stroking them inside and out, teasing her, before his fingers found a resting place inside her lace underwear. Nyah was lost in the moment and he silenced her increasingly loud moans by covering her mouth with his.

"You'll wake up the whole house," he whispered. It was then Nyah remembered where she was.

"We can't do this here," she said, gently pulling away from him, she did not get far, he was aroused and she knew he wanted to finish what she started.

He continued caressing her body, "why not?"

"This is Gran's house; I can't, I'm sorry." She pressed against his chest to push him away and wrapped her dress around her exposed body, "you need to put your shirt on." When he did not move she reached up and touched the side of his face, "I'll make it up to you." He kissed her and rolled over on his back. He reluctantly stood up after a few minutes had passed.

"Where are you going?" she asked.

"You know what you do to me, I'll find somewhere else to sleep," he looked at her with intense longing, "if I can." He rubbed his head and quietly left the room.

When she woke up sunlight was streaming through the blinds. She tucked her bra under her arm and walked into the living room, to see people sleeping everywhere. She looked around for Mark and when she could not find him, she went upstairs to shower and change her clothes. She peeked in on her grandmother who was sound asleep.

"Good morning Miss Nyah," Marjorie greeted her and handed her a cup to pour tea from the teapot as she entered the kitchen. "I'll have breakfast ready in a jiffy."

"Morning Marjorie." The back door opened and Graydon and Mark walked in carrying two big boxes.

"Miss Marjorie, don't worry about breakfast," Graydon said, "we've got breakfast covered; there's donuts, muffins, bagels and coffee, enough for everyone."

"That's sweet boys, I started making breakfast already, but you know you can never have enough to eat, especially with black folks around."

Graydon laughed.

"You know that's right," he agreed, carrying one of the boxes into the dining room.

Mark had changed into a light blue tracksuit and Nyah held her breath as he walked towards her.

"Did you sleep okay?" he asked.

"Did you? I'm sorry about last night."

"I wanted to take you upstairs but I didn't know which room was yours," he whispered, Nyah smiled.

He stretched and she heard the bones in his neck crack.

"Where did you sleep?"

"In the den," he said.

"I didn't hear you come back in."

"You couldn't hear a bomb drop; you were snoring so loudly."

She playfully pushed him, "I don't snore."

He chuckled, "that's what you think."

Graydon returned to the kitchen.

"People are starting to stir out there; I'll help you set up Miss M."

The four of them spread the food out on the table for everyone to serve themselves.

By one o'clock, Gran was ready to kick everyone out.

Mark took Nyah's bags to the car after saying goodbye to Gran and she stood on the front porch with her grandmother, already missing her.

"That one is a keeper," she said pointing at Mark. "Remember what I said honey, the truth will always set you free." She reached up and moved a lock of hair from Nyah's forehead. "I love you baby."

"I love you too Gran," Nyah smiled and hugged her grandmother.

Eleven

Nyah nestled her body into the front seat of the car and kicked off her shoes. She was exhausted, mind and body. The trip to the Big House had taken more from her than she had planned to give. The party, her family, seeing Sean, even having Mark there caused her to expend more mental energy than she wanted to. She rested her head on the back of the seat, facing Mark, grateful that he decided to drive back to Riverdale with her.

Graydon accepted an impromptu interview in New York and could not drive back with her so when Mark offered to forfeit his return plane ticket to be her personal chauffeur she jumped on it.

The music penetrated Nyah's conscious mind before she opened her eyes and realized she had been sleeping for a little over two hours. Sitting upright, she stretched her back, using her fingers to massage a stiff muscle at the nape of her neck. She glanced at Mark who was in his own zone, bobbing his head, tapping the steering wheel, enjoying the music. She wanted to touch him, to reach across the seat and kiss him. Instead, she turned away and stared out the window.

"Where are we?"

He lowered the volume on the stereo reached across the seat and began caressing her thigh.

"We passed through Chicago about ten minutes ago."

"Do you want me to drive?"

"Naw, I'm good." She smiled and tentatively covered his hand with her own.

"It was a nice surprise having you at Gran's party. Did you have a good time?"

"It was nice," he said.

"I know my family can be a little over the top."

"They're cool," he said, "Uncle Junior was a riot."

She laughed and shook her head, "there's no help for him; he's out of control."

"What's the deal with you and your sister?"

"What do you mean?" Nyah's guard went up.

"I don't know, I just sensed some tension between you, and her husband kept watching you all night."

"I can't speak to what you were sensing, but like all families, we have our ups and down," she said curtly.

"Oh, so it's like that, I'll leave it alone." She shifted in the seat and turned her body away from him, sending him the clear message that he had touched on something that she was not willing to talk about.

Unaware that she had dozed off again, the next time she opened her eyes Mark had exited the freeway and was driving down her street. They had been driving for six hours and although the Mercedes was roomy, her whole body was stiff. He pulled into her driveway and left the car running.

"I need to make a quick stop, mind if I borrow your car? My truck is at the airport." She looked at him and rolled her eyes, remembering what happened the last time she gave him her car.

"Sure, but you don't have to ask me, it's your car." He jumped out and raced around to open the door for her.

"And you don't have to do that," she protested, "I can open my own door."

He kissed her, got in the car and sped off without saying where he was going.

Nyah was glad to be home. Even though she enjoyed seeing her beloved grandmother, she, like Dorothy, in the Wizard of Oz felt there was no place like home. She needed a cup of tea so she filled the kettle with water and set it to boil then she checked her answering machine and had fifteen messages waiting. There were two messages from her Women's group, three messages from Sheila, two from telemarketers and eight from Gabby. Everyone will have to wait another day she decided, a hot bath and her bed were calling.

Tea in hand, she was half way up the stairs when the doorbell rang.

"Hey Nyah," Gabby pushed past her into the foyer, "I have been trying to reach you all weekend."

"I just walked through the door and I got the *eight* messages you left on my machine, what's the urgency?" Nyah led the way into the living room.

"No urgency, I wanted us to touch base before school started in a couple of weeks to plan for the New Year, I didn't know you went away?"

"Yes, for a couple of days." Nyah sensed that Gabby was anxious. "Are you all right?"

"Have you got anything stronger than soy milk to drink?" Nyah shook her head and Gabby started pacing back and forth.

"Gabby, what's the matter?"

"I probably shouldn't be telling you this," she paused briefly and then continued. "A few months ago I introduced Mark to a friend of mine, Simone; you met her at the Hakka restaurant. Anyway, she came to my house last night in tears; she thinks that he's cheating on her."

Nyah went into the kitchen and Gabby followed her. "Why are you telling me this, shouldn't you be having this conversation with Mark?"

"I feel responsible; after all, I introduced them. I need you to be honest with me, are you sleeping with Mark?"

"I don't have to answer that," Nyah said defensively.

"You're right," Gabby said smiling, "I don't see you as that kind of person anyway." Nyah wondered what she meant but did not bother to ask her. "I've known Mark for a long time, he's cool but he's wild. I thought that introducing him to Simone would help tame him a little bit because she's definitely his type," she laughed, "but I guess it's hard for a leopard to change his spots."

"This is really none of my business Gabby," Nyah said walking back towards the foyer, hoping she would take a hint and leave.

"So, are you seeing anyone?"

Nyah knew that she was still fishing for information.

"I've got a lot on my plate right now, who has time to date?"

"I'm sure you have to beat men off with a stick, as gorgeous as you are."

"It's getting late and I'm exhausted," Nyah opened the front door, "there's a hot bath upstairs calling my name."

"Okay, we'll catch up later," Gabby stood in front of Nyah and touched her arm, "I'm sorry Ny, you're my friend and I wouldn't want to see you get hurt."

"I appreciate your concern Gabby, but there's no need for it."

Gabby walked through the door.

"Have a good night," she said before she walked to her car and drove away.

Nyah sat on the sofa and sipped her lukewarm tea. Her thoughts were looping; processing over and over the conversation she had with Gabby. She knew that what she had with Mark was not worth writing home about. At best, she was his 'good time girl' until the next woman came along. Being fully aware of how negative and unbecoming that sounded, she knew it would probably end sooner than later, but she wanted to enjoy it while it lasted.

She dragged her body upstairs and set a bath, the kink in her neck had spread to her shoulders. She lit all the scented candles that were around the large soaker tub, and poured lavender oil and bubble bath under the running water. Turning on the CD player, she dimmed the lights, undressed, and slowly submerged her tired limbs into the hot water. The heat penetrated every part of her body, and she allowed her arms and legs to float lifelessly in the water. She closed her eyes, emptied her mind and relaxed.

A few minutes passed before Nyah became aware of Mark's presence at the entrance of the bathroom.

"I hope you don't mind, I used your key to let myself in."

She opened her eyes and saw him leaning, arms folded, against the doorframe. He did not move, he just stood there and watched her.

"Want some company?"

"If you have to ask, then maybe not."

He took off his clothes and threw them on the counter by the sink. In three strides, he stood over the tub.

"Careful, the water's hot," she said and watched him squirm as he stepped in. He sat between her legs and leaned back, using her breasts as a pillow.

"The things you women do," his voice almost a whisper.

"Are you saying men don't take baths?"

"Not like this," he groaned and closed his eyes.
She poured body wash on the loofah sponge and rubbed it on his shoulders then she replaced the sponge with her hands and spread the bubbles across his chest and down his arms.

"I could get used to this," he said pressing his back into her breast.

"Can I ask you a question?"

"Anything."

"Is your relationship with Simone serious?"

"Who's Simone?" Nyah stopped washing his chest and when he smiled, she realized he was joking. The water made waves as he turned to face her. He ran his hands along both her legs and pulled her closer to him.

"No."

"What is it then?"

"Why do you want to know?"

He picked her up and she held her breath as he slowly lowered her so that their bodies joined. He cupped her breasts with both hands, raised them to his lips, and gently teased them with his tongue.

She wrapped her arms around his neck as he kissed her, pressing hard against her lips, prying them apart and taking her tongue into his mouth. He moaned deep in his throat and she held herself back, watching his face, matching his rhythm, waiting for him to peak and when he did he let out a guttural growl and his body jerked splashing water all over the floor. She clung to him and squeezed her legs together, not willing to miss her climactic moment that shook her whole body and caused her toes to tingle. She opened her eyes to find him watching her.

He brushed his lips against hers.

"If I were in a relationship, I wouldn't be here," he said.

Twelve

Nyah massaged her temples, her eyes were sore from staring at the computer screen continuously for three hours but she had to finish her first term report cards. It had been three months since the beginning of the school year and all the teachers were feeling the pressure to get the marks in.

The intercom interrupted her thoughts.

"Nyah, phone call on line 2 and Mrs. Brown would like to see you in her office."

"Thanks Julie," Nyah pressed the button on the phone.

"Hey Auntie," Nikki's voice sounded low almost like she was whispering.

"Hi Nik, are you all right?"

"Auntie, I have something to ask you, please say yes."

"Okay, what is it?"

"Can I come stay with you for a couple of months?"

"Does your mom know you want to leave?"

"I can go to school there; mom said it would be okay with her if it was okay with you. So can I?"

"You know you can stay with me any time."

Nikki sighed heavily.

"Yeahhh, I'll call you next week, thanks Auntie."

She did not have time to process the phone call as she walked to the office; she was more concerned with her upcoming evaluation.

"You wanted to see me Natalie."

"Yes Nyah, come in, have a seat," she said, and her facial expression did not give Nyah a clue what to expect.

"How are you doing?" she asked politely. Nyah smiled and said she was fine. "Well, the reason I called you in here is to discuss your work performance in the last six months, how do you feel about everything so far?" Nyah candidly highlighted strengths, weaknesses, and discussed openly the areas she felt she needed to improve.

"What can I say, you've exceeded my expectations, you have successfully completed your probationary period, here's a copy of your 2-year contract, everything should be in order as we discussed previously." Nyah maintained her outward composure but could hardly contain her excitement on the inside. She quickly skimmed through the contract and signed it right away.

"Congratulations Nyah, and keep up the good work." They shook hands and Nyah left the office smiling.

* * * * * * * **

Nyah called Mark, to share the good news with him but he did not answer his cell so she left a message and he called back half an hour later. She suggested they go to dinner to celebrate; her treat, and he said they would when he returned to town at the end of the week. She did not know he was away; he had not bothered to tell her. When Gabby called and asked if she wanted to go out for drinks and a movie with Sage and Brenda, she jumped on it, welcoming the distraction.

"All men are dogs," exclaimed Brenda as she sat down and took a sip of her drink.

"What about that guy you were just talking to by the bar." Gabby asked.

"That loser, he's got five kids and I bet he doesn't support any of them," her frustration was mounting.

"Well," Sage said, "I find that you get out of a man exactly what you put into him, if you give him love, that's exactly what you'll get."

"What world do you live in Sage?" Brenda asked sarcastically and laughed. "Maybe it's no problem for light-skinned almost white sisters like you three, but for a sweet, dark chocolate sister like me, the pickings are very slim, we don't have as many options as you all do."

"That's ridiculous, color has nothing to do with love," Sage said, "it's your attitude that keeps you single."

"Bullshit, tell that to all our dark-skinned sisters who watch as the brothers pass over them to reach for the light or the white women." Brenda's voice was getting louder. "So you can kiss my attitude Sage Livingston."

Nyah hated conversations about color. She was tired of the *'black get back, white you're alright'* chains that, after so many decades, continued to enslave minds and reinforce the dividing lines between her sisters.

"I agree with Sage," Nyah said, "I don't think men choose to be with women based on color alone. I believe that women are women, regardless of the shade of their skin. There are those who have chosen to buy into varying modes of thought on the issue of color privilege but I've never entertained the belief I was treated differently or better than you or any other woman because my complexion is a shade lighter, why is that even important?"

"A shade lighter?" Brenda snickered, "girl you're practically white, the only reason we see the hint of black in you is because of the way you wear your hair, straighten that and you could pass," she said with a lot of conviction.

"Well I think this issue is so tired," Sage said, "I'm sick of unhappy sisters trying to take their shit out on me. I didn't ask to be born this way; they all need to get a life and that includes you Brenda."

"I know some great black men who date all shades of women, I've been around David for nine years and I have heard him and his friends talk about women. For most men, they say the attraction is seventy percent attitude."

"Yeah and a 100% light skin," Brenda mumbled under her breath. "David's got some fine friends can't you hook a sister up?"

"Brenda, I don't know why you're talking all this trash, you are exquisite. You dress well, you make good money," said Gabby, "I see you with fine men all the time. What are you complaining about?"

"The man she wants," Sage laughed, "does not want her, maybe you're too dark."

"Don't hate," Brenda said, "he's just playing right now, but he'll come around."

"You're not talking about Mark Allen are you?" Nyah's heart skipped a beat when Sage mentioned his name, "he doesn't even know you exist. You know Mark loves the ladies and they love him, the day he settles down, is the day I'll shave my head."

"That could be sooner than you think, so you'd better get the razor ready," Gabby said, looking at Nyah.

Nyah excused herself from the table, went the washroom and Gabby followed her.

"Everything okay Nyah?"

"Sure," she said fixing her hair, "why do you keep asking me that?"

"I saw your reaction when Sage mentioned Mark's name." Gabby came closer to her and touched her back.

Nyah looked at her sternly. "You're seeing things that aren't there."

"What' the big secret Ny?" she asked.

"There's no secret. If you have something you want to say to me, then say it, otherwise, back off. Okay?"

"I'm sorry, I won't say another word," she said and pretended to zip her lips.

When they returned to the table, the conversation had changed to something lighter and Nyah was relieved about that.

"We should go," Gabby seemed agitated, "I want us to get good seats at the movies."

Thirteen

The train station was packed with people who were waiting, coming or going. As Nyah waited behind the gate for Nikki's train to come to a complete stop, a cold breeze blew from the direction of the river and the sun, with all its shining glory did nothing to take the biting cold edge off before it passed through her coat causing her to shiver. She spotted Nikki wearing jeans and a red sweater underneath a leather jacket as she stepped off the train and waved frantically to catch her attention.

"Auntie, you're way too short," she said with a smile, "it's hard to spot you in a crowd."

"Ha ha, you're funny," Nyah gave her niece a big hug.

"Where are your hat and your scarf? It's freezing out here," Nyah tried to zip up her jacket but she resisted.

"I swear auntie, sometimes you act like an old woman, don't forget, you're only twelve years older than me and I know how to take care of myself."

"Okay," Nyah said backing off, "just remember you said that when you catch a cold and you need some tender love and care," she said lightheartedly, "let's get your bags."

"This is it," Nikki said pointing to the overnight bag she carried on her shoulder.

"This is all the clothes you brought with you for two months?"

"Mom gave me some money, I'll get more clothes if I need to," she said plainly.

"Wow, this place is nice," Nikki said looking out the window at the water as they drove along the riverside.

"I like it," Nyah said, "and I think you will too."

When they walked through the front door, Nikki dropped her overnight bag and asked to see the rest of the house. The last stop was the guest room where she would be staying and even though she acted excited, Nyah sensed that she was sad.

"Hey, is everything okay?"

Nikki hugged her, "everything is great."

Nyah registered her in school right away, and before long, they fell into a comfortable routine. After about three weeks, Nyah began to notice changes in Nikki's behavior. She seemed withdrawn, and unresponsive, locking herself in her room for hours at a time after she came home from school. They hardly spent any time together and she shot down Nyah's suggestions to participate in fun extracurricular activities at her school.

"Hey," Nyah caught up with her one Saturday on her way from the kitchen carrying a handful of grapes, "what do you feel like doing today?"

"I don't know," she said, "there's not much to do around here."

"That's not true, we could go shopping at the mall or catch a movie, whatever you want to do and we don't have to stay in Riverdale, we could go to Detroit."

"I think I'll pass, I'm not feeling too hot."

"What's going on Nikki? It's not like you to pass up shopping."

"Everything is fine Auntie; I'll be in my room."

Nyah could not shake the feeling that something was not right but she did not want to press Nikki about it so she called Pamela's cell and left a message on her voicemail.

"Hey Pam, can you give me a call when you get this message, I need to talk to you about Nikki. Thanks." She hung up the phone, went into the kitchen to make up a grocery list, and made a mental note to call Pam again after she returned from shopping, if she did not call first.

She was in the kitchen putting away the groceries when Nikki stormed in.

"Why did you call my mother?" she yelled.

"I called her because I wanted to talk to her." Nyah said.

"About what?"

"Nikki, why are you so angry, what's going on?"

She took a deep breath and her shoulders fell. "Mom is going through a hard time right now, that's why I'm here are you satisfied now?" Nyah was stunned by how abrupt she was.

"Well, if you must know, you seem different, not your usual happy self and I wanted to know why." Nikki sat down on the kitchen stool and began to chew on her nails. "Nikki," Nyah sat down beside her, "you can talk to me, I want to help you."

"No one can help," she said near tears.

"Try me," she said and waited for her to continue.

"Mom keeps getting these bruises all over her body and when I ask her about them, she says she's just clumsy."

"What kind of bruises?"

"I've seen her with marks on her arms and on her legs and across her back."

"So you don't believe her?"

"I don't know what to believe, I'm just a kid."

"Do you want me to talk to her?"

"No!" she shouted, "she'd be very upset with me if she knew I told anyone about it. Auntie," she pleaded with Nyah, "please don't say anything."

Nyah tried to calm her down, "okay, I won't," she said, but she knew she intended to find the underlying cause of it.

"Can I ask you something?"

"What?" she asked.

"How do you feel about your stepfather, do you like him?" She went completely quiet and held her head down. Nyah had touched a chord.

"What do you mean like?"

"I mean, is he nice to you and the boys and to your mom?"

"Why are you asking me that, do you like him?" Nyah sensed her niece did not want to answer the question and wondered why but did not push her any further.

"I don't know him that well," Nyah said turning her head away from Nikki, she did not even want to mention his name after what he did to her and she wondered if he was doing the same thing to her niece. She dismissed that thought right away convinced that Pamela would never allow anything like that to happen to her own daughter.

"Is it all right if I go to Kim's house?"

Nyah had introduced Nikki to Kim, a young girl around the same age as Nikki who lived on the street that ran parallel to Nyah's house with her mother, father and younger brother.

"Sure, but don't come back too late." Nyah felt like a mother.

"We might go to the movies with her parents, Is that all right?"

"I can't see why not, make sure your cell is turned on so I can reach you if I need to."

"Auntie, no offense, but you're beginning to sound like mom," she said and ran upstairs.

Mark called to tell her he was on his way over, and fifteen minutes later, he was standing at her door with a big grin on his face.

"I have a surprise for you."

"A surprise," she said, "I love surprises."

He came through the door and dropped his overnight bag on the floor then he scooped her up and they kissed for a long time. His trip took longer than he planned and she had not seen him in over three weeks.

"You can put me down now," he loosened his hold and allowed her to slide down his body.

"Where's your niece?" he asked, looking around.

"She's gone to the movies," she said and stepped away from him. Whenever he touched her, every fiber in her body ached for him to consume her and it was hard for her to resist him but she had to try. If he could leave town without telling her, she believed she was not very high on his priority list.

"So, how was your trip?" she asked leading the way into the living room.

"Too long," was all he said. "Do you mind if I take a quick shower? I'm sweaty from the plane ride and I have a meeting in an hour."

He kissed her, grabbed his bag and sprinted up the stairs, two at a time. She was happy to see him, to feel him, but at the same time, she did not want to get too caught up in the emotions that threatened to engulf her whenever she was around him.

Nyah made a cup of tea and was about to take a sip when the doorbell rang. She thought it was Nikki.

"Did you forget your…?" Her voice trailed off when she saw Pamela's scowling face.

"Where's Nikki?" Pamela pushed past her and walked into the foyer.

"Hello Pamela," she said trying to ignore her sister's rudeness.

"Cut the bullshit Nyah, I'm just here to get my daughter."

"She's not here right now."

"What do you mean, where is she?"

"She went to the movies with a friend."

"What friend?"

"A girl who lives on the next street over, it's okay Pam, why are you behaving like this, what's going on?"

"Nyah, what happens in my life is none of your business, I sent Nikki to mom's house, how she ended up here is anybody's guess."

"Mom's house? Nikki told me you knew she was here!"

"Why am I not surprised?" Pamela retorted. "Stay the hell away from my daughter and my husband.

"Your husband?"

"He told me what you tried to do at Gran's party; it's too late to come with the innocent act," she accused. "The only person you can fool with that is Gran; the rest of us can read through your shit like a bad book." Nyah stared at her sister; eyes wide with bewilderment.

"You are way off Pamela. I don't know what that snake of a husband told you but he's a damn liar," Nyah's body shook with anger.

"Is everything all right?" Mark walked over to Nyah, put his arm around her and looked at Pamela.

"Mark, you remember my sister Pamela?" She tried to sound calm but her clenched teeth gave her away.

"I do. How it is going?" He extended his hand and shook hers.

"I'm sorry for raising my voice," she said, "I didn't know there was anyone else here. If you don't mind, I'd like to talk to my sister alone," his grip tightened around Nyah's waist.

She leaned against him.

"It's all right," she reassured him with her eyes and he looked from her to Pamela then brushed his lips against hers softly before he left.

"I'll call you later. Call me if you need me," he glanced at Pamela.

"Okay," she agreed and he left.

Pamela began to laugh.

"What the hell was that, does he think he needs to protect you from the wicked step sister? Whatever, I guess you've got him fooled too," she smirked, "I'll wait for my daughter in the car."

"Nikki told me about the marks," Nyah said before she walked through the door.

"What marks?" she seemed surprised.

"The ones on your arms, legs and back."

Pamela laughed.

"Do you see any marks on me?" She lifted her sleeves and the legs of her pants.

"Nikki said she saw them."

"Nikki is a liar, and you need to mind your own damn business." Pamela walked through the front door and slammed it.

Nyah called Nikki's cell phone but there was no answer. At around 11:30, she heard the front door opening and ran to meet her from the living room.

"Hey, did you see your mother outside?"

"Yeah, I just came inside to get my bag," she said nervously.

"Make it quick, we have a long ride ahead of us," Pamela spoke from outside the door. Nikki went upstairs, to get her bags and when she came back down, her face was tear stained.

"Nikki," Nyah hugged her, "you don't..."

"Nikki, let's go!" Pamela stepped inside the door and spoke to her firmly.

"Bye auntie, I love you."

"Pamela, this is ridiculous, I want to help."

"If you want to help Nyah, just leave us alone." Nyah watched as they got in the car and drove away. She felt helpless and a wave of sadness for her sister and her niece washed over her.

She picked her purse up from the counter and opened it to take a pill but the bottle was not there. She ran upstairs and was relieved to find it on her night table. Relief turned to panic when she realized that Nikki might have seen them or worse, what if Mark found out she took pills. She returned them to their secure hiding place and vowed to be more careful in the future.

Later, when Mark came by the house to check up on her, he wanted to know what happened between her and Pamela. She told him it was nothing, just a simple misunderstanding but deep down she knew it was much more than that.

He tried to lighten her mood, to get her thinking about more pleasant things, it worked for about an hour, but when her mind descended from the heights, thoughts of her niece and her sister once again held her captive.

Fourteen

"Are you sure this dress looks okay?" she asked Mark who sat on the bed; watching her model the red dress in the mirror.

"You look amazing," he replied.

"You say that about almost everything I put on."

"Do you want me to lie? You look good, with or without clothes on."

"Me or my breasts?" She asked not really wanting him to answer.

He stood behind her and began to massage her shoulders.

"Baby, you need to relax," his voice soothed her, "the dress looks great, your breasts look great," he grinned. "I want you to have a good time tonight."

"I'm sure I will," she smiled through her anxieties. He looked striking in his dark gray single button suit, white dress shirt that made his eyes sparkle and blue tie that he said felt like a noose around his neck.

She turned to face him and straightened his tie.

"You were right, this was a nice surprise." She reached up on the tip of her toes and kissed him on the cheek. "I'm ready," she said and within a few minutes, they were on their way to Detroit.

Nyah guessed there were about two hundred people in the hall, more than she expected. Mark told her it was going to be an informal occasion with a few business associates but instead they entered a room where everyone was formally dressed in a suit or a gown, naturally she felt underdressed. He held her hand and led her towards a table at the front of the room. Three men stood up and greeted Mark with a smile and a hearty handshake. He introduced her by her name, offering no label for their relationship. After making sure she was comfortable, he disappeared with the three men through a side door.

"Your dress is lovely," Marie said.

"Thank you." Nyah felt light-headed because she had taken two pills before she left her house.

"So, how long have you and Mark been dating?" she asked.

She found the woman's question a bit intrusive but did not want to seem rude by telling her to mind her own business.

"Not long."

"Oh," she said, "well I think you're a lucky girl he's adorable. I've known Mark for number of years and I don't believe I've ever seen him bring anyone to these functions. In fact, as handsome as he is, I thought he was into a different lifestyle if you know what I mean," she nudged the woman beside her."

"He's just private," Lisa, another woman at the table said, "who can blame him, the way people like to gossip."

"What functions?" Nyah asked trying to turn the conversation away from Mark.

"This is the 8th year that my husband and I are hosting this fundraiser. We feel it's so important to help people whose social circumstances are well below average." Nyah looked intently at Marie, who was dripping with diamonds.

"I agree, but I swear sometimes, I don't believe it makes a difference," the other woman at the table said, "these people are just popping up everywhere."

Nyah hoped her face did not betray the disgust she felt in her heart because of that derogatory statement. "What social group do you classify as 'these people'? Women, African American, single parents or youth? People do not choose to be poor, there are social systems in place that contribute to and maintain this way of life for many communities. I believe that organizations like yours contribute more to the problem rather than the solution."

"I don't care what they do with the money, my conscience is clear, once I've made my contribution, I've done my part," Marie said smiling. Nyah realized what she said went completely over their heads. A tap on the microphone prevented her from going any further.

Mark strolled to the entrance of the hall with a broad smile across his face. He embraced an older woman and a young man who came through the door. He ushered them to a table close to the podium; two tables from her, then he rejoined the three men and one woman as they made their way to the platform.

Once seated, the speaker, a black man who Nyah thought was in his mid-to-late thirties sporting long dreads with a round face and a beard tried to get the attention of everyone in the room. He shifted his glasses as he welcomed the audience and thanked them for coming. Then he introduced the evening's host, Mr. Hardwicke and thanked him for caring enough about the youth, especially the black youth in the community to host the fundraiser every year. A tall slim white man dressed in a gray tuxedo approached the microphone.

"Good evening ladies and gentlemen." His voice was warm and engaging. "Every year, we are honored to recognize members of our community who has made significant contributions financially and socially to enhance the way of life for the inner city youth here in Detroit. This year we are continuing to raise funds to build a recreation center in the city so that we can create jobs and provide a facility that supports our growing inner city youth population. It is our goal to raise six million dollars for this project and we are well on our way.

Tonight we would like to recognize three individuals who operate companies here in our community that help to provide jobs and intern programs that foster creativity and open doors for our young people. Brighton Investments, Allen Reid Production Company and the Strong Corporation." He paused while the audience applauded. "Tonight, we will hear from the CEOs of these three companies and why they believe it is important to give back to their community."

He introduced each person and acknowledged their contributions to the youth project. When it was Mark's turn to speak, Nyah hung on his every word and watched every movement he made. She was happy to see that he was contributing more to youth culture than meaningless fantasies of fame and money and proud to be the woman he chose to share this moment with him. He talked about responsibility and presented a check for $100,000 to the project. In return, the organization presented him with a plaque with his company name and contribution amount engraved on it.

At the end of the presentations, the platform party exited through a door on the right side of the room to the sound of thunderous applause. The room started to buzz again with conversation as people began to move around and socialize with each other.

Mark approached the table where he had seated the two people earlier, and the woman hugged him for what Nyah thought was a long time. The young man patted him on the back and they shared some sort of secret handshake. His eyes found hers and she stood up before the three of them reached her table.

"Great speech," Nyah smiled and touched his forearm.

"Not my favorite thing to do," he said turning to the older woman beside him, "mom, this is Nyah. Nyah, this is the love of my life, my mother Sandy." The woman who smiled at Nyah had a beautiful square face, long ash brown hair and green eyes almost like the color of wet grass. She wore a long gray crinkled skirt with a burgundy top and she had a beige scarf hanging loosely from her shoulders. Nyah extended her hand but the woman hugged her instead.

"It's good to meet you," she said. She was almost as tall as Mark.

"And this is my little brother Greg." The young man with spiked black hair stepped out from behind his mother timidly. He was about 18 or 19 years old and dressed in a suit that was two sizes too small for him.

"Hi Nyah," he said mispronouncing her name and shook her hand quickly. "Are you Mark's girlfriend?" Nyah looked at Mark and waited for him to say something.

"Greg, that's really none of our business honey," Sandy said.

"Mom, I need to use the bathroom," Greg started to wander off. Sandy was about to follow him.

"I'll go with him mom," Mark caught up to his brother and put his arm around him. Nyah watched, moved almost to tears.

"So Nyah, that's a pretty name, did you enjoy the presentations?"

"I did," she answered, feeling intimidated by the older woman's presence. "I support change and growth, especially at the community level."

"Absolutely. The speeches were a bit long, but relevant, I suppose." Sandy motioned for them to sit down.

They chatted politely for a while about the presentations and Mark's accomplishments. She asked Nyah about her family and what work she did for a living. Nyah was relieved when Mark came back, she was not comfortable discussing her family with anyone.

"We have to go," Sandy stood, put on her coat and helped Greg with his. "I have some last minute packing to do before we leave in the morning." They walked to the parking lot together. Greg was fascinated by the snow as it fell around him; he reached out and tried to catch the flakes in his hand. Sandy reached up and caressed the side of Mark's face.

"Markie, I am so proud of you, keep doing what you're doing honey. Your father is sorry he could not make it tonight but you know he is proud of you too."

"Thanks mom," he wrapped his arms around her and Nyah could see that they adored each other. For a split second, she wondered what it would feel like to hug her mother like that.

"We'll be back on the 6th of January, why don't you both come to the house for dinner. Call us to confirm." She turned to Nyah, "It was a pleasure to meet you."

"Likewise," Nyah said finding the encounter awkward.

Sandy secured Greg in the truck and waved goodbye as she drove off.

"Markie," she teased, smiling up at Mark.

"Yeah, she still thinks I'm three," he chuckled.

Mark suggested they stopped at his apartment before driving back to Riverdale. With the amount of snow on the ground, the 35-minute drive would probably take over an hour.

Nyah walked through the door to his apartment on the twenty-fifth floor for the first time. There were no walls, just one big open space with an unusual mix of antique and contemporary furniture. She noticed the oversized bed on the far side of the room beside the marble fireplace and wondered how many women had had the pleasure of *sleeping* on it. She felt like she was imposing on his private life.

"This is a really nice place." Nyah took off her coat and handed it to him.

"Thanks, but I had help putting it together," he said, throwing his keys down on a glass table by the door. "I would have been happy in a room with just my piano, but my sister and my mother had other ideas."

He walked over to a bookshelf and pressed a button that moved the books aside to reveal a hidden safe. He opened it and put the plaque and the contents of his pocket inside then closed it all while Nyah watched him. The only light on was the pot light over the bed in the far corner of the room.

"Would you mind if I made some tea?"

"Make yourself at home," he said removing his jacket and tie as he walked toward the part of the room where his bed was.

Nyah plugged in the kettle and reached on her toes to get a cup from the cupboard, unaware the he was behind her until he reached above her head with ease for the cup and handed it to her.

"Thank you." He also gave her the tea bag and the sugar.

"Did you have a good time?" he asked as he opened the fridge and took out a bottle of water. He opened it and offered it to her; she refused it and watched as he drank the whole thing in one gulp then opened a second bottle.

"It was nice, it's a great project."

He sat down on the sofa, put his feet up on the coffee table and turned on the television. Nyah unplugged the kettle and walked over to the window beside the piano to look at the framed pictures he had on the windowsill.

"Is this your family?" he nodded without looking, "your mother is attractive."

"She's gorgeous," he said simply.

"Mama's boy," she teased, but he didn't hear her. He was too engrossed in whatever he was watching. She put the picture down; not wanting to seem too inquisitive and went back to the kitchen to make her tea. Feeling relaxed, she sat beside him on the sofa, and leaned her body against him. Instinctively, he buried his fingers in her hair, gently rubbed her scalp and she dozed off.

Nyah was lying on the bed when she woke up. Mark was not beside her. She got out of the bed and walked towards the harmonious sound of the piano, and as she approached him, he stopped playing.

"That was lovely," she said.

"I hope I didn't disturb you," he said, "just something I'm working on, tell me what you think."

She watched as his fingers passed over the keys in one fluid motion. He began to hum the melody, moving up and down until the tempo slowed and the song finally ended.

"I'm impressed." He reached out and pulled her between his legs. "You have many hidden talents."

"You have no idea," he whispered, burying his face between her breasts. His teeth found one and then the other, playfully biting them through her shirt. He gazed into her eyes with a yearning that tore through her. She lowered her head; taunted him with tiny kisses all over his face, and lingered at his lips. She used her tongue to trace around the edges of his mouth; he moaned and kissed her intensely. She let out a soft cry when he picked her up, walked across the room, and put her to stand beside the bed, waiting for her to make the first move. She coaxed him to sit on the bed and began undressing slowly to music that was playing in her head; removing one layer at a time while he watched with his mouth slightly opened. She danced close enough for him to touch her but she pushed his hand away each time he tried.

She straddled him, brushed her lips against his biting them gently. Pushing against his chest, she told him to lie down, and used her mouth and hands to explore every inch of his hard body watching his face distort with pleasure. In one swift movement, he turned the tables on her and she moaned sweetly when he returned the favor.

At first, he was gentle, handling her like a delicate glass flower, he did not want to break but when he slid inside her, his passion intensified and his movements slowly pushed her body to the edge of the bed. When she could no longer contain herself, she threw back her head and every ounce of vigor flowed from her body at the same time his limbs stiffened. After a few minutes passed, he rolled onto his back, drew her to lie on top of him, and held her so tightly she could hardly breathe.

"You give sweet love, Miss Parsons," he said. "I'm not the only one with hidden talents." She closed her eyes and inhaled his intoxicating scent of sweat and the ocean.

She took everything he gave her because she felt it would not be long before he would move on to his next conquest.

* * * * * * * **

"Hey, I'm going to the gym for a couple of hours," Nyah heard his voice but his words did not register immediately. She felt the dampness of his lips as he pressed them against hers but she was too tired to respond. She tried to open her eyes but could not focus so she turned away from him, pulled the covers over her head to block the sunlight, and went back to sleep.

Fifteen

"Don't hate me Trace," Sheila begged Nyah when she walked through the front door of her house. Mark followed behind her carrying the coffee and croissant sandwiches they bought for lunch. Nyah thought she was behaving like a naughty child who had done something wrong and did not want to get a spanking. When she saw Mark, she straightened up.

"Sorry, I didn't realize we had company." As he walked past her she said, "Hello, I'm Sheila, Tracie's best friend."

"I met you at the party a few months ago." He smiled at her and disappeared into the kitchen.

"I guess you've both come up for air," Sheila said loud enough for him to hear.

She went into the living room and Sheila followed her.

"You have been keeping secrets," she said.

"No I haven't, you haven't been around," Nyah said.

"That face, that body, is that who I think it is?" Nyah stared at her blankly. "I guess you guys are way past one-night-stand?"

"How is your husband?" Nyah asked her, trying to change the subject.

She sat down on a chair and let her arms dangle over the sides.

"That dead beat, mom always said '*if you lie down with dogs, you're bound to get crabs*' and boy was she ever right."

"You have crabs?" Nyah asked trying to conceal a smile, "I take it then, the marriage is over?"

"It's a figure of speech and don't change the subject, I'd rather talk about you and stud muffin."

"Since when do you want to talk about me?" Nyah's tone was sarcastic.

"Since you have been getting some on the regular," she said, waiting for confirmation. "What do I need to know?" Nyah joined Mark in the kitchen, he had put the croissant sandwiches on a plate and when she entered, he held the plate but she refused.

"He's polite too, I'm so jealous." Sheila took a croissant and sat down beside him at the table. Nyah decided to make a cup of tea. "So where is this going?" Nyah looked at Mark, then at her friend and scoffed.

"Sheila, behave."

"You spend an awful lot of time together, how are you single, or maybe you're not." He chuckled.

"Sheila, stop it." Nyah's voice was stern she was not amused.

"It's impossible to find kind, good-looking unattached men these days, so my best guess is you're either married or you're bi and you are taking my girl for a joy ride."

"Okay, that's it," Nyah grabbed her friend by the arm but she pulled away, "you are way out of line."

"Relax Tracie, I'm just checking. Your skin is all glowy and shit, and our friend here needs to know I got your back."

"I'll consider myself warned," Mark said, clearly enjoying Sheila's tirade.

Nyah turned off the kettle, no longer interested in making tea and went upstairs to change her clothes.

When she came back downstairs, dressed in tights and a long blouse, they were still sitting around the table in the kitchen. He stood up and smiled when he saw her.

"Ready to go?" he asked.

"I am," she said, "Sheila, I will talk to *you* later."

"Let's do this." He took her hand and they walked out the door. "Take care Sheila," he shot over his shoulder before pulling the door shut.

* * * * * * * **

Nyah scolded herself for allowing nervous energy to control her thoughts and affect her body when they parked his truck on the side of the road two doors from Gabby's house. She knew she was opening herself up to scrutiny by going to Gabby's Christmas brunch with Mark. After he got the reminder call from Gabby on the way to her house earlier, he suggested they go together and at that time, she said yes because she was still riding high on the after effects of their blissful night together and had not thought the proposition through carefully. Even as they walked up the driveway holding hands, she did not see herself as his woman. The only time she felt at ease with him occurred when they were alone and naked.

He rang the doorbell and every nerve in her body told her to turn and run but it was too late, Sage opened the door and stared at them.

"Hey, Nyah and Mark, fancy seeing the two of you here, holding hands." Sage emphasized her last few words and she seemed genuinely surprised.

"Hey Sage." Mark hugged Sage then he touched her back and asked if she needed anything to which she quickly responded she would get something later. He bent down and kissed her before walking off to join his friends.

Nyah found herself in a mental space, that made her uncomfortable but she was determined to make the best of it.

"What is this?" Sage could hardly wait to interrogate her.

"What?" she asked innocently and at the same time, Gabby came down the stairs with folded towels in her hands.

"Hey, Nyah, I didn't know you were here."

"Oh she's here all right." Sage said, bursting to tell Gabby what she saw, "she came with Mark."

"That's nice," Gabby said.

"No, you didn't hear me, she came *with* Mark," Sage repeated with more emphasis the second time, "as his date."

Gabby's eyes widened, "Aha, I knew it, I knew it."

She grabbed Nyah's arm and pulled her into the kitchen away from prying ears. Sage followed on their heels.

"Since when?" she asked, "how long has this been going on?"

"That's what I would like to know," Sage interjected.

Nyah fidgeted with her scarf.

"We're just friends," she said.

"Friends, right." Sage made no effort to hide her sarcasm. "You were holding hands and he practically chewed on your face in front of me."

"You're exaggerating Sage, it was just a friendly peck," she said.

"I invited Simone," Gabby said sheepishly, "I didn't know you would be here with Mark and she begged me."

"I guess Brenda and Simone are shit out of luck," Sage said.

"Please, Brenda was never in the running," Gabby chimed.

"I don't think it's that easy," Sage said, "don't you two have history together?" She looked at Nyah.

"We met in high school, we hung out for a while but we lost touch over the years."

"That's not what she said; you've conveniently left out some key information."

"What are you two going on about?" Gabby asked as she chopped potatoes.

"Apparently, miss thing here, has a habit of stealing Brenda's men."

"What?" Nyah was stunned. "Is that what she told you?"

"Sage, you're ridiculous," Gabby said, "Mark is a free agent and he can screw whoever he wants; Brenda will get over it." Nyah was annoyed at Gabby's choice of word, but she did not comment, instead, she asked if she could help.

"Sure, you can make a garden salad; the veggies are in the fridge."

"I hope so, I hope she can get over it and to tell you the truth, I'm glad I don't have a man that you can steal," Sage said as she left the kitchen.

"Ignore her, I do," Gabby said and Nyah smiled gingerly. "I hope it won't be too weird for you with Simone here."

"Hello ladies." Edward walked into the kitchen and when he saw Nyah, his smile widened.

"Hey Eddy, I didn't hear when you came in. I'm glad you could make it." Gabby embraced him, "you remember Nyah?"

"How could I forget such a beautiful..." his voice trailed off when he hugged her. "It's great to see you again."

"We were just talking about you." Nyah glared at Gabby. "I'll get you something to drink." Gabby left them standing there.

"So, Eddy, how are you?" Nyah cut through the awkward silence.

"I'm great, now that I've seen you again." Gabby returned with two drinks.

"Why don't you two sit and have a drink together?" She handed them the drinks and nudged them in the direction of the sofa.

"Edward, would you excuse me please?" Nyah pulled Gabby through the back door onto the patio away from everyone else.

"What are you doing?"

"You told me you weren't seeing anyone, Edward is a great guy, very stable and he's a doctor for goodness sakes. Know how many women would kill for a man like him?"

"You are trying to set me up with Edward?" Nyah asked.

"I'm sorry, I didn't know you were coming with Mark," she said. "He wanted to get to know you better and I thought this would have been the perfect opportunity."

"Gabby, you really need to mind…"

Sage poked her head through the back door and chuckled, "this should be interesting."

Simone called out from the kitchen and Gabby pulled Nyah back inside.

"We'll talk about this later," she whispered. Simone hugged Gabby excitedly," thank you, thank you," she was almost jumping out of her skin. "How do I look, think he'll like it?"

Gabby smiled.

"Very sexy, that's just the right amount of cleavage. You remember Nyah?"
Simone looked at Nyah from head to toe.

"Yeah, from the restaurant, right?"

Mark walked over to where the women were standing but before he could say anything, Simone asked to talk to him in private and Nyah watched as they disappeared through the side door, closing it behind them.

"I would give anything to be a fly on the wall right now," Sage said mischievously. Nyah handed her drink to Sage and headed for the bathroom. She leaned against the sink, closed her eyes and breathed deeply to steady her runaway thoughts. She consoled her heart by reminding herself that she meant nothing to Mark outside great sexual chemistry. People who had sex, sometimes held hands and it wasn't that uncommon for them to attend parties together so maybe today was the day she would become the nameless, faceless orgasm and that was fine with her.

She was also not going to run away like a cowardly child, she certainly was not going to give Gabby, and Sage anything further to gossip about, she knew Mark was not committed to her and she was determined to have a good time despite how heartbroken she felt. She went into the kitchen and continued to make the salad.

"Nyah, are you okay?" Sage asked.

"I'm fine," she answered in her cheeriest voice.

"I'm sure she's fine," Gabby said without looking at her. "You guys are just friends right?"

"That's right," she said. "Is there anything else you want me to do?"

"You didn't come here to work in the kitchen. Let's dance." Sage took her hand and led her into the living room.

Nyah discretely watched the door as she talked to Rick and Trey. She even agreed to dance '*The Christmas Song*' with Edward. When Mark and Simone finally came back inside the house, he had his arms around her, and she looked like she had been crying. She sat down on sofa and he went into the kitchen to get her a drink.

Having had enough, feeling like a third wheel, she thanked Gabby for the invitation discreetly announced to everyone that she was leaving and made a quick exit before Mark had a chance to come back into the room.

When she walked out into the crisp evening air, Nyah realized she had left her purse in his truck so she didn't have any money to take a cab home but she was not about to go back inside and ask him for it, so she decided it was a great evening for a walk.

****

Nyah opened the front door, walked back to the living room. Mark came in with her purse under his arm and closed the door behind him.

"You left the party without telling me."

"I'm not obligated to tell you what I'm doing, besides you were busy," Nyah took up a magazine and started flipping through it.

"Are you going to tell me what's wrong or do I have to guess?" He sat beside her on the sofa not bothering to take off his coat.

"I knew it was a bad idea going to that party together, I'm sure it gave everyone the wrong impression," she said, taking her purse from him.

"Why are you so concerned with what other people think?"

"I don't fool myself about us, this, whatever it is, but when other people get involved, then it becomes crazy and I don't like crazy."

"Believe me, you're not the only one. How did you get home?" he asked concerned.

"It's a nice evening, I walked." He rubbed his head and Nyah knew he was frustrated. "You don't have to worry about me; I'm not your responsibility." Her voice was cold and aloof. He stood up and walked to the front door. She watched him from the entrance of the living room.

"I'm glad you're okay," he said as he walked through the door and left it open. His tires skidded as he drove off and after closing the door, Nyah leaned against it, wanting to cry out of sheer frustration but the tears would not come, she took a deep breath in its place.

"Where's mister man?" Sheila asked from the rail at the top of the stairs.

"Where did you come from? Didn't you hear the doorbell?" She thought Sheila had left because she had to use the spare key that was hidden in the flowerpot on the front porch to get inside the house.

"No, I was on the phone, that deadbeat husband of mine is trying to give me a hard time."

Nyah walked up the stairs and paused briefly to hug her friend.

"I think I'm going to turn in early, I'm overdue for a good book."

"Is everything okay Trace?"

"Oh yeah, everything is great." Nyah went inside her bedroom and closed the door.

* * * * * * **

When she got up, around two o'clock the next day, Nyah decided at the last minute to go Christmas shopping with Sheila. She bought twelve $150 gift certificates from Talbots and sent one to Pamela and to each of her children, her three aunts, Marjorie and her three friends. Gran was in Florida and insisted she did not need anything so Nyah just arranged to have purple lilies sent to her hotel. She also spent five hundred dollars on clothes she knew she would wear only once or not at all.

"So, I'm leaving in the morning, I need to get the ball rolling on this divorce with my lawyer," she said.

"It's really over?" They sat around the table eating the apple pie Sheila bought.

"Yeah, he's apparently moved on to his next victim. Would you believe the jerk was broke, I should have known when he told me there was a fire at his house and he asked if we could stay at my sister's house for a while."

Nyah was not surprised, she suspected something was not right with him that first night when Sheila said his car was in the shop and she had to drive him to that other party.

"Go ahead; I know you're dying to say *I told you so.*" Nyah was not used to seeing Sheila so sad even though most times she believed her friend's attitude was just a front to mask things she did not want to face about herself.

"I'm sorry things didn't work out with this guy," was all she said.

"That's life, isn't it?" she murmured before going upstairs to the guest room.

Nyah sat down to watch television when the doorbell rang. Gabby stood at the door with a cheesecake in her hand and a sheepish grin on her face.

"Peace offering?" she held up the cake.

"I didn't know we were at war," Nyah said dryly. "Come in."

She began to gush.

"Nyah, I had no idea that you and Mark were dating, I had asked you before and you said you two were just friends. Edward asked me if you were taken and I told him no, because that's what you told me." Nyah took the cheesecake from her and went into the kitchen. "I'm sorry for interfering."

"Look Gab, it's fine, no harm done. I left yesterday because I was tired," she lied.

"Did what happen with Mark and Simone upset you?" she asked.

"No, let's just leave it alone."

"Nyah, I've known Mark for nine years, he is a private guy, pulling teeth is easier and less painful than getting him to open up about his personal life. He only tells us what he wants us to know and when I saw you at the party together, I was surprised yes, but I was also very happy because I think the two of you fit together."

"Let's just have some cheesecake," Nyah smiled at her, grateful for the reassurance.

Gabby stayed for a little while and then left because she had plans to go to the movies with Brenda. She almost bumped into Mark, when she opened the front door.

"Hey," she said and hugged him, "I was just leaving." She turned around to look at Nyah and smiled, "I will call you later," she said and walked down the driveway, "or tomorrow if you need more time," she shot over her shoulder.

In three steps, he was standing in front of her. She reached up on her toes, wrapped her arms around his neck and kissed him. He pulled her closer and they continued kissing as he lifted her off the ground, her feet dangling and walked with her to the sofa. When he sat down, he pulled her with him, and she sat on his lap.

'I'm sorry I left the party without telling you," she said.

He brushed his lips against her ear.

"I'm sorry you felt you had to. I took a week off work, I think we should go away together for Christmas," he said.

"Really, isn't this kind of sudden? Where would we go?" she asked; intrigued by the idea of having him completely to herself for one whole week.

"Anywhere you want to go, I hear Fiji is nice this time of year."

"Sounds wonderful," she said.

"Are you game?" he asked burying his face in her hair, she nodded and he made reservations for the next day.

Nyah did not tell anyone that she was going on vacation with Mark, not even Sheila. When she left the house, Sheila thought she was going to his apartment to spend the night.

"Well I'm leaving in the morning so I might not see you," she said.

"Call me on my cell when you get home, lock up before you leave." Nyah hugged her friend and then she left with Mark.

* * * * * * * **

The plane left Detroit Airport at 8:25 on Christmas morning. They made their first connecting flight in Houston and the second in Honolulu and finally arrived in Nadi just after 12:30 in the morning Fiji time. They were too exhausted from the plane ride to notice anything about the resort so they undressed and slept until close to 12:00 the next afternoon.

Nyah was having a great dream, or so she thought. She woke up to find Mark searching for buried treasure between her legs, she tried to push him away but he would not budge.

"At least let me clean my body," she said covering her morning breath, feeling conscious that she had not showered the night before.

"I'm not complaining."

He continued his trek up her body and lingered at her breasts. She reluctantly tore herself away from him and ran to the bathroom with her overnight bag to brush her teeth and take a quick shower he followed her and her ten-minute shower turned into forty-five minutes of screaming and wasted water. He carried her back to the bed and they lay side by side completely satiated.

"I'm starving," she said, "what time is it?"

"I'm in heaven," he said as he raised her hand to his lips and kissed it.

"I wasn't ready for everyone to know that we were sleeping together," she said. He turned on his side and propped his head up using a pillow. "The questions, the stares, what Gabby did with that girl; it was awkward for me."

"Are we still on that?" he asked, "I thought we were on vacation."

"I just wanted you to know how I felt."

"Okay, now I know but you can't trip every time you see me with another woman. You either trust me or you don't. You didn't see me freaking out when that guy tried to make his move on you."

"What guy? Edward? He wasn't hitting on me." He rolled on his back, drew her close to his side and threw his leg over her, pinning her down.

"He never took his eyes off you once."

"And how would you know that, you were preoccupied."

"Well, he can give it his best shot," he said light-heartedly, leaning over her. "But he's not the one on this beautiful island, on this beautiful day, in this beautiful cabin, in this big beautiful bed, with the most beautiful woman in the world," He kissed a different part of her face after each statement and Nyah's heart fluttered when he began singing the lyrics to the song *'you are so beautiful to me'*.

She smiled and they kissed passionately for a long time.

For six days, she enjoyed being the center of his attention doing almost everything together. They went dancing, scuba diving, fishing, she beat him at tennis and found out he could bench-press just below two times her weight. She found however that it was not so easy to convince him to take a seaweed spa treatment with her; he did not relish the thought of being covered from his neck to his toes in green slime. She noticed however, that he did not complain about the softness of her skin when she allowed him to stroke, prod and work his wonders on her body every chance he got.

On their last day at the resort, they went on a day tour to see the sights and paid a staff member to follow them around and take pictures with five disposable cameras. They spent the first evening of the New Year; the last night of their vacation dancing on their private deck to oldies music, afterward, they enjoyed each other in the hot tub.

They sat on separate chairs at the edge of the deck staring at the moon-glazed water. The only audible sounds were the cricket, the night owl and the faint sound of music in the distance.

"I can't believe it's been one week already," Nyah said trying to savor the moment with him.

"Did you have a good time?" She could hardly hear his voice it was so low.

"I had an amazing time; you are quite the 'feel good' man Mr. Allen." He laughed deep in his throat.

Later that night, Nyah was having a hard time falling asleep so she quietly left the bed and stood at the edge of the deck. The moon's brilliance caressed the surface of the water as she stared absentmindedly into the stillness.

"Can't sleep?" His voice was low and she could hardly hear him. She shook her head but she did not turn around. He stood behind her, opened the front of his robe and captured her in his embrace, she leaned into it and he held her for what seemed like an eternity. She loved the smell of bergamot and spice that mixed with his natural scent. There were no words between them as they gazed at the water, just a silence that ushered her into unfamiliar territory. She wondered if he could hear the escalated rhythm of her heart every time he came close to her, feel the knots in her stomach when he touched her, sense the utter weakness in her knees when he kissed her, see the complete and unreserved mindlessness she experienced when he made love to her.

They woke up around eleven o'clock on the day of their departure after a night of unprecedented passion. Nyah had no idea her body could withstand such pleasure. She reluctantly packed and got dressed; knowing if they missed the boat another one would not be available until the next morning and they would miss the plane.

Their first vacation together was etched forever in her memories.

Sixteen

A week after being back from their vacation, they sat in his truck in the driveway of his parents' home. The reality of their separate lives was beginning to sink in. Mark was away in Atlanta for three days and Nyah spent time getting her classroom ready for the New Year.

"Are you sure you want to do this? I don't want you to feel any pressure." His voice was tender.

She smiled and said, "This was planned so it's okay." He got out of the truck, walked around to her side and opened the door. An older man who was not much taller than Nyah answered the door. His face was golden brown and wrinkled; his eyes were dark and round. He had a short black afro with a receding hairline.

He was genuinely excited to see Mark and greeted him warmly.

"Son, it's good to see you, Happy New Year." Mark returned the sentiment. "And you must be Nyah?" He smiled at her and shook her hand.

"Nice to meet you sir." She found his mother more intimidating.

"Please, call me Daniel. Come in, my wife is in the back." He took her elbow and led her through the house. "The only time we get to see our son in on special occasions," he said grinning. Mark laughed. He led her down a long hallway and into a huge family room. The room was painted a pale yellow and that gave it an airy feel. The ceiling was high and vaulted and Nyah could see his mother's personality and appeal in the room. There were two sofas facing each other and four chairs strategically placed to form a semi-circle around an antique arched fireplace. Mark's mother entered the room. She greeted her son with a kiss and an affectionate hug. Then she did the same with Nyah.

"Welcome to our home Nyah," she smiled and led them outside to a glass enclosed deck that was attached to that room. The sun had gone and it had started to snow.

"This is my favorite room. I love to watch the sky fall from in here," Sandy said as they all sat around a half moon lounge chair. The wooden deck was heated and it was easy to see the snow falling through the clear plastic enclosure. "Dinner is ready; we'll eat as soon as Cindy gets here."

"Where is Greg?" Mark asked.

"He's probably trying to find something suitable to wear," she said.

"I'll go check on him," Mark disappeared inside the house.

"Greg is autistic," Sandy volunteered, "and making decisions can be a bit of a challenge for him."

"So, my dear," Nyah looked at Daniel. "I understand you are an elementary teacher; what grade do you teach?"

"I teach grade 7 at Canberry Middle School," she said.

"Do you still live with your family?"

"Daniel, stop questioning the young woman," Sandy scolded leaning her head on the back of the chair. "She'll tell us what she wants us to know when she's ready."

Daniel smiled and began to tell her about his life before he decided to retire early. He was born and raised in the Bronx with very humble beginnings. When he was thirteen, his parents died in a car crash and left him to care for his three younger sisters. He worked odd jobs, and sometimes stole to provide for them. When he was 16, he dropped out of school and began to work for a small company doing construction. Two of his sisters went to live with distant relatives in Florida and the other got married and moved to Sacramento, California. At 28, he ventured on his own and started a small construction business. He met Sandy 4 years later, when he hired her to help him with the administrative work. She was 19 years old.

"I retired two years ago because of my failing health. I had to sell the business."

"Nyah, he's not telling you the whole story. He met me, and my two children. Cindy was three, and Mark was one and a half when I started working for Daniel. He felt sorry for me, so he married me 6 months later. We celebrated our 31st wedding anniversary last month. He is the only father my children have ever known, the only man I have ever truly loved, and who's managed to love me despite how broken I was. When I was a girl, I lacked direction because my mother lacked direction. A little colored boy told me he loved me and I believed him so I had Cindy. I later found out he also loved many other girls so that did not work out. A few months later, his friend Tyrell, a boy from the same neighborhood told me he loved me and Mark came along. I never saw either boy again." She spoke without hesitation.

A young woman with short dark brown hair walked into the room. Sandy stood up to greet her. "Cindy, I didn't hear you come in. Where's Paul?"

"He's talking with Markie in the front hall," he said and looked in Nyah's direction.

"Cindy, this is Nyah, Mark's lady friend."

"Hello, good to meet you Nyah, you're so pretty and so tiny." She smiled at Nyah and hugged her parents.

"Now that we are all here, let's eat." Sandy led the way into the dining room where the table was formally set. Mark and Nyah were seated across from each other; Cindy was seated beside Mark and across from Paul, who she recognized as the dread from the fundraiser she attended with Mark, before they went on vacation.

Nyah enjoyed the meal and the conversation flowed easily and was not pretentious. She watched Mark interact with his family and saw a completely new side of him. He was attentive and funny, at least his mother thought so. They all went into the family room and played The Game of Life. Greg won and spent the rest of the evening, gloating. Nyah believed they let him win. When it was time to leave, she thanked his parents for a lovely evening and they extended an invitation for her to visit more often.

****

"Nyah Parsons, the doctor will see you now." She got up when the nurse called her name and followed her into another office in the back room to wait again. Shortly after, the doctor walked into the room. This was her first time sitting in a doctor's office since she moved to Riverdale and her first time meeting the doctor.

"Miss Parsons, I'm Dr. Hoyt, we have not received your files from Dr. Maynard's office yet, I hope you don't mind if I ask you some preliminary questions to bridge the gap until they courier the files from Wisconsin?" He opened a file folder containing a blank sheet of paper and began to write her answers to his questions. "What can I do for you today?"

"I haven't been feeling well. I've lost my appetite and I'm tired all the time, I think I might have caught a bug from the kids in my school or something," she said.

"How long have you been feeling this way?"

"It's been about a week."

"When was the last time you had a physical?" he asked and motioned for her to sit on the examination table.

"Almost two years ago," she answered.

He proceeded to take her blood pressure and used his stethoscope to listen to her heart.

"You are 26..." The doctor glanced at the file and continued to probe her ears and throat.

"Yes."

He nodded and wrote something else in the folder.

"Your blood pressure is a little high, 130/90, have you been experiencing headaches, nausea or fever?"

"Sometimes I get headaches," she said.

"So far, nothing jumps out at me except for the blood pressure and a bit of congestion in your lungs, what's your diet like? Perhaps you should cut down on your meat intake."

"I don't eat meat at all."

"I see, with your permission, I would like to draw some blood and do a complete physical just to get a full picture," he said, she agreed and for the next half hour a technician drew eight vials of blood from her and accompanied by a nurse, the doctor checked her body inside and out. "If you don't hear from us in a few days, there was no cause for concern," they left the room, giving her time to clean up and get dressed.

Nyah did not get the sense that anything was wrong outside a flu bug so she did not bother to ask the doctor any probing questions.

On her way home from the doctor's office, she called Gabby and arranged for them to see a movie together realizing they had not done anything outside school since before the Christmas brunch at her house.

Mark had been very busy with work for the last month and a half since they returned from vacation. He pregnant because Mark was very militant about using protection.

She took the test in the washroom, and they waited for the plus or minus sign, it was the longest minute of her life. She asked Gabby to read the results because she was too wound up to do it herself.

"Oh my God, congratulations." Nyah stared at her friend in disbelief. Pregnant, she was pregnant with Mark's baby. She should have been jumping for joy but instead, she sank to the floor and began sobbing quietly.

'Ny, what's the matter; this is good news, right?" Nyah did not answer, she leaned her head against Gabby's shoulder, grateful that she was not alone and kept crying.

"Mark is going to freak out, it is his baby right?" Gabby asked.

Nyah straightened up and dried her tears with the back of her hand, "what kind of a question is that?"

"I'm just asking, you know men, it takes more than a baby to keep them around," Gabby said.

She stared at Gabby questioningly.

"You think I'm trying to trap Mark with a baby?" Nyah began to laugh, "I'm tired. I'm going to lie down, see yourself out."

"Nyah, I wasn't implying..." Nyah stopped her in the middle of her sentence.

"Thanks for your help, I'll talk to you." Nyah walked her to the door and when Gabby stepped outside, she closed it.

Pregnant, she was pregnant with Mark's baby. Her head began to spin so she went upstairs and crawled into her bed. She was so wound up, she had to take two pills that night to help her calm down. She tuned everyone and everything out; she did not want to think because for her, thinking meant planning and planning meant action.

* * * * * * * **

On Friday, when she met Mark at the airport he gave her a long 'I'm happy to see you' kiss.

"I missed you," she said clinging to him.

He held her tight, and she winced in pain, her breasts were sensitive but she did not pull away from him, she needed to feel his arms around her. As they walked to the car, he began talking about his trip.

"Good news," he said, "we may be doing the score for a movie," she could tell he was excited. "They want us to present three sample pieces by the end of next month."

"Congratulations, but is that enough time?" she asked and her cell phone interrupted the conversation.

"This is Dr. Hoyt's office, is this Nyah Parsons?"

"Yes," she said and stepped away from Mark, not wanting him to hear the voice on the other end.

"Miss Parsons, the doctor wants to see you as soon as possible, when would be a good time to come in?"

"I can come tomorrow afternoon," she said, glancing sideways at Mark.

"Does tomorrow at four work for you?" The secretary's cheerfulness annoyed Nyah.

"Yes, four is fine."

"We'll see you then, bye." Nyah hung up the phone and felt Mark's eyes piercing a hole through her.

"Who was that?" he asked.

"My dentist," she lied; she was not prepared at that moment to tell him about the pregnancy and face his reaction.

They barely made it through the front door of his apartment before Mark was all over her. She knew when she picked him up, she could not refuse his advances especially since they had been apart for so long. She tried to clear her mind of everything except how happy she was to see him and to be consumed by him. It worked, and before long, she was mindlessly screaming his name.

"Maybe I should go away more often," he teased, "I love the way you welcome me back."

She lay on top of him and rested her head on his chest; he buried his fingers in her hair and gently massaged her scalp.

"What do you think about us living together?" he asked nonchalantly.

Her mind froze and for a brief moment, she was speechless. She knew they had been dating for almost a year, they had had many sexual encounters, they had even taken a vacation together, but never in all that time had he once told her he loved her. For her, living together was not an option. His proposition brought her back to the beginning of their relationship and her heart sank. She was grateful that he got up to use the bathroom before she could answer.

His cell phone began to vibrate.

"Mark, your phone is ringing," she said.

"Answer it baby," he shot back, "I'm waiting for an important call."

"Hello," she had never answered his cell phone before; whoever it was hesitated and hung up.

"Who was it?" he asked climbing back into the bed and snuggling up beside her.

"I don't know? They hung up." He took the phone from her and tossed it to the other side of the bed.

"Then I guess it wasn't very important."

He positioned himself on top of her. She was having difficulty breathing; her breasts were sore and her stomach was hurting. "I hope you're not tired," he said playfully as he kissed a different part of her face between each word. "There's more to come."

Seventeen

Nyah's visit to the doctor confirmed what she already knew.

"According to this chart, you are about five weeks pregnant, Congratulations."

"Thank you," she said.

"However," he continued, "there is cause for some concern. The blood tests revealed traces of benzodiazepines in your system, are you taking any medication right now?"

Nyah reached up and shifted a lock of hair from her face nervously.

"Sometimes I get a bit anxious so my previous doctor prescribed some tablets for me to take as needed."

"What kind of tablets, Valium, Ativan?"

"I take Xanitol," she said, took the bottle from her purse, handed it to the doctor; he read the label and made notes in her file.

"How long have you been taking them?"

"Almost a year." The doctor's questions made Nyah uncomfortable; she felt like she was a child being scolded for doing something bad.

"And when was the last time you took them?"

"I took two a few nights ago, is something wrong?" she asked.

"Miss Parsons, I'm recommending that you reduce and then stop your intake of Xanitol as soon as possible for your safety and the safety of your unborn child. It is unfortunate that you have been taking this medication for so long and without proper monitoring. May I ask why you were prescribed Xanitol in the first place?"

Nyah hesitated.

"I was attacked," she said knowing that was only partially true, she has never told anyone what really happened; not even her doctor.

"How long ago?"

"I was nineteen; seven years, four days," Nyah rolled the exact date off the top of her head.

"I see. I am sorry to hear that. Have you tried other treatment options to help you cope?"

"Before my doctor prescribed Xanitol, she sent me to a therapist but it didn't help to talk about it. I cope just fine; I'm not a victim."

"Miss Parsons, in light of your pregnancy, I must advise you that your use of benzodiazepines can greatly affect the life expectancy of your baby. I know you've indicated that you have tried before, but perhaps enough time has elapsed and you can try talking to another therapist." Nyah could feel her mind shutting down; she had not planned to have a baby right now. She felt her relationship with Mark would not be able to survive him finding out about her pregnancy. She did not want him to believe for one moment that she got pregnant on purpose to trap him as Gabby suggested.

"Dr. Hoyt, you have given me a lot to think about," she said. "I'll let you know what I decide to do," she got up and left.

When she got home, she turned off the ringer on the phone and went straight to bed.

* * * * * * * **

Gabby was waiting for her by her classroom door when she got to school on Monday morning.

"Hey," she said, "how are you feeling?"

"I'm good," she unlocked the door and walked past Gabby to put her bags down on the desk.

"So, how did Mark take the good news?" she asked excitedly.

"I didn't tell him," she said.

"Don't' you think he has a right to know?" she inquired.

"Gab, can we talk about this later?"

"I'm sorry about what I said the other day." She walked over to Nyah and gave her a hug then she touched her belly. "Sorry I can't help myself, I'm so jealous," she said and left the room.

Nyah sat behind her desk and used her fingers to massage her throbbing temples. She avoided seeing Mark for the whole weekend by telling him she had papers to grade. As far as she was concerned, their relationship had no foundation, the fact that he suggested they live together confirmed her belief that she was nothing more than his sex partner. She believed there were enough children born in dysfunctional situations, and she was not willing to ruin another child's life. Nyah sighed heavily and distracted herself by planning her lessons for the day.

When she got home, she returned Graydon's call; he had just finished an art exhibition in Boston and wanted to know when they could get together. She told him that she was very busy right now but it would be soon. She did not tell him about the pregnancy because the fewer people who knew about it; the less stressed she would feel if she decided to terminate it. Her heart sank at that thought and silently rebuked herself for thinking such a morbid thought. She called Gran, but there was no answer so she left a message with Marjorie for Gran to call her back. Finally, she called Pamela. When Sean answered the phone, she hung up quickly.

Nyah was hungry but was afraid to eat because she knew it would just come up so she made a cup of weak tea. She was about to sit down and drink her tea when the doorbell rang. Mark stood at the door with his hands in his pocket. He bent and gave her a quick kiss before he walked past her into the foyer. He seemed anxious and Nyah thought that was unusual for him.

"We need to talk." She felt a knot forming in her stomach wondering if he knew about the pregnancy. He took her hand and led her to the living room. She watched his face intently as he searched for the right words to begin.

"Are you okay?" he asked with concern in his eyes.

"I'm fine" she said, "Mark, what's this about?"

"About eight years ago, I met a girl, we dated for a couple of years, everything was going great and then one day she was just gone. I never heard from her again, I tried to find her but I couldn't, well until yesterday, she's back in Detroit and she has my son."

"Your son?" The words stopped in her throat. Nyah felt as though someone had slapped her across her face with the back of their hand, "you have a son?"

"Apparently so," he remained calm, showing no outward emotion as he told her the story.

"How old is this child?"

"He's almost six, his name is Jason." There was a long pause between them. "Say something."

"What do you want me to say?"

"Anything. That you will be patient with me while I sort this out, figure out what to do."

"This is big, you have a child, it's not like you can give him back?" Nyah started picking at her nails, "are you sure he's yours?"

"Why would she lie about something as important as having my child?" He seemed disappointed that Nyah questioned his paternity. Did he expect that she would take the news like a good little girl and give him a big hug?

"You have to do what feels right for you." She sat on the sofa and he sat beside her.

"This won't change anything between us, unless you change it."

She could feel anger rising within her, "unless I change it? This has nothing to do with me, this is your story; you're telling me about some woman you supposedly got pregnant, who conveniently disappeared then reappeared six years later with your child. You would have to be blind or stupid not to see how news like this can change a situation." She stood up, walked towards the door, and opened it, "I guess you have stuff you need to sort out."

He stopped in front of her but she turned her head away, he brought her hand to his lips and kissed it. "I love you, I'll call you later." She sank to the floor and started crying. She had been waiting to hear him say those three words for a long time. On any other day her heart would have screamed for joy but not this day, not after being told that the man whose baby she was carrying had another family, a child with another woman. Joy was the farthest thing from her heart.

****

Nyah ignored the phone the first time it rang, she looked at it the second time, finally, she picked it up to stop the annoying ringing. It had been a week since Mark told her about his ex-girlfriend and their son, the wound was festering and that left her in a bad mood. She went through the motions at school because she had to, but she sealed herself off from almost everyone and everything else. He called her several times but she did not know what to say to him so she did not answer the phone.

"Hello," she said abruptly.

"Auntie, it's me Nikki," her niece sounded distraught.

"Nik, is everything all right?" Nyah immediately softened her tone and put aside her troubles.

"No, I can't take it anymore."

"Take what anymore? Honey, calm down and talk to me."

"Please can I come and stay with you for a while?"

"Nik, where is Pamela?"

"She's not feeling well," she said, almost stuttering.

"Just let me speak to her."

"She ain't here, Auntie, please come and get me."

"Listen," Nyah said, running up the stairs, "stay put and I'll get the next flight to New York. Do you have a friend who can stay with you for a few hours?"

"No Auntie, I'm all alone." Nyah's heart was beating very fast; she knew something was wrong. Nikki sounded desperate and Nyah felt completely helpless being so far away.

"Nikki, I will get there as soon as I can." When her niece hung up, she called Graydon. She told him about the phone call from Nikki and that she was going to New York, he said he would meet her there. She quickly threw some clothes and undergarments in an overnight bag and called Pamela's house again, as she got dressed. There was no answer, so she dialed 911 and told them about her concern for her niece, she gave them the address and they said they would send a police car to check it out.

The drive to the Detroit airport seemed longer than usual and when she got there, the attendant said her flight was not leaving for three hours. The wait was torture, she could not stop thinking about Nikki and how desperate she sounded on the phone.

She arrived at JFK airport in just over two hours, hailed a cab and within 35 minutes, she was knocking on Pamela's front door, there was no answer. She continued to knock louder until she heard a voice behind her.

"They ain't home," an elderly woman with no teeth spoke to her.

"Do you know the people who live here?" she asked.

"Yeah, the man, that prissy woman, a young girl and three little boys."

"Yes," Nyah said, "have you seen any of them?"

"Last I saw of the prissy one was when they took her away in an ambulance last night."

"An ambulance, was she sick?"

"How should I know, I try to mind my own business."

"Have you seen the young girl today?" she asked,

"You mean the little troublemaker, yeah, I seen the little ho." Nyah felt like she was getting nowhere with the woman. "Last I saw her was last week sometime."

"Thanks," Nyah said and started dialing 411 to get the phone numbers for hospitals in the area. She called every hospital number she received and asked for her sister by name, but they said they had no one by that name admitted there. She spent an hour calling hospitals but Pamela was not registered at any of them. Graydon exited the cab and ran up the stairs two at a time.

"Gray, thank God you are here," she hugged him. "I've been here for over two hours and I can't find them anywhere. The woman next door told me she saw Pamela leave in an ambulance last night and I've called every hospital in the area but I couldn't find her. I think something is terribly wrong."

"Where's Nikki?" he asked.

"I don't know, but we have to find her."

Nyah turned to leave and suddenly everything went black.

When she woke up, she was on a stretcher in the emergency room.

"Gray? Gray?" she was disoriented.

"I'm here," he said standing beside the stretcher.

"What happened?"

"You fainted," a young nurse said while taking her blood pressure.

Nyah tried to get up. "I have to go; I need to find my niece."

"Miss, what you need to do is remain calm, your blood pressure is a little high and the stress is not good for the baby, I'll get the doctor," she said and drew the curtain.

"Gray, I know something is wrong," she said trying to divert attention from what the nurse said.

"Why am I just finding out now that you're pregnant?"

"I haven't really told anyone."

"How could you keep something this important from me?"

"I'm still trying to wrap my head around it," she said honestly, "I'm a single woman, what am I going to do with a baby?"

"Mark seems like a good guy, I'm sure he's got the ring picked out already."

"I called the police before I left home, maybe they know something," she said trying to change the subject.

"Stay put Nyah, I'm not joking around, I'll be right back." He left the room just as the doctor came in to check on her. He warned her to take it easy and within two hours, she was released. She waited in the room until Graydon returned and he took her to his place where she showered and he made pasta for himself and she had dry toast.

"Wanna know what I don't understand, where's Mark? Why does he have you running all over New York by yourself?"

"What kind of a question is that? Mark is not my keeper," she said defensively. Her voice softened, "he has a lot to deal with right now."

"What could be more important than you and his baby?"

Nyah continued to pick at her bread, "he doesn't know that I'm in New York."

"He does know you're pregnant, right?"

"There you go again, what is with you and all these questions? I don't want to talk about this right now, we should be focusing on finding Nikki," she pleaded with him and he backed off.

Graydon would not let her go to the police station with him; he told her if she did not listen, he would tell Mark she was pregnant. Even though she did not believe he would betray her like that, she was not about to take that chance. When he came back, he said he found Pamela at Mount Sinai Hospital. Visiting hours were over, but they planned to go first thing in the morning.

Morning couldn't come soon enough for Nyah, they took a cab to the hospital and the information clerk directed them to the sixth floor. When they entered the room, they saw Pamela sitting on a chair by the bed, when she saw them; she had a look of dread on her face.

"Pam, we've been calling all the hospitals looking for you," Nyah rushed to her side. It was then that she noticed Nikki lying in the hospital bed with tubes coming from her nose and mouth. Nyah could not tell if she was unconscious or asleep. "What is going on here?" she questioned; her tone was accusing.

"Shhhh! Keep your voice down," Pamela walked out of the room and they followed, "what are you guys doing here?" She sounded very annoyed.

"What happened to Nikki?" Graydon's voice was worried.

"She got hurt," Pamela said.

"Who hurt her?" Nyah questioned accusingly.

"Look, she's going to be fine, this is none of your business, you've caused enough trouble for us."

"What does that mean?" Graydon asked.

"When you called the cops yesterday, you have no idea what you did," she accused Nyah venomously.

"From the looks of things, that call might have saved Nikki's life," Graydon said.

"We don't need saving, just leave us alone," she said and turned to walk away, Nyah stopped her.

"Nikki called me yesterday afternoon, and she sounded very upset; she wanted me to pick her up right away. Today I find her lying in a hospital bed. Either you give me some answers or I will get them from the police."

Pamela walked over to the waiting area and sat down.

"Nikki tried to kill herself yesterday," she confessed and started to cry.

"What?" Nyah was stunned.

Graydon sat down beside Pamela and wrapped his arm around her shoulders; Nyah stood looking at them in a daze. "She's got some serious mental issues and we'll see that she gets the help she needs."

"What issues? She's fourteen years old, are you saying this is her fault?" Nyah was so angry her face was burning, "you or Sean had nothing to do with it? We're talking about suicide Pamela; she was obviously hurting. How could you not see that? You're her mother!"

Graydon looked at Nyah and grew concerned, "calm down Ny," he said, hinting at her condition.

"No, I will not calm down," she said hotly, "Nikki is a child and when a child tries to take her own life, it's a serious cry for help. She didn't get here on her own, and you and that dreadful piece of shit you married have to take responsibility for what has happened to her."

Pamela got up and stood directly in front of her, "screw you Nyah, don't throw your moralistic, better-than-thou attitude at me. I have four kids to take care of and I work my ass off to make sure they get what they need. You have some nerve talking to me about responsibility, where were you? If you cared so much, where were you? You weren't so concerned that my husband was a piece of shit when you were screwing him."

Nyah slapped her across the face so hard, the palm of her hand turned red and began to tingle. Graydon got up quickly to step between the two warring women. Nyah blinked to remove the tears that were blocking her vision; she could not control the rage that was building inside her. "Me, screwed your husband? I wouldn't touch that piece of shit with a ten foot plunger." Graydon had to use all his strength to keep the shouting women apart.

"He rejected you so you went running with your tail between your slutty legs to some god forsaken town to hide."

"I was there; I have always been there for Nikki and for the boys. You were the one who came and took her from my house, and look at where she is now, this is you, Pamela, not me."

A small crowd was starting to gather and a man in a suit along with three hospital security officers walked briskly down the hall towards them.

"I'm sorry, we're going to have to ask you all to leave, this is a hospital facility and we cannot tolerate this kind of disruption."

"I'm not going anywhere, my daughter is in there," she pulled her blouse down and tried to straighten her hair, "she should leave." Two security guards stood beside both women. "Why don't you get the hell out of here and go back to your perfect little life," she was screaming as she lunged at Nyah.

Mark positioned himself between both women and Pamela's blow caught him in the back.

"Trace, let's go for a walk," he said but she did not move; her chest was rising and falling quickly. Mark nudged her and being no match for his strength, she allowed him to lead her into a room and he closed the door. She paced back and forth for a while and then she turned to face him.

"What are you doing here?" Her voice still sounded angry.

"You need to calm down," he said.

"I don't need to calm down. Why does everyone keep telling me to calm down? My niece is lying in a hospital bed after she tried to kill herself and that..." She stopped talking and screamed before closing her eyes; the tears began to flow again. He wrapped his arms around her and she buried her face in his chest.

"I tried calling you last night, I went to the house and you weren't there. When I couldn't reach you, I got worried so I called Graydon and he told me that you were here with him."

"What else did he tell you?" she backed away from him.

"That he was worried about you, now I can see why." Nyah didn't realize that she was holding her breath until she exhaled.

"This is such a mess," she said relieved that he made no mention of the baby. "I can't leave Nikki alone Mark; she needs me right now. I might be here for a while."

He kissed her gently on her forehead, "I'll stay for a few days."

She looked into his eyes and was comforted, a couple of days with him were better than nothing.

Nikki stayed in the hospital for four days and the social worker would not allow Nyah to talk to her. When they released her, she could not go home with Pamela and Sean. The children's aid society placed her in foster care and continued to investigate her home situation. They took Graydon's name and contact information as next of kin for emergencies.

Mark left after staying with them at Graydon's apartment for two days; he had to sign a new client. Nyah asked to see Nikki again but the social worker said she did not want any visitors. After a week passed, nothing changed and Nyah needed to get back to her classroom. The day before she left, Nikki asked to see her; Nyah was overjoyed.

"Hey, Nik," Nyah was aware that they were being supervised.

Nikki hugged her weakly.

"Hey Auntie," Nyah did not know what to say to her. She had lost a lot of weight and she still had the bandage wrapped around her head. They sat for a while, neither of saying anything.

"I'm so happy to see you," Nyah said trying to hold back the tears, "I'm so sorry I couldn't get here fast enough but, I'm here now, everything is going to be all right, I promise." Nyah smiled to try to reassure her, "I love you, always remember that."

"I'm sorry I stole your pills," Nikki whispered.

"What pills?"

"The ones I saw you taking all the time, I only took three."

"Nikki, why…"

"I'm sorry ma'am, your time is up," the social worker came over and stood closer to their table.

"It's not five minutes yet," Nyah looked at the woman in frustration.

"I'm sorry ma'am," she said again, "time's up." Nyah thought the woman should have been a prison guard instead of a social worker.

She hugged Nikki tight and kissed her on the cheek.

"Everything will be okay Nik," Nyah reassured her.

Eighteen

Mark insisted on picking Nyah up from the airport. She stayed at his apartment that night and being sympathetic to her plight, and thinking she was still upset about her niece; he gave her all the free space she needed. She listened while he talked about his son Jason, how smart he was, how well he took to his grandparents, how happy he was that he finally got the son he wanted. The more he talked, the more she realized that the child she was carrying would always be second to his son and that was not good enough for her; she wanted all or nothing.

When she woke up the next morning, he was not in the apartment, she assumed he went to work and saw no reason to wait for him to come back to take her home. She stood under the shower with her eyes closed, enjoying the feel of the hot water on her skin, wondering if it was too hot for the baby when she heard his voice behind her. Startled, she turned around quickly and reached for the shower curtain to hide her belly but missed it and stumbled forward. He reached out but not fast enough to prevent her from falling; she hit her stomach on the edge of the tub. The pain shot straight to her head but she ignored it; not wanting to draw attention to her exposed body. She sat down in the tub, pulled her knees into her chest and wrapped her arms around them.

"Are you okay?" Nyah had never seen him so anxious.

"I'm fine," she said, "just clumsy." He tried to help her stand up but the pain in her belly intensified and she brushed his hands away.

"I just need a minute," she said, also realizing that if she stood up, he would definitely see the changes in her body. Her breasts were bigger, at eight and a half weeks, her waist was beginning to expand, and she was determined not to tell him about the pregnancy until she was ready.

"Can I get a towel please?" he hesitated; looking at her with concern in his eyes then he left the bathroom and returned seconds later with a large white towel. He wrapped it around her, picked her up and carried her to the bedroom.

"Maybe we should get you checked out," he said laying her on the bed and using the towel to dry her off. "I didn't mean to scare you; I went out to get you some breakfast." Nyah was moved by his tenderness and was tempted to tell him about the baby; she resisted, remembering he already had the one he wanted.

"I'm okay, see," she wiggled her fingers and toes and the pain in her belly was beginning to subside. "Can you take me home?"

"I'd feel better if you stayed here," he caressed the side of her face with his fingers.

"I haven't been home in a while," she smiled, "I want to make sure my plants are still alive." She sent him to make her some tea and while he was gone, she got dressed quickly, joined him in the kitchen, and had to reassure him that she was fine.

On the way to her house, he got an emergency call to meet with an irate client in Atlanta. She could tell by the expression on his face that he did not want to leave her alone, but the client requested him and would not accept anyone in his place.

After taking her bag upstairs and making sure she was settled, they stood at her front door.

"I'll only be gone for a few days, are you sure you're gonna be okay?"

"You need to stop, I'm fine." He kissed her tenderly, "call me if you need me," he whispered and then he left.

* * * * * * * **

Her senses were heightened to the changes that were taking place in her body and in her mind because of the baby. She began reading the pregnancy book she had bought a week earlier and started taking folic acid and vitamins to ensure she was getting enough nutrients that she would not otherwise get from her vegetarian diet. She made a conscious effort to fill her mind with positive thoughts about the baby, and although having a baby was not a part of her well-laid plans, she was willing to learn all she could about raising the baby on her own; comforted by the knowledge that many women had done it before her.

At two o'clock one morning, she laid on her back, wide-awake, staring at the ceiling. She tried to read a book but could not get her mind to focus on the words. She got up and went downstairs to make some tea but as she walked through the living room, she glanced at the piano and wondered if she could still play. She sat down on the black stool and lifted the dusty cover, placed her fingers on the keys and noticed that they were trembling. She closed her eyes and enjoyed the sound of the keys as her fingers pressed them. The music flowed through her like a waterfall and except for a few missed notes; she managed to play an extended version of *Mary Had a Little Lamb* in A minor. She smiled at her accomplishment, went upstairs to her bed and fell asleep with her hand resting on her belly.

The next morning, she called Graydon for an update on Nikki and he told her that she was having a hard time with her recovery and that the CAS was still investigating Pamela and Sean but he did not tell her why.

Pearline called to tell her that they decided to put Gran in a nursing home for her own good, so that she could receive care around the clock. Of course, Gran was livid and Nyah wondered how they managed to get her to leave the Big House without putting up a fight.

Nyah called the school and requested two months' leave of absence; she needed some time to adjust to everything that was going on in her life. They scheduled her return in May. With extra time on her hands, Nyah went to see Gran.

When she walked into the nursing home, the pungent smell that greeted her was a combination of dirty clothes, disinfectant and urine. Nyah hated the place immediately and could not believe that Pearline had put her grandmother in there, the only plus being it was close to the Big House.

"Hey Gran," she said quietly. Matty turned off the television and smiled at Nyah when she entered the room.

"Nyah, honey," then her face got serious. "I hope you didn't have nothin' to do with putting me in this hell hole?"

"No Gran, I didn't, Pearline told me and I came to see how you're doing."

"Good, then, I'm happy to see you." Nyah hugged her. "What's on your mind; you look like the cat ate your supper."

"I'm good Gran, everything's fine," Nyah said but Gran gave her a disbelieving stare.

"You is lying child, I can see it all over you," she said.

"Gran, I came here to see you, to make sure you were okay not to talk about me."

"Nonsense. I can sum up my whole life in two sentences. I was born, now I'm old. They put me in this old folk's home and I hate it. End of story," she said.

"I hope they are treating you all right in here?"

"It ain't no palace but, I eat, bathe and sleep. I'm as good as I can be. God sustains me, he keeps me going." She started to cough. Nyah rubbed her back and held a glass with water to her lips but Gran wouldn't stop coughing long enough to drink it. She pressed a button beside the bed and moments later, a nurse entered the room.

She told Gran to lie in the bed and asked Nyah to leave the room while she checked Gran over.

A few minutes later, the nurse told Nyah she could go back in but only for a few minutes because Gran needed to rest. The nurse put a breathing mask over Gran's face.

"Don't look so worried child; it's just a little cough. They got me taking some pills to make it go away but them pills ain't worth a damn." She laughed and coughed briefly. Gran looked at Nyah intently. "How is that handsome young man of yours doing?"

"Gran, are you feeling sick?"

"No, I just swallowed too much air." She looked at Nyah and smiled. "Don't worry."

"He's fine," Nyah answered her question about Mark.

"He sure is," she said laughing, "he seems like a nice fella. When are you all getting' married?"

"Married?" She was taken off guard. Marriage was the farthest thing from her mind where Mark was concerned.

"Well, you're expectin' aren't you? I'm guessin' the baby is his?" Nyah shifted uneasily, amazed at her grandmother's ability to sense things.

"Who told you I was pregnant?" she asked.

"Ain't nobody got to tell me nothing, I can see it all over you, you don't weigh but twenty pounds and I can see the belly pushing out. Besides, I had a dream about fish last night and here you are, in the flesh smelling like one." Gran wanted to laugh but she coughed instead, "how far along are you?"

"I'm just past nine weeks."

"I knew it was just a matter of time, the way that boy looked at you and all. Is he planning to marry you and take the shame out of your eye?"

Nyah broke down and told her grandmother the whole story, about Mark's ex-girlfriend, his long lost son, also, how she believed it was bad timing to tell him about the baby. Gran didn't buy it.

"A man has got the right to know he has a child coming. You are selfish if you think you can keep it from him, I'm sure you don't want to make the same mistake your mother did. Now, in God's eyes, having a child out of wedlock is a sin but He is a good God, a forgiving God and he can reset this situation. Promise me you'll tell your young man about the baby and give him a chance to do the right thing." Gran began to cough again and the nurse came in the room and told her it was time to leave. They hugged and Nyah promised to visit her again soon.

Nineteen

Graydon called Nyah to let her know that the social worker moved Nikki from foster care into a group home because she had started to act out. She wanted to visit Nikki again but she was experiencing a lot of cramps. The gynecologist said it was just her body adjusting and making room for the growing baby. At almost twelve weeks, she could hardly find clothes to fit anymore. Mark was away in Atlanta for almost a week and she was relieved because she was running low on excuses why she was not in the mood.

Nyah kept thinking about what her grandmother said and decided to tell Mark about the baby when he returned from his recording session in a couple of days, even his worst rejection would not be bad enough because she was reconciled to raising the child by herself.

Gabby dropped by the house unexpectedly to take Nyah to lunch, she reluctantly agreed.

"You are positively glowing," Gabby whispered to her as they walked up to the entrance of the restaurant where Sage was waiting for them.

"Hey Nyah," Sage said and hugged her. They walked in together and a host seated them at a booth with a view of the river.

"I love the hair," Nyah said to Sage; admiring her new cut and honey brown color.

"I thought it was time for a change," she said.

They ordered lunch and the waiter brought their food in about fifteen minutes. Nyah had not been feeling nauseous for a few days and thought she would try a simple pasta dish.

"So Nyah, I hear Mark has a son, have you met him?"

"Not formally," she said, trying to remain cool as she kept eating.

"That must be hard for you, no?"

Nyah looked at her squarely, "not as hard I'm sure as it is for Mark and Jason," she hoped her tone sent the clear message that she was not going to discuss Mark's business with anyone. A sudden sharp pain in her abdomen caused her to topple over.

"Ny, what's wrong?" Gabby asked.

"I don't know, I have been having sharp pains in my belly but the doctor says there's no need for concern. Excuse me." She stood up and took one step towards the washroom when she heard Sage cry out.

"Oh my God Ny, you're bleeding."

"Bleeding?" Gabby got up quickly, knocking over the chair and rushed to her side, "We have to get you to a hospital now, I'll get the car." Nyah thought the flow she felt was a heavy discharge.

She doubled over in pain, unable to stand up straight.

"Maybe you need an ambulance," Sage said and Gabby asked the waiter to call for one. Nyah fell to her knees clutching her stomach the pain was unbearable. Within minutes, the ambulance came and the paramedics secured her to a stretcher and wheeled out of the restaurant.

"Sage, could you pick up the check and meet us at York General?" Gabby said trying to take control of the situation.

* * * * * * **

The emergency room was crowded with mostly children and elderly patients, but Nyah bypassed everyone, they placed her in an examination room right away. The doctor on call entered the small space, and when Dr. Hoyt saw her, he was visibly surprised.

"Miss Parsons; what's happening here?" He asked the attending nurse and she handed him the chart. "I haven't seen you since our last visit in my office."

"I know," she said, "and I'm sorry, I've had family emergencies to deal with."

He took her blood pressure and used his stethoscope to listen to her heart and the baby's heart beat.

"Prepare an IV right away and get her into the ultrasound room stat," his tone was urgent. It was not long before Nyah had a tube in the back of her hand, and was wheeled by an attendant to a room with a computer and a large monitor. The technician squeezed a warm gel across her abdomen, moved the instrument across her belly and stared at the monitor.

"Is my baby alright?" She asked, trying to read the expression on the technician's face but couldn't.

"I can't answer that," she said, "the doctor will have to discuss that with you."

The technician left the room and returned a few moments later with the doctor who also examined the monitor closely. The look on the doctor's face created a hollow feeling in the pit of her stomach.

"Miss Parsons," he said, "I'm sorry, but we are unable to locate a heartbeat, the fetus shows no sign of life. I can't tell for sure how long it's been deceased but I suspect a few days, a week at most." Nyah's chest tightened and it was difficult for her to breathe. She heard the doctor's words, but she could not believe them.

"The baby is dead? How?" Her voice was shaky.

"That's hard to determine right now," he looked at her chart, "you're about eleven and a half weeks is that right?" She nodded. "Miscarriages can occur for any number of reasons, usually before entering the second trimester. We will need to prepare you for a Dilation and Curettage procedure as soon as possible; your uterus has begun the process and this procedure will make sure all the deceased fetal tissue is removed. I'll get the nurse in here to prep you for the surgery, I'm sorry."

Nyah saw his lips moving but she could not focus on his words. All this time, she had Mark's baby growing inside her, now it was gone, and he didn't even know. Dr. Hoyt left her alone and she felt numb.

Gabby walked into the room carrying all her belongings.

"Are you all right, is the baby okay?"

"Baby? What baby?" Sage came in behind her. "Nyah, you're pregnant?"

Nyah stared blankly in front of her, not looking at anything in particular.

"Was pregnant."

"You lost the baby? Maybe, it's all for the best." Gabby said.

Sage pushed past her.

"That's so insensitive Gab. Nyah, I'm really sorry."

She remained silent.

The nurse prepped her for the short surgery and afterward they placed her in a recovery room for a few hours. When the anesthesia wore off, she longed to hear Mark's voice. She knew he was still out of town, but she was sure hearing his voice would make her feel better so she called his cell phone. She didn't know what she would say to him but at that moment she needed him, she needed him to call her beautiful, to brush his lips against hers and tell her she smelt good, at this point, she was willing to take anything she could get. When his phone went to his voicemail, she did not bother to leave a message. She planned to call him back later but she never got around to it.

The doctor decided to keep her overnight for observation and when Gabby picked her up from the emergency room the next morning, she wanted to go to Mark's apartment; to surprise him when he returned from his trip. She wanted to be around anything that reminded her of him, to feel like she was a part of him and to find comfort being in familiar surroundings.

"For as long as I've known Mark, this is the first time I've been to his place," Gabby said as they walked through the door. "Let me fix you some tea, I can stay with you for a little while," she said. Nyah curled up on the sofa and fell asleep; the sound of a high-pitched voice woke her from a tormented dream. She opened her eyes and saw a woman clutching a little boy, who had buried his face in her side.

"Who are you and how did you get in here?" The woman seemed startled, Nyah's mind began to focus and soon she was able to determine who they were.

"Who are you?" Gabby asked.

"I live here." The woman looked Latino or Mediterranean, with an exotic square face, brown eyes and long black wavy streaked hair.

"What do you mean you live here? This is Mark's apartment." Nyah sat up quickly.

"We live here together," she said still holding the little boy.

"This is my boyfriend's home, there must be some mistake."

"Oh, you must be Nyah," she mispronounced her name. "I'm Meaghan and this is Jason." Nyah dialed Mark's number again but there was no answer. "If you are trying to reach Markie, he's at a session and he won't be back for a few days."

"Markie?" Nyah got off the sofa; felt a numbing pain in her lower abdomen but she pushed through it. She walked over to where the woman was standing with her child; feeling anger rising in her with each step. "I'm not sure what's going on in your head, but let's be clear so there is no mistake. I know where Mark is, I know what he is doing and I know when he is coming back." Nyah was aware of the child, but she did not look at him.

"Where the hell did you come from, what are you doing here? It has been six years for god's sakes. Shit." Nyah could feel her whole body trembling. She had been through an ordeal losing the baby only to find out that Mark was shacking up with some woman and their child. All his talk about loving her, and wanting her to be patient while he sorted things out was all bullshit. Liar, she hated him.

"You know what, you stay, I'll go," she said in a very composed voice then she picked up her sweater and calmly walked out of the apartment. When they sat in the car, Nyah screamed at the top of her voice.

"That son of a bitch," she could not control her anger. "All this time he had me believing he cared about me, he loved me and he's living with another woman."

"Nyah, you shouldn't jump to conclusions." Gabby tried to reason with her.

"I know what I saw; she had a key to his apartment."

"I have a key to your place."

"Okay, stop it," Nyah snapped, "that's different and you know it, he's a man, my man."

"What does that mean? Look, all I'm saying is, how do you know you can trust her? If I were you, I'd wait to hear Mark's side." Nyah rested her head on the back of the chair, closed her eyes and began to breathe deeply. Her body craved her pills and she looked around for her purse but realized she left it in the apartment.

"I left my purse upstairs," she said.

"Relax, I'll go and get it." Gabby looked at her. "There has to be an explanation for all this. I did warn you about him."

They drove home in silence. Whenever Gabby tried to talk to her, Nyah would abruptly cut her off. Feeling safe in her home, she refused Gabby's request to stay with her and went upstairs, fell across her bed and cried until she fell asleep. Her house phone and cell phone rang several times but she did not want to talk to anyone.

When Mark called her later that night, she did not want to talk to him so she let the answering machine take a message and then replayed it when she was in a more receptive frame of mind. His message said he would be back tomorrow and he was anxious to see her.

When he came to the door, she was reluctant to let him inside, she didn't want to see him, or talk to him. She moved aside and he entered the foyer and turned to face her.

"Are you okay?"

"How do you think I am?" she snapped, her arms folded defiantly across her chest.

"What happen at my apartment yesterday?" He asked pointedly, his tone sounded accusing. She did not respond and he continued. "Meaghan called me, very upset, she said you shouted at her in front of Jason and tried to kick them out of the apartment."

"So she was able to talk to you. I called you all day yesterday and the day before and I couldn't reach you."

"You know I turn off my phone when I'm in the studio. She left a message, and I called her back. What were you thinking?"

"What was I thinking? I thought that I was your girlfriend, that you cared about me, but I was a fool for believing that. No, the question is, what were you thinking; living with some woman behind my back? How long has this been going on Mark?"

"There is nothing going on."

"Right, and you expect stupid little naive Nyah to believe that."

"What has gotten into you, why are you acting this way? Tracie, you know how I feel about you, you are my first priority; I told you when I first found out about all this that I needed some time to work through it," he said.

"Some 'time' as in space?" she asked.

"No, time as in 'time', don't put words in my mouth. I need you to trust me on this. They'll be staying with me for a little while and I don't want you to freak out about it."

"So you want me to accept the fact that you are living with another woman and her son."

"Our son," his words cut through her like a knife. In the last 48 hours, she had been to hell and back, she had lost their baby and he was rubbing another woman and their child in her face. For Nyah, that was as much as she was willing to endure.

"You can take all the time you need," she said, "I have nothing more right now. This whole situation also what's going on with my niece is a big deal for me, I hope you understand."

"Did something else happen with Nikki?" he asked, but she did not feel like talking to him anymore.

"No," she said.

He drew her closer to him, bent and kissed her lightly, to her, it felt like goodbye.

"I'll call you later," he said and left, and when he called her, she refused to answer it.

Nyah spent the next couple of days in bed; giving her body a chance to heal from the surgery. She ignored all Mark's calls and it wasn't long before he stopped calling, she felt like a lost soul.

Twenty

The drive to see Gran was very relaxing and Nyah took the time to enjoy the scenery along the coast. When she left Richdale, the roads were clear but as she drove through Chicago, the driving conditions had changed and the roads got slippery from heavy rainfall. It had been over two weeks since she lost the baby and she was having a hard time moving past the pain.

Planning this trip to visit Gran was just the joy she craved in her life right now; she needed to get away from Richdale for a while. She felt vulnerable because Gabby knew too much about her personal stuff and she was convinced that her relationship with Mark was over. When she told him she was taking the trip to Wisconsin, he offered to drive her, but she refused; saying she wanted to be alone. She realized that it was in his nature to rescue wounded souls, to be their savior and she was determined not to be his damsel in distress. He made a choice and it was clear that choice did not include her. She stopped at the Big House before going to the nursing home, Marjorie answered the door and Nyah greeted her with a warm hug.

"Miss Nyah, this is a nice surprise, I wasn't expecting to see you, no one told me you were coming."

"I didn't really tell anyone I'd be here I decided to visit at the last minute."

"I'll need some time to get your room ready for you."

"That's okay Marjorie, I can stay at a hotel, there's no problem," she said.

"Rent a room?" she said with disdain in her voice. "Not while I'm alive, this is your home, I'll get your room ready right now," she said and Nyah got the feeling there was no point arguing with her.

"I can do it myself," Nyah offered.

"I'm happy to do it, there hasn't been much to do around here since Miss Matty has been gone."

"Okay, if you insist," she smiled and Marjorie was almost running up the stairs. The house felt cold and empty without Gran in it and as she looked around, a wave of sadness almost stifled her.

Nyah took a shower and changed her clothes.

"You hungry Miss Nyah?"

"No. I want to get to the nursing home before it gets too late, maybe when I come back I'll have something," she said when she saw concern in Marjorie's eyes.

"Okay, what do you feel like eating?"

"Anything is fine," she said as she went through the front door.

It took her fifteen minutes to drive to the nursing home.

Gran was sleeping when Nyah entered her room, not wanting to disturb her peaceful slumber, she sat in a chair beside the window and watched her chest as it rose and fell gently with every breath she took. Even as she slept, Nyah thought her Gran's face looked tired. Memories of her childhood with her grandmother flooded her thoughts and her heart fluttered and filled with emotion.

Forty minutes passed before Gran stirred and slowly opened her eyes. Nyah walked over to the bed, fixed

Gran's pillow and adjusted the purple scarf that she used to keep her wig in place.

"Hey sugar, when did you get here?" her voice sounded hoarse.

"Just now Gran, how are you doing?"

"'I'm still breathin'," she said trying to sit up but she couldn't.

"Everything all right?" she asked.

Nyah sighed.

"Everything all right?" Gran asked again, this time in a more forceful voice.

"Ah Gran, life hurts."

"Life is what you make it," she said.

Before Nyah could stop herself, she told her about losing the baby.

"I'm sorry to hear that, but God knows best, He knows why he took that baby from you, I lost six babies before I had your mother, you're still young, you'll be all right."

"It still hurts," she said.

"And it will, maybe for a long time, but, this too, shall pass," she said squeezing Nyah's hand. "Right now, I'm praying for this family. It breaks my heart to see everyone walking around with their own piece of hurt. You all care about your own self more than you care about each other, but the time is coming for healing and restoration. You all need to make your way back to one another, in the end all you got besides God, is family." She paused and closed her eyes.

Nyah saw the tears running down the corner of her eyes. "You know, I remember when you were a little girl right after your mother dropped you on my doorstep, I discovered very quickly you didn't like to have your hair combed. All I had to do was show you the comb and you would make a big fuss. It's not like your hair was nappy neither, it was soft, you just didn't want anyone to touch it. I'd watch you play dress up with your little friend down the street, what was her name again? You know the little white girl that lived with her mother."

"Lydia," Nyah said smiling at the memory.

"Yeah Lydia, I wonder whatever happened to her? Anyway, when she would put all the pretty ribbon in her yellow hair, you didn't want none of that, you were okay with your golden curls, you had your mind made up, you were your own person and no one, not even me could change it." Gran paused and moaned as if she was in pain and Nyah touched her hand. "I remember you use to have three dolls and you never combed their hair either." Gran laughed softly. "Wherever you went, if you couldn't take all three of those dolls with you, you didn't want to take none at all. You loved them dolls as one, you treated them like family. What your mother did to you was not nice, but she did what she believed was right at the time."

"Gran, she didn't want me, she threw me away."

"Hush, all she did was throw you into my arms, and didn't I catch you just fine? Sometimes it's hard to be sure, but I believe I did the best I could with what God gave me, I hope that was enough. Baby, I'm tired, can you come visit me tomorrow."

"I will," Nyah kissed her grandmother tenderly on the cheek, fluffed her pillow and tucked her in then left the room.

She visited Gran every day for two weeks; bringing her fresh purple lilies every other day. Gran told her to stop because the room was beginning to look like a purple graveyard. Some days, all they did was listen to music, other times Nyah read to her until she fell asleep. The stories her grandmother shared with her, reminded her of better times.

"What's going on between you and Pamela?" Gran asked unexpectedly as Nyah was getting ready to leave one afternoon. "She came by to see me a few times and whenever your name comes up; she gets madder than a bull in chains."

"She thinks I slept with her husband."

"Well, did you?"

"Gran, how can you ask me that?" Nyah raised her voice by her grandmother for the first time since she was a little girl, "no, I didn't."

"Then tell her."

"That's easier said than done Gran."

"You two are sisters, nothing should ever come between sisters, I wish to God I had one," Gran said with a reflective look in her eyes. "Don't forget, I saw the way you reacted at my birthday party back in August when they came up beside you. Now I may be wrong, but I know you left Wisconsin because something scared you real bad and I think it has something to do with that man, I just don't know what that something is. Tell you the truth; I don't want to know. Now, I've looked at you this past year and I've seen changes in you that break my heart; you are sitting on some shit and you need clean that mess up."

Nyah started to cry.

"Gran, I wouldn't know where to start."

Gran's voice was firm.

"Hush your cryin'; it's only good for cleansing the soul, not for self-pity. Now you listen to me," Nyah cried silently and fixed her gaze on her grandmother, "you're stronger than you think you are. You act all big and bad, like you don't need nobody, hiding behind your fancy words and your degrees; well, no man is an island and your best to remember that. There's no shame whatsoever in asking for help when you need it. You remember that. Will you be here tomorrow?"

Nyah nodded, she felt anything but strong. She believed her whole world was crashing down around her.

She hugged her grandmother and turned to leave the room.

"Baby."

"Yes Gran."

"True love and forgiveness go hand in hand, they're partners, you can't have one without the other. Try it out on yourself first, it's liberation'; then when you have a handle on that love thing, give it away without expecting a return and see what happens."

Nyah snuggled up against her grandmother.

"I love you Gran."

"I love you too sugar."

Twenty-one

Nyah left the nursing home and headed for the mall, on her way there, she spoke to Graydon and he told her that he was coming to Wisconsin to do a mini art show and to spend time with Gran.

She walked into a clothing boutique and sifted through the racks hoping to find something that her grandmother would like. She noticed that Gran was not smiling as much as she used to and thought that a new outfit would cheer her up.

The next morning, when she arrived at the nursing home, she did not get to see Gran because she had gone for testing and the nurse said it would take a while so Nyah stayed long enough to straighten up her room and folded the purple dress that she bought for her and placed it neatly on her grandmother's pillow.

When Nyah returned to the Big House, she spent the rest of the day cleaning the house from top to bottom amidst heavy protest from Marjorie but Nyah told her she needed to keep busy so that the time would go by faster. That evening, she was too tired to eat; she just fell across her bed and went to sleep.

At around 2:30 in the morning she woke with a jolt, as if someone threw a bucket of cold water on her back and there was a sharp, prickly pain in her right breast that would not go away. Nyah picked up the phone to call Mark but changed her mind half way through dialing his number thinking he was probably not available.

She went downstairs to make a cup of tea, thoughts of her grandmother alone in that place weighted heavily on her mind she had to do something. The only thing that she could think of doing was selling her house and moving back to Wisconsin to take care of her grandmother herself. She wanted Gran moved back into the Big House and she was determined to make it happen while she was in Wisconsin.

After she made her decision, Nyah managed to get a few more hours sleep and in the morning, she could hardly wait for the flower shop to open so she could bring Gran lilies and tell her the good news. When she got to the nursing home around ten o'clock, she was surprised to see her mother sitting in the waiting room.

"Mom, what are you doing here?"

"I'm here to see you," she said and used a tissue to wipe her nose. She wore no makeup and her hair was in a ponytail.

"How did you know I was here?" Nyah thought her mother's behavior was a little peculiar, but she did not know her long enough to determine if that was normal for her.

"That doesn't matter, we need to talk."

"Mom, I'm here to see Gran right now; can we talk later?"

When Nyah walked into her grandmother's room, the first thing that she noticed was the dress, still lying on the pillow exactly as she left it the day before. She inserted the new flowers in the same vase with the old ones, and thinking Gran was in the bathroom she called out but there was no answer so she went to inquire at the nurse's station.

"May, I help you," the nurse asked without looking up from a chart on her desk.

"Mrs. Janssens is not in her room, has she been moved?"

"What room is she in?" the nurse asked.

"She's in the room at the end of the hall, 214."

She looked at Nyah and got up from her chair. "I'll get the doctor for you."

"The doctor?" Nyah's heart began racing; she was beginning to get worried. "Is she alright?"

"I'll be right back." The nurse disappeared into an office at the end of the hall and returned with a woman in her mid to late forties.

"Hello, I'm Dr. Bridgewater." Nyah had a sinking feeling in the pit of her stomach. "Are you related to Mrs. Janssens?"

"These are my children, Graydon and Nyah, you and I spoke earlier."

"And I guess you haven't had a chance to tell them."

"Tell us what?" She was starting to shut down. "She's dead isn't she?" Nyah's voice was barely above a whisper. Graydon put his arm around her when the doctor looked at Pearline and then back at Nyah.

"I'm sorry, Mrs. Janssens died of pneumonia early this morning," she said. Graydon let out a loud cry and walked away. Nyah's heart ached; she felt as though someone had reached into her chest and ripped it out. It was getting harder and harder to breathe.

"I'm sorry honey," Pearline said through her tears. Nyah could no longer hear what was going on around her; she walked down the hall into Gran's room, her mother tried to console her, but she shrugged her off. She climbed in the bed; pulled her knees into her chest and lay motionless.

The next few hours were a blur for Nyah. There was a lot of chatter but she just wanted everyone to go away and leave her alone.

"Nyah, I'm Dr. Sheard, a psychiatrist with the nursing home." Nyah did not respond. "I'm so sorry for your loss. Maybe I can help."

"You can't," she said.

"I understand that losing a loved one is never easy for anyone to cope with. I'll leave my card on the table just in case you or anyone in your family would like to talk." She put the card down and left the room. Nyah must have fallen asleep because the next time she opened her eyes the hall lights were on and it was dark outside.

"Ny," Graydon's voice was low, "let's go."

She could not answer him. The words would not come.

"Nyah, you can't stay here." Pearline's voice was shaky.

Her grandmother's face flashed across her mind, and she closed her eyes to preserve the memory.

"She didn't give me any warning; I wasn't ready, she didn't tell me she was going to leave me." Nyah's voice was hoarse. She forced herself out of the bed, picked up the dress, as many lilies as she could carry and walked slowly out of the room.

When they made it back to the Big House, it was filled with people; the news of Gran's death had reached her church congregation and they were ready and willing to offer their support. She heard their words and she felt their touch, but she didn't look at or respond to any of them. Wasted tears, she thought, crying would not bring her Gran back. Graydon held Nyah close to his side as they walked through the crowd of people and upstairs to her room. When she was alone, she bolted the room door and shut everyone out, she was alone and she wanted it that way.

For three days she stayed in her bed, even when Graydon broke down the door because they thought something happened to her, she remained silent, trapped in her own little world.

"Miss Nyah, it's me, can I come in?" Marjorie entered the door-less room with a bowl of soup on a small tray and a wooden box under her arm, "you need to eat something, or you'll get sick. I made you some pea soup." She put the tray on the night table next to the bed. "Nyah, I need you to drink this soup." When Nyah did not acknowledge her presence she continued, "Miss Matty told me to give this to you if she died. There's something in there I think she wanted you to read." Nyah didn't move. Marjorie walked around to the other side of the bed, lifted her arm and placed it over the box.

"Please have a little something to eat; you'll need your strength to say a proper goodbye."
Nyah's tears had soaked her pillow and Marjorie gently lifted her head to replace it with another one before she left the room. Shortly after, Graydon came in, put the box on the floor and sat on the bed.

"Ny, please drink the soup."

"I don't want any soup," her voice was no more than a whisper, "leave me alone." Her heart was in pieces and she didn't know what to do.

He stood over her, "you're not the only one in pain, you're not the only one who loved Gran and miss her, we all loved her and we all miss her, you don't have to go through this alone," he turned to leave.

"Gray," she said and he turned around. She could hardly open her eyes and her throat was dry. His eyes were red and swollen, he had been crying, "I'm sorry." He returned to the bed and sat down. "It hurts, really bad."

"I know," he said and hugged her, it was the first time in three days she allowed anyone to touch her.

"I think you should open a window and get some fresh air in here. When was the last time you showered?"

"Do I smell?" she asked quietly.

"A little, I'll set a bath for you." He looked around the room, saw empty Kleenex boxes everywhere and used Kleenex tissues all over the floor. "You've been by yourself in this bed for the past few days, why don't you come downstairs and sit with us. Everyone has been asking for you."

"Where's Pearline?" she asked.

"She went to meet with the funeral director to make arrangements for the funeral on Friday."

Nyah could feel the tears swelling up again.

"Gray, I can't believe she's gone. I'm so alone."

"You're not alone, we are all here and we all miss Gran." She did not respond, he didn't understand. "Get cleaned up, I'll set the bath, but first, drink some of that soup, one death in the family is all I can handle right now."

She got up slowly and went to the bathroom. She stared at her face in the mirror and could hardly recognize it. It was puffy and her eyes were swollen from crying. She tried to run her fingers through her hair but she could not get past the knots. She undressed and lowered her body in the tub resting her head on the ledge, closed her eyes and breathed deeply but it hurt to breathe.

Twenty-two

The evening before the funeral, Nyah drove in the limousine with Pearline, Graydon and Marjorie to the funeral home for a private viewing. When they got there, she could not will herself to get out of the car. She was paralyzed. She didn't want to see her grandmother in that tiny box. Everyone else went inside but she was unable to take that first step.

She felt a draft as the limousine door opened and Mark slipped in beside her.

"How are you holding up?" he asked. "Why didn't you call me?"

She turned her head away from him, "what do you care?"

"How can you say that to me?" Nyah heard the hurt in his voice. She did not respond, "Do you want me to leave?"

Tears filled her eyes as she looked at him. She was angry with him for not being there when she needed him. She was angry with him for choosing some woman and her son over her. She was angry with him for so many reasons she thought were important, but at that moment, she needed him.

"No," she said.

He reached over and touched her hand. "I'm sorry about your grandmother she was cool."

They sat in silence for a while before she began to sob. He reached across the seat and took her in his arms. She closed her eyes and allowed the tears to flow as he stroked her hair.

"Do you want to go inside?" he asked.

"No."

"Okay," he said and continued to hold her. She raised her head and looked into his eyes.

"Thank you. You can go in if you want," she said and pulled away.

"Let's go together. I'll be right there with you." He convinced her to go in with him.

The sadness in the air nearly choked her. Pearline was sitting on a chair with Spencer's hand resting on her shoulder. Graydon stood over Gran's body wiping his eyes with a handkerchief. Nyah wanted so much to reach out to them but she couldn't. She could not see beyond her own pain. She refused to look at her grandmother lying in the casket so she stood in a corner of the room finding solace in Mark's arms, watching people pay their last respects to Gran, wondering if she had any more tears left to cry.

The Big House was overflowing with people; some were getting the house ready for the wake after the funeral tomorrow. Some of the women were singing, some were decorating the house and others were cooking in the kitchen.

Nyah sat with her family downstairs more for the company than the conversation before Mark followed her upstairs to her room, relieved to see the door had been replaced.

"Where are you staying?" she asked hoping he would stay with her.

"I have a room at the hotel."

"Okay," she acknowledged, but what she really wanted to do was beg him to stay with her and hold her all night.

"I'll let you get some rest, call me, if you need me," he said and walked to the door. Nyah was not surprised that he wanted to leave but she was disappointed. "I know this might not be a great time, or what you want to hear right now, but everything happens for a reason." He closed the door on his way out. No, it wasn't what she wanted to hear but coming from him, it wasn't so harsh.

* * * * * * **

Nyah woke up with a headache. She hadn't been sleeping very well for a while and her vision was blurry. She drove with Mark in his truck while the rest of the family went in the limousine. There wasn't enough room in the church for everyone who attended Gran's funeral. The church officials had to turn people away for safety reasons. Immediate Family members sat in the first three rows on both sides of the church. The rest of the pews were filled with her friends from all phases of her life. Mark sat with her and held her hand. She was touched to see how many lives Gran affected. The ceremony began with a prayer and Gran's favorite song, a choral rendition of 'I Shall Wear a Crown'.

Nyah listened, as people spoke kind words about her grandmother. They talked about her love and her generosity. She didn't know that Gran sponsored 14 impoverished children all over the world, that she had at one time been first elder at her church, and that her mentor was author and poet, Maya Angelou. The thing that amazed Nyah the most was, her grandmother was a Jazz pianist in the early 40's. Pearline finished the eulogy and after being silent for so long, Nyah felt compelled to say something. She stood up and her head began to spin.

She paused for a moment to steady her body, determined not to let the moment pass without telling Gran how she felt about her.

She walked to the casket and stood there, looking at her grandmother's lifeless body, wanting desperately to remember the happiest moment that they shared together but her mind could not conjure up any one memory, there were too many. Nyah smiled, Gran's face looked so peaceful, just like that day she walked into her room and watched her chest rise and fall as she slept.

"I have been lost, my guide and mentor, decided to leave me without giving me any warning not even a chance to say goodbye." She paused because the tears were flowing and the words could not come out. She glanced over at Mark and his eyes reassured her and gave her the courage to continue. "I miss her so much. I was blessed to be with Gran a couple of nights before she...when she told me the best kind of love is the one you give away without expectation of return. Gran loved unconditionally, she never minced words, she said what she meant and she meant what she said. Who's gonna love me now Gran?" She paused to free the words that were caught in her throat. "My heart desires one thing, and that's to be just a fraction of the woman she was. Gran was my hero and for as long as I live, I know that I will carry a piece of her love, her strength and her wisdom with me. I love you Gran, rest in peace."

Going to the burial plot crushed Nyah to the very core. When they lowered Gran into the ground and threw on that first bit of dirt, Mark had to hold her up. She cried until her body was lifeless. At that moment, everything stood still and the finality of her grandmother's death hit her like a brick wall. She stayed at the graveside for about an hour after everyone else was gone. Mark stayed in the truck to give her some grieving space. She knew he was there in the shadows, watching and waiting for her if she needed him. It began to rain, he brought an umbrella to cover her head, and she walked with him back to the truck. Nyah sat in the front seat and stared out the window, watching the rain fall silently on her grandmother's grave.

"Can you take me away from here," her voice was barely a whisper. As though sensing her desire for peace and quiet, he took her to his hotel room instead of to the Big House. She did not bother to take off her clothes or shoes; she just rolled up in a ball on the bed and fell asleep.

When she opened her eyes, there was stillness. Mark was lying behind her, wearing only his boxers, his body fitted to hers. His breath was even and that's how she knew he was asleep. She got up quietly and went into the bathroom, turned on the hot water and stood motionless under it trying to wash off the scent of the funeral. Closing her eyes, she allowed the events of the past few weeks to flow from her mind.

When she was finished, she wrapped her body in a towel, walked over to the bed and nestled against Mark's warm body. He pulled her closer; she rested her head on his shoulder and placed her arm across his chest.

"Are you alright?" his voice soothed her.

"No."

"You will be."

In the middle of the night, Nyah stirred. Having Mark so close to her, being in his arms ignited a longing within her. She used her finger to trace down the center of his face and lingered around his lips. She gasped when he parted his lips and drew her finger into his mouth and playfully bit it. She nibbled on his ear, he moaned softly, and slowly turned his face to kiss her tenderly. She shifted her body to lie on top of him. And there, in the dimly lit hotel room, she opened her heart and soul to him, as she had never done before and at the right moment, they experienced a sweet release together.

Nyah lay in his arms and was comforted, but she knew that being in this place was not enough to erase the hurt he caused her over the past few months.

Twenty-three

Mark stayed in Wisconsin for three days after the funeral and then he had to go and Pamela arrived at the Big House with her three boys the day after the funeral.

It was the first time in a long time that Nyah was able to be in the same room with some members of her family without feeling uneasy and disconnected. Everyone openly talked about their memories of Gran; they cried and swapped stories about her life. She wanted to ask Pamela about Nikki, but felt the time was not right.

As they sat around the dinner table in the kitchen, the doorbell rang Floyd went to answer it. When she heard the voice, Pearline stood up, knocked over her chair and ran from the kitchen up the back stairs to the guest room. Seconds later a man entered the kitchen behind Uncle Floyd.

"Hey everybody looked what the cat dragged in," he said with what Nyah thought was a lot of sarcasm. The man greeted everyone at the table but they all averted their eyes and their welcome was very chilly.

"I know I probably shouldn't be here right now," he began.

"You got that right, you have some nerve showing your face..."Pamela was clearly angry with him but he cut her off.

"Regardless of how you all still feel about me after all these years, when I heard about Matty's death, I wanted to come and pay my last respects."

"You've done that, now you can go," Pamela's tone was icy. Nyah sat quietly watching the exchange that was taking place between the man, who she thought was very handsome, in a rugged way and her family. His pale face was oval shaped with a square chin and mesmerizing green eyes. He had a small nose, which she thought was unusual for the size of his face. His reddish-brown hair was wavy and long enough for him to have it up in a ponytail. He looked at Nyah and smiled showing even white teeth.

"Hello Nyah," he said and walked up to her to shake her hand. All eyes in the room followed him as he approached her and she heard some murmuring when she shook it.

Pearline came back into the kitchen, her body seemed tense and a frown creased her forehead.

"Keith, what are you doing here?" Her tone was angry.

"It's good to see you Pearl, you're looking well."

"You can keep your compliment; you have no right being here, this occasion is for friends and family only."

"Well I would say under normal circumstances I could be both but today, I'll just claim the family part."

"Family," Pearline scoffed and began to laugh. "You lost that privilege when you slept with my best friend 20 years ago." Richard, Gail, Floyd and Graydon got up and left the room.

"Now is not the time for this foolishness. Miss Matty is probably turning in her grave," Floyd said before he walked out of the kitchen. Pamela and Nyah stayed with Pearline.

"Pearl, I'm not here to cause any trouble, like I said, I just wanted to pay my last respects and to talk to Nyah."

"Over my dead body Keith," she was adamant.

"Why don't you give her a chance to decide for herself?" He looked at Nyah," can I talk to you for a minute?"

Pearline stepped between them. "It's too late, 27 years too late to be exact."

"Mom, what is going on?" Nyah finally spoke; she wanted the bickering to stop.

"Nyah, I'd like you to meet your dead beat father," she spat out vehemently. He did not respond to her anger, he simply looked at Nyah and asked if she could give him a few minutes of her time.

She looked at the man who Pearline claimed to be her father, meeting him seemed so anti-climactic, until that moment she never had a desire to know who he was or to meet him.

"Sure," she said and noticed that Pearline was visibly upset.

"I'm coming with you."

"Not this time," he told her. Nyah noticed her mother's tears but that did not stop her from leaving the house with Keith.

* * * * * * * **

They drove to a coffee shop close by and sat down at a table in the back by the window.

"What is this about?" she asked.

"You've grown into such a beautiful young woman," he said, when she did not respond, he continued. "Nyah, I don't know what your mother has told you about me but I'd like to give you my side of the story." She didn't feel the need to tell him that up to that moment, her mother had never spoken of him, at least not to her. "Let me begin by saying I'm sorry and I hope someday you can find it in your heart to forgive me for not being the father I should have been to you. I don't know how much she's told you and frankly, it doesn't matter. What I hope is that we can move past all that and start fresh."

She had no idea what he was talking about and she let him know.

"Keith, it's not my intent to be rude but you are a complete stranger to me. Until today, I would have passed you on the street and not known who you were. I don't want to discuss my mother with you. If you have an issue with her, I think it's best that you talk to her, not to me."

He paused and she got the feeling he was trying to choose his words carefully.

"I've always wanted to be a part of your life Nyah but I couldn't because your mother wouldn't let me and I was a coward, I made a mistake, and I handled the whole thing very badly. I wanted to visit you when you moved to Riverdale, but I didn't want to interfere in your life."

"Why are you telling me all this now?" she asked.

"Because I believe you deserve to know why I was absent from your life for all these years," he said.

"Look Keith, I appreciate the fact that you took the time to come and pay your respects to Gran, that was very thoughtful, but I'm not interested in any of this right now. I'm not a child anymore, I don't want to know about you or your past indiscretions, and I don't want to know about your failed relationship with my mother, I'm sorry." She got up and left the coffee shop. He didn't try to stop her.

* * * * * * **

Pearline called a family meeting. She opened the floor for discussion on what to do with the Big House and the restaurant. She said a lawyer would be coming to the house at four o'clock that afternoon to read Gran's will and the lawyer wanted the whole family present for the reading. Nyah was in her room when Graydon came to tell her that Mr. Smythe was downstairs. As she entered the family room, they were all discussing among themselves what they thought was in Gran's will. Pearline, her two adopted brothers Richard and Floyd and their wives, and Pamela all sat waiting for the lawyer to begin. Graydon and Nyah shared a chair in a corner of the room.

"Good afternoon everyone. As most of you know, I am the Attorney appointed by Mrs. Mataline Janssens to prepare her last will and testament and present it at the event of her death. These are her words as she asked me to read them in a letter.

'You are all here together because I'm dead. I guess that was the only way to bring the family together. Floyd, get a job and stop mooching off everybody, you can have the car. Richard, you need to stop sharing your family's business in your sermons. I know Gail liked that painting in the study so she can have it. Pearl, it's about time you let go of the past and stop blaming everyone else for your one mistake'.

Ms. Jenssens' will reads as follows:

This is the last will of me, Mataline Elaine Janssens currently of 310 Oak Lane in the state of Wisconsin.

1. *I revoke all former wills.*
2. *I give the Big House, all its contents to Nyah Parsons 100%.*
3. *The restaurant and all its contents to Nyah Parsons 50% and Graydon Wright 50% equally.*
4. *The total sum of my life insurance and all investments Nyah Parsons 100%.*
5. *The contents of my bank accounts Nyah Parsons 30%, Graydon Wright 20%, Pearline Ried 10% (that should cover the expenses for all the parties you planned for me) Pamela Wright 10%, Nikki Smith, Byron Jeffers, Sean Jeffers Jr. And Shane Jeffers equally 10% (held in*

trust until age 18) Mt. Zion Baptist Church 5%, Marjorie Andrews 15%.

That's it," he said and closed the document.

All at once, every eye in the room turned to look at Nyah.

Floyd was the first one to speak. "Well ain't that a peach, I've done so much for that woman and all she left me was a half dead piece a crap car."

"You are so ungrateful Floyd, you've lived here in the Big House, rent free for the last four years, it's a wonder she left you anything at all," Richard said.

"I guess now I know for sure how she felt about me." Pearline said.

"I will have papers drawn up for the distribution of the will within the next week." Mr. Smythe gathered his belongings. "Miss Parsons, our office will be in touch within a week or two with the final figures," were his last words before he left the house.

Nyah got up and went into the kitchen to make a cup of tea. She could hear the rest of the family arguing about how unfair the will was. She heard someone say they needed to contact their lawyer.

"Bunch of vultures," Graydon said as he walked into the kitchen. Nyah sat down at the table cradling the hot cup in her hands and he sat on the chair across from her.

"How are you?"

"Just great!" She knew her tone was sarcastic. "My grandmother is dead, my family is fighting over her estate, and nothing I can do will bring her back to me." He came around and rubbed the back of her head.

"Hey," he said brightly, "let's go spend some of that money Gran left you."

Nyah looked at him and smiled weakly.

"Maybe later and you're buying."

Twenty-four

After the will was read, the mood in the Big House changed for the worse, tempers flared, and even though no one said it outright, Nyah believed they all thought she influenced Gran's will somehow. She decided to drive home needing to get as far away from their bickering and pettiness as possible and to coddle her broken heart in peace. Graydon decided to stay in Wisconsin and guard his newly acquired assets.

The house was dark and musty; she had not been there for almost five weeks. She opened all the blinds to let in the last bit of daylight and cracked the windows to allow fresh air to pass through. She put the wooden butterfly necklace inside the treasure chest and closed it quickly, she did not want to see the contents and she did not want to read the note that was folded inside. She put the chest in the guest bedroom and covered it with Gran's purple scarf.

She tried everything she could to soothe her spirit; cleaning had become her favorite pass time but nothing she did could fill the large void in her soul.

She woke up around noon on Sunday went down stairs to make breakfast, and checked her answering machine. Gabby and Sheila both left countless messages; she called Sheila first and expected to see her in two hours, Gabby was at her house in less than fifteen minutes.

When she opened the door, Gabby hugged her so tightly she coughed.

"Hey, I'm so sorry to hear about your grandmother. Mark told David he was going to the funeral, I tried calling but I couldn't reach you."

"Thanks."

"How are you holding up?" She asked, "Is there anything that I can do for you?"

"No, just sit and talk to me, how are things with you?" They sat in the living room and Nyah hugged a pillow to give her hands something to do.

"Things are great," she said. Nyah could tell she was excited about something and realized what it was, when she flashed her left hand. "I'm getting married."

"Yeahhhh," Nyah cheered, "congratulations. So when's the big day?"

"I'm thinking a June or July wedding," she said beaming, her joy lifted Nyah's mood and for a brief moment, her pain was not front and center. "I'd love for you to be one of my bridesmaids."

"Me? Sure, I'd love to," she said.

"Sage is throwing a spring party next week at her place I want to do something different with my hair, do you feel up to going for a drive?" She stood up and headed for the front door, "please come with me."

"You mean today, now?" Nyah asked.

"No time like the present, besides, you could probably use some serious cheering up."

"Beauty salons aren't open on Sundays," she said.

"You don't know my girl Cynthia, she's open twenty-four seven, now let's go before she gets too busy."

* * * * * * **

Nyah walked through her front door a little past seven o'clock.

"I have been waiting here for you for over an hour, I told you I was coming," Sheila walked into the foyer to meet her at the door, "where have you been?" She looked at Nyah's hair, "what did you do?"

"I washed it," Nyah said.

"It's completely straight, it does not look good Nyah, I'm used to seeing you with the curls."

"It doesn't matter," Nyah shrugged, walked past her friend and headed upstairs to take a shower, Sheila followed her. "I can shower on my own Sheila."

She put her bag on the bed and Sheila started looking through it.

"I met this guy and I think he's hot, a lot better than that deadbeat I married." Nyah went into the bathroom and started taking off her clothes. Sheila kept on talking, "I can't stay tonight, I'm meeting a friend in Chicago."

Nyah stuck her head out the bathroom door, "don't let me stop you." She turned on the water and stepped into the shower.

Sheila walked into the bathroom; holding up the bottle with her pills.

"Hey, what's this?"

"What?" Nyah saw the bottle through the glass enclosure, rushed out of the shower and grabbed it from Sheila, "what are you doing, searching through my bag?"

"Why are you taking Xanitol? Isn't that for mental people?"

"What I do is none of your business," Nyah snapped.

"You're touchy today, what's your problem, I'm just asking. And why is your face so long, did somebody die or something?"

"Gran died almost 3 weeks ago," Nyah said quietly.

"So the old woman finally kicked the bucket," Sheila said casually and Nyah stared at her in disbelief. "What?

She was old wasn't she? She's been old since we were twelve."

"Sheila, sometimes you can be such an insensitive bitch," she said.

She looked at Nyah innocently, "what did I say?"

"Get out and leave my house key on the bed," Nyah said pushing her into the bedroom and slamming the bathroom door shut.

"What is your issue today? Maybe you should take one of them pills you have hiding in your bag." Nyah heard the bedroom door slam. She got dressed and went downstairs to find Sheila in the kitchen.

"I thought I told you to leave," Nyah said.

"You did, but I'm not ready yet. I needed to get something to eat, and I want to know why you are taking drugs?"

"Did someone put you up to this? Why were you searching through my bag?" Nyah was more annoyed than angry.

"If you must know, I saw that crap the last time I was here and I wanted to get a closer look. I know some people who've used Xanitol once or twice to help them chill at a party." Nyah took a bottle of water from the fridge, walked into the living room and sat down on the sofa; Sheila stayed in the kitchen and made an egg omelet with cheese then sat on the chair across from her and began to eat.

"Girl, you know how I am, I push through, I may not be the cookie cutter friend, but we've been together a long time, you've helped me through some rough spots over the years and I am here for you, so talk."

There was a long pause.

"Sean raped me." That was the first time Nyah made the admission aloud.

"What? Who the hell is Sean?" Sheila put the plate down and wiped her mouth.

"Sean is Pamela's husband."

"Pamela, your sister Pamela?" she asked.

"Yes," she felt very vulnerable but she continued. "It happened eight years ago when I went home from school for the Christmas holiday. I was usually the first one there, but this year, Pamela, who was pregnant at the time and Sean got there before me. Gran was late putting the annual food baskets together and when they were done, she needed to get them to the church right away but the deacon said the church van was not working. She asked Sean and Pamela to take them over because their van could hold everything. Pam was not feeling well, and she could not go, so Gran asked me to go with Sean.

We got to the church and unloaded the baskets. On our way back, he said he had to stop at a friend's place to pick up something. I told him I would wait for him in the truck. He told me it was a rough neighborhood; he wasn't going to take long but to be safe I should go with him. I followed him down an alley and through the side of an old house. He called out to someone named Scales or Scar, I can't remember." Nyah's heart started racing and her mouth got dry. She paused and took a deep breath and Sheila sat beside her on the sofa.

"You don't have to talk about it if you don't want to," she said.

Nyah began to cry and when Sheila sat beside her and hugged her, she pushed her away. "The next thing I remember is feeling like my insides were on fire and tasting a salty hand over my mouth. The room was dark so I couldn't see anything, I know I smelled Sean's cologne, but I didn't know who the other guy was."

"Sean wasn't the only one?" She asked her eyes wide with bewilderment.

"On the drive back to the Big House, he said that if I told anyone, his friend knew where Gran lived, and to cover himself, he told Pamela that I had seduced him into having sex with me. When we got back to the house, I ran upstairs to take a shower but no matter how hard I tried I couldn't wash away the blood…" Nyah stopped, unable to continue. "I was such a coward, I didn't fight, I didn't run, I did nothing."

"Are you kidding me, how does one woman fight off two men? That son of a …" She picked up the phone and started to dial.

"Who are you calling?

"Who do you think? I'm calling the police." Nyah wrestled the phone from her friend's hand.

"What are they going to do? It's been eight years, besides; it's my word against his."

Sheila wiped away her tears with the back of her hand. "Listen, I can get someone to put him in the hospital or worse. We can find that…" She struggled to find the word, "those swipes and jack them up good," she said and Nyah believed her.

"What good would that do now?" Nyah rested her head on the back of the chair. "Don't they say time heals all wounds?"

"Except you're not healing, you're hiding. Isn't that why you're taking the drugs?"

"The pills help me to not freak out all the time."

"I think you should talk to someone, like a professional or something."

"I've tried, nothing helps except the pills." Nyah said.

"You know you can get hooked on that stuff.

"There's more," Nyah told Sheila about the baby and the situation with Mark's lost and found son.

"What the hell are you talking about Nyah, when were you pregnant and why didn't I know? And I find out today in passing that your grandmother died. How could you keep all this, a secret from me?"

"I didn't want to burden you; you were going through so much with your divorce…"

"Burden my ass, and I thought my life was screwed up, if your shit can fall apart, there's no hope in hell for someone like me." Nyah leaned against Sheila's shoulders. "I'm glad you told me and I'm sorry that I haven't been a better friend, but you know this sister's got your back."

Twenty-five

"Why won't you answer any of my calls?" Mark asked impatiently.

"When did you call?"

"I have been trying to reach you since I got back from the funeral, are you avoiding me?" he asked.

Sheila told her he called, several times but she could not bear the thought of opening herself up to further rejection when he found out about her rape. It was enough that he left her for another woman, and he was not *available* when she lost their baby and all his energy had shifted to his long lost son. She was tired of fighting to keep something that was never really hers from the very beginning.

"I have left messages on your cell, your house phone, I came here yesterday but Shiela said you weren't home."

"Sheila didn't tell me you came by; and I'm not avoiding you," she said, I've just been busy.

"Can I come in?" He was still standing outside the front door.

"Sure," he stepped inside and she closed the door. When she turned around, he was standing so close to her, she almost bumped into him. He did not move so she stepped back and maneuvered around him. He held her hand to prevent her from walking away.

"Trace, what's going on with you, talk to me," he was almost pleading with her.

"What do you want me to say Mark, what can I say? You've already made your choice." He released her hand and she walked into the living room.

"What choice Nyah? Why are you turning this into such a big deal?" It was the first time since she'd known him that he called her by her first name, and she thought that was significant.

She didn't feel like explaining how she really felt about everything.

"It's not a good time for me right now." He stared at her with a puzzled look on his face. She wanted more than anything to soothe his heart, to say she would wait for him to sort himself out and that she trusted him, but she could not get past the fact that he chose to live with another woman. The thought of him loving and touching her was more that Nyah could bear.

"How is your son?" He seemed surprised that she asked.

"He's doing alright."

"Good." Nyah said through a feigned smile. "Are you going to Sage's spring party?"

"I don't think so. I'm working on some new material; the deadline is next week. Are you going?"

"No, I think that I'll just stay home and read a good book." He nodded to acknowledge what she said but his eyes were distant.

He turned and walked slowly to the front door, paused and turned to look at her.

"You know I love you right."

She smiled weakly, not saying a word and then he was gone.

So you say, she thought as the tears streamed down her cheeks.

* * * * * * **

Nyah glanced out the window again, everything seemed so small and insignificant from high in the sky. She did not feel like driving for six hours to Wisconsin so she took the plane and rented a car from the airport to the hotel. She decided not to stay at the Big House especially now that Gran was not there. Gran's lawyer scheduled a meeting to tie up all the loose ends involving the will. Two weeks had passed since the reading and she had not spoken to anyone in the family except Graydon. Her mother called a couple of times but Nyah avoided speaking to her. She figured that they were all still upset with her because Gran left her about 70% of her estate. Graydon has been staying at the Big House with Uncle Floyd and Patsy, Nyah believed he wanted to keep a close eye on the restaurant, and he did not want them running off with anything from the house. The house was hers but it meant nothing without Gran in it.

She went straight to the lawyer's office from the airport.

"Miss Parsons, it's good to see you again." Mr. Smythe greeted her and motioned for her to sit down in the leather chair in front of his oak desk. "Can I get you something to drink?"

"I would appreciate some tea, thank you." He called his secretary and told him to bring her some tea.

"You're looking well," he said. Nyah knew he meant she looked better than the last time they met. The secretary came in and put the tea on the desk in front of her.

"Thank you," she said smiling at him and took a sip.

"Let's get started. Miss Parsons, we have had an opportunity to review your grandmother's estate and have come up with the final figures. We've already met with the other members of your family to let them know their portion of the estate, now it's your turn." He read from the papers in front of him Nyah's share of Gran's will. "The house was appraised at $4.8 million dollars. The restaurant at 50% is $775,000. The life insurance is $2.5 million; investments cash value today $935,000 thousand. Finally, the bank account $97.5 thousand bringing the total value of your portion of the estate to $9.1075 million dollars. The will is iron clad and even if someone wanted to contest it, that process could take years, you are a very rich woman Miss Parsons."

Nyah was speechless. As far as she knew, Gran lived a very simple life. She never did anything that led Nyah to believe she had so much money. She drove the same car since 1979, she never owned anything that belonged to an animal or wore any piece of clothing she could not buy at K-Mart.

"We would be happy to create a will for you if you do not currently have one, we would also like to recommend a financial management firm to assist you with handling your portfolio. If you provide us with a bank account number, we can wire the liquid assets of ninety seven thousand to your account within 24 hours. We will coordinate with the insurance company and send you those funds when our office receives them." He stood up and gave her a business card. "My secretary will help with the details. Do you have any questions?" Nyah shook her head and Mr. Smythe extended his hand, "a pleasure Miss Parsons."

Nyah left the lawyer's office in a daze trying to process what had transpired. Of course, she thought of calling Mark but they had not spoken since the time she saw him briefly at her house after the funeral. It was clear to her that he had moved on. Sheila called her almost every day since she told her about the rape but Nyah felt exposed, not relieved like she thought she would feel after sharing the burden with someone else. She reopened a wound that had been festering like an open sore for the last eight years and now bitterness and anger were threatening to consume her. When she got back to her hotel, she was surprised to find Pamela waiting for her in the lobby.

"I need to talk to you."

"Is it about Nikki?" Nyah asked.

"No."

"Then we have nothing to say to each other." She walked past her sister towards the elevator.

"I promise I'll be quick," Pamela insisted. Nyah looked at her and sighed. "Just five minutes, please." She followed Nyah to her room.

Nyah turned to face her sister and waited for her to talk.

"I know there is no great love between us, and if I had another choice, I wouldn't be here but I need your help."

"What do you need Pamela?"

"I need twenty-five thousand dollars, but I can't tell you why."

Nyah began to laugh. "You are kidding right? Why me, why not mom or Gray?"

"Do you think this is easy for me to ask you for money, the person who has caused me the most pain in my life?"

"Pamela, I'm not going to get into this with you. You're free to believe whatever you want to."

"How could you do that to me? I'm your sister." Tears were rolling down Pamela's face and Nyah felt helpless. She knew it was easier for her sister to believe she slept with Sean and be heartbroken than to know the truth about the man she married and be completely devastated. "Can you help me or not?"

"Banks are closed now, but I'll go first thing when I get home." Nyah said.

"Thank you," she sounded relieved. "Here is my account number," she handed Nyah a piece of paper, "I'm sure it's easier to put that amount of money in my account than it is to write me a check, I promise I'll pay you back." Nyah watched her as she walked through the door and closed it behind her.

She was back in Riverdale by noon the next day and she went straight to the bank to transfer the money into Pamela's account.

Twenty-six

Going back to work in late May provided a welcome change for Nyah and with all the money Gran left for her, she knew she didn't have to work but teaching was the only thing in her life she felt she had control over.

It was Friday afternoon and while preparing her lesson plans for the next week, Gabby walked into her classroom.

"Ny, a few of us are going out to dinner tonight, do you want to come? Mason's at 8:00."

"Sure," she said, anything was better than the sad memories that had been haunting her thoughts lately.

"Now I have to warn you, Edward will be there," she said gingerly.

"That's fine," she said, "how is Edward?"

"I guess he's good," she said, "I haven't seen him since the spring party."

"Sorry, I wasn't able to make it to that," she said apologetically.

"That's completely understandable," she did not leave right away, she stood and watched Nyah who sensed there was something else she wanted to say.

"What?" she asked. Gabby said it was nothing and left the room.

When Nyah arrived at the restaurant, Sage, Julie, Trey, Nick, David, and Dwight were there. The whole gang, except Brenda and Mark. She was disappointed but she figured he had better things to do with his time. Even though they had not seen or spoken to each other in almost two weeks, Nyah could not shake the hollow feeling she had in her heart. It had been a while since she socialized with his friends and she felt a little self-conscious, especially now that she and Mark were no longer together.

Gabby knocked her glass to get everyone's attention.

"We have an announcement to make. You are all a part of our wedding, and we wanted you to know we've changed the venue for the wedding. Instead of getting married here in Riverdale like we originally planned, we wanted to try some place more romantic and give you all an opportunity to decide if you still wanted to be a part of our special day."

"Why do you have to turn everything into such a mystery Gab, spit it out," Sage said.

"We want to get married in Jamaica," David said,

"We figured since we were going there for our honeymoon, we would kill two birds with one stone," Gabby added smiling at David.

"You guys have been together for 10 years, how much more honeymooning do you all need?" Rick commented.

"Hey everyone, sorry I'm late," Edward sat on an empty chair between Julie and Nick. "What did I miss?" He was dressed in black pants and a gray polo shirt buttoned to the collar. His hair was newly trimmed and he sported a thin mustache. "Hey Nyah, I didn't know you would be here."

"Liar," said Gabby, "I told you."

"Well yes," he said, "but I didn't think you were actually going to show up."

"Are you ready to order?" The waiter went around the table with her eyes and left after everyone ordered food and drinks. They spent the rest of the evening dividing wedding jobs; Nyah's job was to help with the wedding invitations. Gabby said she needed to send them soon so that people could start saving, if they had to, for the trip to Jamaica.

She had a good time but was glad when the evening was over.

She was just about to get into her car when she heard someone call her name. Edward walked up to the car and stopped in front of her.

"It was great seeing you again, you look amazing."

"Thanks."

"Listen, I was wondering if you're free next week, if you would like to accompany me to a movie or something," he seemed nervous.

"Next week," she said thoughtfully, "I don't know, can I get back to you?"

"Sure, sure." He took a business card from his wallet and handed it to her.

"I have your number, I'll call you," she said and drove away.

"You do that!" he shouted after her.

* * * * * * * **

Graydon flew into Detroit the next day and she picked him up from the airport. He had a fresh tan and a big smile on his face.

"Where did you go?" she asked him.

"We went to the Bahamas," he said.

"We?"

"Just a young woman I've been seeing for a few of months," he beamed.

"And you took her to the Bahamas? Is it the same woman we met at the funeral?"

"Yeah, and this trip was on her." We got his bag off the conveyor and started walking towards the car. He put his arm around her. "It's so nice to see you smiling again," he playfully touched her cheek.

"It's fake," she joked.

"Fake or real, it was hard for me to see you so broken over Gran's death."

"Is that why you didn't call me?" she asked, "because you thought that I was in pieces?" Nyah knew she was not the easiest person to comfort, when she zoned out, people had to wait until she decided to let them in.

"I called you, several times. You didn't call me back, you shut yourself down," he said. They finally reached the car and drove out of the airport. Graydon was hungry so they stopped at the diner to get something to eat. "I had no idea Gran was a miser." Nyah assumed he was talking about the will.

"I prefer the word 'frugal,'" she said, "miser sounds like Mr. Scrooge."

"I knew she had the restaurant but because she didn't talk much about it, I didn't remember. Have you been there lately?"

"I haven't been there at all," she said, "is it nice?"

"There's lots of space, and it has a lot of potential. What do you think we should do with it?" He asked, chewing on his burger.

"Gray, to be honest, I haven't really thought about what I want to do," she said.

"That's cool. It's generating steady income and I haven't really made any changes, I think you should take a look at it and then we should decide if we are going to keep it and fix it up or sell it."

"Well, I'm back at work and I really don't want to take any time off before summer so..." he interrupted her by putting an envelope on the table.

"I thought you might say that, so I brought some pictures, here, check these out," it was hard to miss the excitement in his voice. Nyah picked up the pictures and skimmed through them. The furniture and fixtures had a sixties look. There were saucer-like lights hanging from the ceiling above each table. Maybe Gran and Granddad were going for a space setting. She put the pictures down and rested her chin in the palm of her hand.

"It's a beautiful place," she said, "I can see Gran's eccentric personality all over it." She pushed them towards Graydon.

"Listen Ny, I'm sorry, if this is too soon, we can..."He began to say but she stopped him.

"It will take me a while to not react whenever I hear Gran's name mentioned, but I'm trying to move forward. I have to get my report cards ready so I'm tied up for the next two weekends but I promise I will fly down to Wisconsin to look at it with you the second weekend in June." He smiled and put the pictures back in the envelope.

"So, is it serious with this girl you're seeing?" She asked changing the sad mood that hovered like a dark cloud above the table.

"She's doing it for me Sis; she is gorgeous, fine and beautiful. Just the way I like them," he said with a grin across his face.

"Those are all physical traits Gray, but I haven't heard you talk about a woman like that in a while, will I ever get to formally meet her?"

"Whenever you're ready Sis," he said as they got up to pay the bill at the cashier. "I'm hoping she won't turn psycho on a brother." They laughed and walked out of the diner, arm in arm.

Twenty-seven

The plane landed at the Manley Airport in Jamaica at one o'clock on Thursday afternoon, two days before Gabby's wedding. As Nyah walked out of the plane and down the stairs with Gabby and Sage onto the runway, the humidity made it difficult for her to breathe and the intense heat clung to her skin. She was grateful to have her straw hat and sunglasses to shade her head and eyes from the merciless rays of the late June sun. Gabby asked her to help with last minute preparations and she welcomed the chance to take a vacation, even if it was only for a weekend. The rest of the bridal party, David and Gabby's sister, who was her maid of honor were all scheduled to arrive the next day.

Within twenty minutes, they were driving along the coastline towards their resort in Negril.

"This place is gorgeous," Gabby said staring out the window, "look at it, the water is so blue and it' nice to breathe fresh air for a change."

"I just want to take off all my clothes and take a dip in that salt water." Sage said.

"Mi know just the right spot fi dat," he said grinning, "Mi can show you a good time."

"What?" Sage could not understand him because his accent was very strong.

"I think he means he'd be happy to take you to his own private beach." Gabby laughed.

"In his dreams," she said grimacing at him.

Nyah ignored the playful chatter and welcomed a feeling of serenity as she gazed absentmindedly at the blue-green water that evoked memories of the vacation she took with Mark in Fiji. She closed her eyes and halted her thoughts, knowing that to linger there would only remind her of what she no longer had.

The cab pulled up to the entrance of the private resort Gabby reserved for the bridal party. To save on costs, everyone doubled up but Nyah paid the full price to get a room by herself. To share a room meant that she would have to share space, time, conversation, things she did not relish doing on this trip. She wanted only peace and quiet and if it cost a thousand dollars extra, she was willing to pay for it. Waiters holding trays ladened with champagne greeted them at the door, and attendants took their bags to their rooms. After settling in, she went shopping with Gabby to buy island souvenirs for the bridal party and then they took a cab up a narrow hill to pick up the bridesmaid dresses. As they entered a small room, a white fan that was sitting on top of a table, oscillated hot air in one area of the room where a plump woman sat around a sewing machine. She said hello, but she did not stop sewing.

"Are you Mrs. Johnson?" Gabby asked.

"Yes."

"We are here to pick up the bridesmaid dresses."

"What's the name?"

"Gabby Monroe."

"I have some last minute tings to finish up on the dresses so you'll get dem by tomorrow mornin'," the woman said in a monotone voice without looking up.

"I was told they'd be done by this afternoon," Gabby raised her voice slightly.

"It's not afternoon yet, you can't tell time?"

"Excuse me, could you stop sewing for a minute?" Gabby said impatiently and the woman stopped the machine, turned her head slowly and glared at Gabby.

"Is there a reason why the dresses aren't finished yet?" Gabby was visibly getting angrier the more she spoke to the woman, Nyah thought she was overreacting. "When we paid the deposit, we were told that the dresses would be ready on Thursday, today is Thursday.

"Look, I'm doin' the best I can, you can't expect me to sew and look at you at the same time. I won't be able to get the work done on time if people like you keep coming in here and interrupt me." She mumbled something under her breath and started sewing again. "I'll try to get dem ready for later, you can come back if you want or you can wait, it's up to you." Nyah could sense the tension between the two women mounting.

"Mrs. Johnson, is there somewhere around here I can buy a drink?"

"What kind of drink you want? Hot, cold, wine, beer?"

"Just a pop," Nyah said.

"When you go through the door, turn right, you will see Mas Danny cart, 'im sell everyting." Nyah had a hard time understanding her but wanted to leave the room before Gabby hit the woman.

"Thank you," she said pulling Gabby with her outside.

They were hardly out of the room before Gabby started ranting about how rude the woman was. Nyah coaxed her into going for a walk and they found a man selling snacks and cold drinks from a cart. Nyah changed her mind about the pop and bought three coconut waters in the shell instead. Nyah told Gabby to wait under a tree in front of the woman's store and she went back inside.

"I got this for you," Nyah handed her the coconut water. The woman looked at it and then at her before she took it.

"Tanks."

"Sorry about my friend, she's just nervous about her wedding," Nyah said smiling, "how much more time do you need."

"Not long, just a hour or two," she said throwing the empty coconut shell in the garbage. "That just hit the spot, tanks again." The woman smiled and returned to her sewing.

"Okay, we'll come back tomorrow," Nyah said and rejoined Gabby outside.

"The dresses won't be ready until tomorrow," she told Gabby who started walking towards the door. "The girls won't be here to fit them until then anyway."

Gabby stopped and sighed heavily.

"It's about the principle. People should do what they say they are going to do and be more considerate of others and their time." Nyah sensed there was more to her statement than being upset about the dresses but she did not press her.

They got back to the resort just past 6'oclock worn-out from all the walking they did. They ate supper together in the resort dining room and agreed to retire to their rooms early.

Friday morning Nyah convinced Gabby to accept a total body spa treatment as a pre-wedding gift before meeting the other five bridesmaids at the airport and going to fit the dresses.
Brenda gave her a chilly reception and Nyah tried her best to stay out of her way. It wasn't until late in the afternoon that Nyah had a chance to relax by the pool and read a book.

David, some of the guests and three of the groomsmen arrived later that evening, there were hugs all around and excitement replaced anxiety.

"Where are Dwight and Mark?" Gabby asked. "I thought you guys were all coming down together."

"They are coming in on a later flight," David said, "they'll be here, don't stress."

"Hey Ny," Sage sat on a chair beside her. "We really haven't had a chance to talk, how are you? I was sorry to hear about your loss."

"My loss?"

"Your grandmother," she said. "How are you holding up?"

"I'm fine, much better," she said, gluing her eyes to the book, but not reading a word.

They were having supper on the balcony when David turned off his cell and announced in a boisterous voice that his best men were on their way to the resort. Everyone at the table had been drinking champagne except for her, something she hadn't done since she began taking her pills, so they were loud and very giddy.

Nyah's heart began to race; she had not seen Mark in close to three months and still got butterflies in the pit of her stomach whenever she heard his name. When she saw them walking up the driveway, her first instinct was to get up and run to her room but a part of her wanted to see him. She used her fork to push around a piece of broccoli on her plate wondering if he was going to say anything to her. Gabby ran to meet them, hugged Mark and kissed him. When they got close to the table, the groom stood up to greet them and the excitement grew.

"Hey Trace," he said.

She looked up at him and smiled.

"Hey yourself." Her head was spinning and her heart was beating so loudly she was almost certain everyone could hear it.

He held his arms open for a hug. She got up and stepped into his familiar embrace and all the feelings she had been trying to keep buried, engulfed her.

"I still don't bite," he whispered so that only she could hear. She looked into his eyes and smiled shyly.

"Can I get some love too?" Dwight was standing beside Mark with his arms opened. He released her; she quickly hugged Dwight and went back to the comfort of her broccoli.

"I'm syked," he said excitedly rubbing his hands together. "In the words of Mr. Gaye, *'Let's get it on'*."

"First we eat then we celebrate," Dwight said referring to the bachelor party they had planned for David that night.

Having Mark so close and being unable to touch him was unbearable for Nyah. He seemed so content laughing and joking with his friends. Occasionally their eyes met but he did not give her any clues about his feelings for her, if he still had any. After dinner, walking back to her room, she knew that if her life were a movie, she would have won an academy award for her performance that evening. She did everything she could to appear happy and fulfilled. She wore the mask well.

****

She lay across her bed, closed her eyes and wished, with all her might to be somewhere else.

There was a tap on her door.

"Come in," she sat up as Sage walked into the room.

"Are you okay?" she asked.

"I'm fine." Nyah got up, walked over to the sliding door, and opened it. "Why do you ask?"

"I figured maybe it was weird for you being around Mark." Nyah smiled and leaned against the door, staring out at the water.

"Nyah, I know we're not best friends and I know you've been through a lot this past year but you're okay in my book." Nyah turned to look at Sage and noticed concern in her eyes. Sage inhaled and exhaled slowly as if she was trying to weigh her next words. "I think you should be careful what you tell Gabby. I know the two of you are close but it's best if you keep your info to yourself, especially, if it's about Mark."

"Why do you say that?" Nyah's interest peaked.

"I also think you should know that she is good friends with Meaghan, they've known each other since middle school."

"Meaghan, Mark's Meaghan?"

There was another knock on the door and Gabby stuck her head in.

"Hey Ny, so this is where the party is," she entered the room and closed the door. "We're getting ready to head out…"

"Gabby, Sage just told me that you know the woman we saw in Mark's apartment. Is there something you want to tell me?" Nyah interrupted her, still not quite believing, needing confirmation.

"Something like what?" Nyah saw the women exchange piercing looks, "what have you heard?"

"I told her about Meaghan, she had a right to know the truth," Sage said.

"What truth? What are you talking about Sage?" The silence that followed was deafening. When she did not deny it, Nyah walked over and faced her squarely.

"You told that woman how to find Mark." A light went off in Nyah's head. "She showed up right after you found out I was pregnant, why did you do that?"

"I don't have to justify my actions to you or anyone else, I haven't done anything wrong. Meaghan and I have been friends for a long time, Mark knocked her up, and it was only fair that he took responsibility for that child first."

Nyah stared at her blankly.

"I knew you were sleeping with Mark long before you had the balls to admit it. I saw you kissing him at the side of the house the night I had the surprise party for Linda and I saw when he got in your car. I knew all about your grandmother's birthday party, and how he flew down to surprise you, I even knew about your little trip to Fiji. All that shit was fine, he's a man and you threw yourself at him, what man do you know who would refuse such easy access."

"So you spied on Nyah and sabotaged her relationship with Mark, for what?"

"I didn't sabotage anything, it was doomed from the start; you're not his type. I let you into my life, I befriended you and you couldn't even be honest with me. How many times did I ask you about your relationship with Mark? You kept saying you were just friends. You are a liar, and *that* speaks to your character, or lack of it. The day I found out you were pregnant with Mark's baby, I knew I had to do something drastic so I called Meaghan she owed me a favor. Then when you lost the baby, I believed it was a sign that maybe I still had a chance."

"Oh my God Gabby, what the hell are you saying?" Sage looked at her friend in disbelief. "You're in love with Mark?"

"There's no shame in admitting that. I've known him for nine years and in less than a year, you came on the scene and you were going to have his baby; that was hard to digest." Nyah felt goose bumps all over her body. The only thought flowing through her mind was how someone that she cared for and trusted so implicitly; someone she truly thought was her friend could have deceived her.

"If you were in love with Mark all these years, why didn't you just tell him?" Nyah asked.

"I did, he said we were better as friends," she laughed. "So, we're friends and I won't let anyone mess with that."

"If you can't have him, nobody can, is that right? Why are you even marrying David tomorrow?" Sage wanted to know, "this shit is right out of a movie," she said shaking her head.

"I know why," Nyah said. "As long as you're with David, you get to see Mark."

"Please, don't kid yourself. I can see Mark anytime I want to, I don't need David for that. Mark's a true friend."

"Do you have any idea how crazy all this is?" Sage was baffled.

Nyah sat down on the bed and stared at her, "I shared so much with you Gabby. I thought *we* were friends."

"They say keep your friends close and your enemies even closer," Sage said absentmindedly.

"You're not my enemy Nyah, I have nothing against you."

Nyah felt her body tense.

"Really, you could have fooled me and I guess you did," she said, "well you got what you wanted and at least now I know where you stand," Nyah felt mentally drained.

"I'm sorry if I hurt you," Gabby said, "I didn't mean to." She left the room, closing the door quietly behind her.

Nyah sat on the bed staring blankly at the floor, tears streamed down her cheeks, not because of what Gabby did, but because at that moment she felt utterly alone.

"I'm sorry Nyah, and for whatever it's worth, I've known Mark for a long time too, and I have never seen him happier than when he was with you." Sage hugged her and left the room.

* * * * * * * **

Nyah sat in her room, unable to move for about an hour before she called the airport and tried to get an early morning flight out of Jamaica, but they were all booked. The walls began to close in around her so she walked down the hall, through the sliding doors onto the balcony into the fresh night air. She froze when she saw Mark sitting on the step, staring into the night and was tempted to turn around and go back to her room. Instead, she touched his shoulder, startling him.

"Can I join you?" She asked softly.

"Be my guest," he motioned to the spot beside him.

"Why are you sitting here all by yourself, shouldn't you be at the bachelor party, partying?"

"The night is still young. I could ask you the same question."

She tried to smile but her heart was not in it. She was not about to tell him the real reason she was sitting on the balcony steps with him and not at the bachelorette party.

"You look good," he said. Nyah was grateful that he could not see that her eyes were red from crying.

"So do you," she said fidgeting with the ring on her thumb.

They sat without words for a few minutes and the only sound she could hear was the loud thumping of her heart. She stood up and started walking towards the water, he called her name and she stopped. He stood behind her, ran his hands down her arms, intertwining their fingers, and buried his face in her hair.

"I miss you," he said, his breath warm against her head.

"You look like you're doing just fine."

"Looks can be deceiving."

Feeling like his comment was aimed at her; she freed her fingers from his, stepped away, and turned to look at him. Memories of the past six months flooded her thoughts. "Mark, when I needed you, you weren't there. You chose to be somewhere else with someone else doing something else. I can't just forget that." She looked at her hand that was still tingling from his touch.

"Why didn't you tell me you were pregnant?" he asked, his words halted her thoughts and she stared into his eyes.

"I wasn't prepared to be pregnant. I did not know what kind of relationship we had, or if we had a relationship at all. I couldn't tell if you wanted anything more from me besides sex, and when you told me about your girlfriend and your son, I thought the timing was off so I never got around to it."

"It wasn't your decision to keep something like that from me; you should have told me when you first found out. Everything I did showed how much I loved you."

"Sex isn't love Mark," she said softly, "and *that* was the foundation of our relationship." Nyah felt the tears beginning to well up again.

"It was just sex for you? Even if that's what you thought, I would never have agreed to an abortion."

"What?" Nyah was stunned his words pierced her through the heart. "You think I aborted your baby."

"I know it's your body, you made that clear from the very beginning and I can't tell you what to do with it, but you should have at least given me a chance to try."

"What you wanted was for me to wait in the wings for you to choose between me and another woman, well I made it easy for you. I knew it wasn't a part of the deal because you weren't mine, but I didn't want to share you with someone else," she said.

"What sharing? She was a woman I used to date a long time ago."

"But she had your son, something that you wanted, you said it yourself."

"What I wanted was your support and a little time to sort things out, not for you to bail on me when the going got a little tough," his tone was accusing.

"A little tough? It was more than a little tough." Nyah wanted to scream at the top of her voice how she felt when he told her about Jason, constantly talking about how wonderful he was. How she felt when he was not available to comfort her after she lost their baby and when she found out he was living with his ex-girlfriend but after what happened with Gabby earlier that evening, she had lost the will to fight. Her mental energy reserves were depleted and she had none left to decode the meaning in his words.

"Mark, what we shared was fun, there were times I almost believed it was real but it ended just like I knew it would and now we are on two different paths. I don't want to be forced to remember anything about that time, it doesn't matter anymore, I'm sorry." Nyah turned abruptly and there was only darkness.

Twenty-eight

Nyah heard a sound; it was muffled and far away. She reached her hands out and grasped at the air, it was so dark she could not see anything. She heard the sound again, this time it was louder, right in front of her. She opened her mouth to speak, to cry out for help, but the words were stuck in her throat.

"Miss Parsons, can you hear me?" Nyah could not tell if she was dreaming or if it was real. "Miss Parsons." This time, the voice was more distinct. When she opened her eyes, Nyah was staring into a bright light, she tried to shut her eyes but she could not, something was forcing them to stay open.

"Where am I?" her voice was hoarse and her throat was very dry. She had a throbbing pain at the side of her head.

"You are in the hospital, I am Dr. Hartley." Nyah stared blankly at the tall man standing over her.

"How did I get here?"

"Your husband brought you in."

"My husband?" The last thing that she remembered was talking to Mark on the beach.

"Apparently, you passed out and you've been out cold for the past 20 minutes, we needed permission to draw some blood and he was willing to sign the papers." Nyah felt too groggy to explain to him that Mark was not her husband. "We're just waiting for the results."

"Did I hit my head? It hurts," the bright lights made it worse.

"I'll arrange to have a look at that."

"Hopefully, we'll get the results of your blood test within the hour. I'll send your husband in," before she could protest, the doctor left the room.

Nyah managed a weak smile when Mark entered the room and stood by the side of the bed; she could tell he was worried.

"How do you feel?"

"Except for this headache, I feel fine. What happened?"

"One minute we're having a conversation and the next you're falling for me," he chuckled.

"I've already done that," she said and immediately regretted it. He pulled up a chair beside the bed and sat down. Dr. Hartley came back into the room.

"Miss Parsons, the form your husband filled out was almost complete; we just have a couple more questions before we can proceed." She glanced at Mark and wondered why he did not correct the doctor's assumption about him being her husband. "Do you have any history of heart problems?"

"No," she said.

"Do you currently take any medication?" Nyah hesitated; she knew if she lied, her blood test would reveal the truth.

"Yes, I take Xanitol." She could feel Mark's penetrating gaze.

"How long have you been taking it?"

"On and off for almost 2 years," she said quietly.

"And when was the last time you took it?"

"Almost two weeks ago, why are you asking me all these questions? My family doctor prescribed the Xanitol; she said it was safe for me to take."

"I understand that, but that kind of drug should only be taken for one or two months at the very most and in conjunction with some form of behavior therapy. I won't know for sure until we have done more tests but I think your body is beginning to go through withdrawal and that's probably why you have the headache."

"What kind of drug is it?" Mark asked and she wished he was not there, "what's it used for?"

"Xanitol is a tranquillizer, used primarily to control severe panic attacks or to help victims to cope with post traumatic stress, it's also very addictive. Miss Parsons, do you have the pills with you now?"

"They're in my hotel room," she said as tears streamed down her face. She felt exposed, the secret she tried so carefully to conceal all these years was uncovered and now Mark knew she was not as together as she wanted him and everyone else to believe.

Vivid images revived painful, buried memories from the dark recesses of Nyah's soul causing her to physically relive that night eight years ago when she was raped, the loss of her baby, the death of her beloved grandmother, the only person she believed truly loved her, and her mind began to slowly shut down. She turned her body away from both men and began to sob uncontrollably; neither of them could console her. The throbbing in her head merged all the sounds in the room; threatening to drive her to the verge of insanity. She tried to get up and run away, but she did not get very far, her legs were weak and they betrayed her, throwing her to the ground. She would not allow anyone to touch her.

"Stop, you're hurting me, don't touch me, I have to get out of here!" She knew she was screaming but she could not stop herself, her mind had disconnected from her body. She felt like a trapped animal and began to fight wildly using her arms, her legs, her teeth. She was being attacked, she had to protect herself, and she did not want to be raped again. This time she would fight back. She used all her energy to free herself, screaming and kicking and when she lost her voice and she had no more will to fight, she stood at the edge of the cliff staring at the jagged rocks below, she was all alone, and then everything went black.

****

When Nyah woke up she had to blink several times before her eyes could focus on anything, her head was no longer throbbing and she did not feel anxious only groggy. The bed felt hard against her lower back and the white cotton sheets were cool against her bare legs. A nurse walked into the room carrying a clipboard in one hand and a tiny cup in the other. She put both down at the foot of the bed, walked over to the window and pulled the two curtains apart. Nyah used her hand to shield her eyes from the fierce sunlight that streamed into the room uninvited and unwelcome.

"Good morning, how are you feeling today?" It was a rhetorical question that she had gotten used to hearing asked by well meaning nurses and doctors over the past couple of days. The nurse pushed a button and raised the bed so that Nyah was in a sitting position, took her temperature and blood pressure then noted the results on the clipboard. Nyah knew by the woman's accent that she was not in Jamaica anymore, she didn't remember leaving, but there were lapses in her memory and she was not able to sequence the events that happened in the last couple of weeks. "Here, take this," the nurse handed her the cup.

"What is it?" Nyah stared at the tiny pill.

"It's Xanitol; you have to continue taking small doses daily until we can stop your treatment completely." She did not recognize the drug because it was a different shape and color from the one she was used to taking. She placed it on her tongue; it dissolved quickly. The nurse then poured cold water from a pitcher into a glass, told Nyah to drink it and she obeyed.

"You have a visitor, should I send him in?"

"Do you know who it is?" Nyah did not recognize her own raspy voice.

"I'm not sure, but he said he was a family member. When you feel up to it, we need a urine sample, the bottles are in the washroom," she said and then left the room. The nurse was not discourteous but Nyah thought she was not very warm.

She glanced around the small room frowning at the pale yellow walls. There was a rolling table beside the bed and an uncomfortable looking armchair in the corner. She swung her legs over the edge of the bed using the rails to support her weight, slowly rolled her head to relieve a kink in her neck and stretched to release the soreness in her back. She tried to stand up just as Graydon entered the room and he lengthened his strides to reach her before she was on her feet. He put down the flowers he had in his hand on the table, put his arm around her waist and she leaned against him for support.

"Where do you think you're going?"

"I'm going to pee in a cup, care to join me?"

"If that's what you need."

She looked at him with her nose turned up, "I was joking."

"I wasn't."

She leaned against his arm and they walked to the bathroom. She managed to fill a quarter of the bottle, placed it on the ledge, walked back to her bed and climbed in, this time refusing his help.

Graydon sat beside her on the bed and rubbed her calves through the blanket.

"I'd feel better if you did that to my neck," she said and turned her back towards him.

"You scared the hell out of all of us," he said gently pressing his fingers into her shoulders.

"Really, how do you think I felt? Crazy can be scary."

"You're not crazy Sis, but you look like crap," he said jokingly.

"Thanks," she said trying to run her fingers through her hair, "and today is a good day."

"Ny, I'm so sorry," Graydon stopped massaging her shoulders and wrapped his arms around her from behind.

"For what, that I'm a druggie?" Nyah said through a weak smile.

"What kind of brother am I if I couldn't see this coming? I had no idea what you were going through, none of us did, I'm sorry." She turned to face him as he stood by her bedside.

"What are you talking about? You're not a mind reader, I should have said something."

"Still, I should have…I let you down."

"Guilt is a bitch Gray, don't do that to yourself."

Her eyes shifted from Graydon to the door when she heard Sheila's voice.

"Try and stop me heifer, that's my sister in there." Sheila burst into the room with the nurse right behind her. "Nyah, this nurse is trying to tell me I can't come see you because I'm not *immediate family*, can you set her straight please?"

"It's all right, she can stay; she's my sister."

"Hospital policy states that each patient can have only one visitor at a time," the nurse said.

"Well I'm not leaving," she looked at Graydon, "Gray, you need to make another appointment."

"Do you need anything?" he asked.

"No, "she said, "but I promise to let you know if I do."

Graydon kissed her on the forehead.

"I love you."

"I love you too," she squeezed his hand.

"Sheila, why do you have to be so loud all the time, you have no decorum."

"You can kiss my decorum Graydon," she said and hissed at him.

He pulled her weave when he walked past her and she tried to kick him.

"You two are so juvenile."

Sheila hugged Nyah for a long time.

"It's all good, that's my future husband, he just don't know it yet. So I hear you went to Jamaica and lost your mind."

"Hello Sheila, nice to see you too."

"Don't hello Sheila me, look at you, you're falling apart and you still look good." She pulled a big tooth comb from her purse and began running it through Nyah's hair. "Don't you ever scare me like that again."

"You told Gray what I told you didn't you?"

"Yes, I told him what that asshole did to you, I told all of them, your mother, your sister, the son of a bitch was living the high life and you were in pain, I don't think so." Nyah knew there was no point in getting upset with her friend; she could not change what was already done.

"Sheila, I need to know that I can trust you to keep what I tell you just between us."

"And you can, I swear, but I wasn't going to let him get away with that shit. You taught *me* to speak against shit like that. Now, you need to hurry up and get out of here so we can go on a vacation."

"That sounds wonderful."

Sheila hugged Nyah's head, "you know how I feel about you right? I don't need to spell it out." Nyah smiled. She knew exactly how Sheila felt even if she could not say it.

"I have so much to tell you." Sheila talked until Nyah dozed off.

* * * * * * * **

She sat in the therapist's office three days later; fidgeting with her fingers.

"Can I call you Nyah?" she asked.

"Sure."

"So Nyah, where do you want to start? Is there anything you want to share with me?"

"Like what?"

"Anything, let's begin with your childhood, where were you born?"

She had agreed to talk to a therapist, knowing it was a big part of her recovery but she was not ready to dig deep into her suppressed memories.

"I know you want to help me but I need more time." Nyah got up and left the doctor's office.

When she got back to her room, Mark was waiting for her. She knew she was not in top form but she hoped she looked better than the last time he saw her.

"How do you feel?" His gaze penetrated her feeble attempt at showing a strong persona.

"Much better," she said, "how are you?"

"I'm okay, worried about you," he said burying his hands in his pocket.

"Don't be, I'm fine, I've got Gran's blood running through these veins," she said fidgeting with a lock of hair at the back of her head. "I never got a chance to thank you." She smiled. "So, how was the wedding?"

"I wouldn't know."

"I know you weren't there, and that was my fault, sorry, but did they get married?"

"Yeah." The silence that followed was awkward for Nyah, she knew he was there because he rescued her but she wasn't sure if he was convinced she was not crazy. She was relieved that everything was out in the open, that he saw the ugliness of her pain, and she no longer had to carry around the heavy burden of deception that nearly ripped her mind apart. She was free and even if that freedom cost her her dignity and any kind of a future with him, what they shared was enough to last her a lifetime.

"Thank you for taking care of me," she said without looking at him, determined not to be a burden to him any longer. "I don't know what I would have done if you hadn't been there but I'll be fine, I'm sure you have more important things to worry about, I'm not your problem anymore." She turned her face to the window, away from him so he couldn't see the tears welling up in her eyes.

He reached across the bed and touched the side of her face, wiping away a single tear that streamed down her cheek.

"Call me when you need me," he said and left the room.

Twenty-nine

When Nyah walked through the front door of her house, she felt relieved; happy to be in the one place where she was not being observed or judged. The ordeal she experienced over the last six weeks made her appreciate her own space even more. She did not call anyone to pick her up, and since her *meltdown*, everyone wanted to be her savior and frankly, all the attention was stifling; she just wanted to find her way on her own. She made a cup of tea and was about to take a sip when the telephone rang.

"Hey Auntie."

"Nikki," Nyah was happy to hear her niece's voice. "Hey, how are you?"

"Okay," she said.

"Where are you?"

"Oh, I'm still here, at the group home but I think I'm ready to go home, they just won't let me. I can have unsupervised visitors now, well from everyone except Sean, will you come see me soon?"

"I'll come first thing next week, okay?" They talked for a little while longer about her progress and then she had to go to a group counseling session.

Nyah spent most of the next week rearranging all the furniture in her house, throwing away everything that evoked negative memories or that took up too much space.

She was pleasantly surprised, by a visit from Natalie who brought her a beautiful bouquet of flowers and a relaxation CD. They visited for a while and Natalie assured her that her job was still there if she wanted it. Nyah was grateful, but deep down she was not sure if she wanted to continue working at the same school as Gabby.

* * * * * * * **

Nyah stopped in New York on her way to a meeting she had with her lawyer in Wisconsin, she was anxious to see her niece but she wanted to make sure it was alright with Pamela first, so she went to her office. Nyah thought she looked great in her dark blue suit but her face was sad, even through her half smile.

"I'm surprised to see you," she said sitting behind a big glass desk. "I thought I would be the last person you'd want to see."

"Why would you think that? You're my sister."

"If you're here for your money, I don't have it yet," she said.

"I'm not here about the money Pam; I told you you don't have to pay me back. I was on my way to Wisconsin and I promised Nikki I would stop in to see her, I hope you don't mind."

"No, I don't mind," she said quietly and stood up. "Nyah…"she stopped. "We are in the middle of a huge acquisition right now, so I don't know how much time I can spend with you."

"I'm just here for a day or so not long enough for us to really hang out." Nyah said trying to keep the conversation light. "Did you get my letter?"

"I did," Pamela said, averting her eyes away from Nyah.

"I hope you can make it." Nyah was about to leave but Pamela stopped her.

"I'm so glad you're okay, you look great."

"I'm getting there," she said and left the office.

Nikki had lost a lot of weight. Her face was gaunt and her eyes looked weepy. Nyah hugged her niece and they sat on the sofa.

"The one good thing about being in here is, I look good, I wear a size four now." Nyah smiled because she knew exactly what her niece was saying. She couldn't find anything to fit her when she went home from the hospital. "And talk about boring. ' Use I words'; that's all I'm hearing every day," she imitated the counselor. "I this, I that; who really talks like that?" Her spirits seemed lighter and Nyah was happy for that.

"Do you feel like telling me why you tried to hurt yourself?" Nyah asked gingerly.

"It was more than that, I tried to kill myself, I wanted to die," she said boldly. "I don't know, it seemed the only way out at the time."

"The only way out of what?" she asked.

"It's so hard for me to talk about it. Have you ever felt so alone you didn't know what to do or where to turn?" she asked and Nyah could see she was going to cry so she sat beside her and put her arms around her. She knew exactly how Nikki felt, it took her a week of trying with her own therapist before she could open up and talk about her pain.

"It's okay honey, we don't have to talk about it now. I will be there whenever you are ready, and I do know that feeling. The important thing is that you understand you have a family who loves you, and you can depend on us to be there for you anytime."

"That's a relief," she said with a sigh.

"You know you can trust me right?"

"You're cool Auntie," she said and gave Nyah a tight squeeze.

Nyah smiled and changed the subject.

"Listen, when you get out of here, we are going shopping and I will buy you whatever you want."

"Word?"

"Scouts honor," she said raising her right hand.

* * * * * * * **

Nyah waited impatiently for Edward to show up. She returned from Wisconsin to find four messages on her answering machine from him. He had called her an hour after she settled in the house and she did not have the heart to make up another excuse so she decided to meet him for lunch. She knew he was not a bad person he just tried too hard to impress her.

"I'm so sorry I'm late Nyah. I had one patient who just kept the complaints coming," he seemed flustered as he sat down.

"No worries, I haven't been waiting long," she said trying to put him at ease; making it seem like twenty minutes was not long.

"You look great," he said. She smiled and he motioned for the waiter to come to their table. They spent the lunch hour talking about his children, and about how his ex-wife was trying to take him to the cleaners by making unreasonable support demands because he was a doctor. Nyah listened and at the appropriate time, she would nod and sympathize but she had no interest in listening to a man whine about his ex-wife being a bitch. Finally, the lunch date ended and he walked her to her car. She turned to face him.

"Thanks for lunch," she said.

He moved closer to her and when she saw his face getting closer to hers, she turned her head, his kiss landed on her cheek.

"Can I call you sometime?"

"I don't think so, you're a great guy, but I'm not attracted to you in that way."

"I hear you, but a guy can hope." He took her keys and opened the car door; she thanked him and quickly sat down in the driver's seat. "Mark's a lucky man."

"Take care Edward," she said and drove off.

Thirty

Sheila did not have to twist Nyah's arm to get her to go to Leah Blaque's CD release party in Cleveland, she agreed without hesitation. The summer was almost over and she wanted to have some fun before returning to the classroom in a week. She decided to go back to her old job, at least until her contract ended. She had been living without the pills for over two months and started feeling like her old self again.

They entered the venue, and Nyah immediately sensed the excitement in the room, it was buzzing with people who were anxiously waiting for Leah to come on the stage. She looked around and recognized the faces of a few artists she had seen in interviews and wondered if Mark was there.

"Wow, this is so exciting," Sheila said, and she agreed. "There's our spot." They walked to a table at the front of the room. "Benefits of association," she said and started to chant Leah Blaque's name; instigating the crowd.

"Is everybody having a good time? LET ME HEAR YOU SCREAM!" The MC tried to pump the crowd and it worked. The audience screamed. "PUT YOUR HANDS TOGETHER AND WELCOME TO THE STAGE RECORDING ARTIST SENSATION, ALL THE WAY FROM LONDON, ENGLAND, MISS LEAH BLAQUE!!" The room resounded with applause, Leah bounced onto the stage, and began to sing her new single 'It Ain't Over.' Nyah lost herself in the music and sang along with the lyrics. When the song ended, Leah sang another song that had the crowd on their feet.

"Wow," she is amazing," Sheila could not keep still. Leah started singing a song Nyah vaguely remembered hearing before, it was a nice fusion of Jazz and R&B. She hung on every word, every note, it was almost as if the lyrics and the melody spoke to her. Sheila left her briefly to visit with some of her friends but Nyah was too engrossed in the music to notice.

"Hey everybody, I'm glad that you all could make it here tonight to share this special occasion with me, thanks for your support. I loved making the new album; I worked with some wonderful musicians who co-wrote some wicked tracks for the project. I'd like to mention one guy in particular, he wrote five of the songs and produced the album, he's supposed to be here somewhere." She shaded her eyes and tried to find him in the audience. "Mark, where are you darling?" Nyah followed her fingers as she pointed towards the back of the room and saw him standing with a group of young ladies at the bar. "You are a musical genius my friend, give him some love everybody." The room resounded with applause, he raised his glass and smiled, then he leaned against the bar and started talking in the ear of one of the girls. Nyah turned away only to see Gabby standing by her table.

"Isn't she amazing? I absolutely adore her, but you know that already." Nyah had not seen or spoken to Gabby since the night before her wedding.

"She's got a great voice," Nyah said.

"Nyah, we need to talk."

"I don't think there's anything more to say." Nyah said and walked in the direction she last saw Mark.

He was still standing at the bar when she approached him; he had a drink in one hand and his arm on the shoulder of a shorter man. He leaned his head sideways in an attempt to hear the man.

"Hey," she said loud enough for him to hear her over the noise in the room. The man left and she was standing face to face with her heart.

"Hey yourself," he put down the glass and buried both hands in his pockets, "wow, look at you, how are you?"

"I'm good," It took all the courage she had, to not turn and run away, "I enjoyed your new song."

"Thank you," he said, "that was the song..." His voice trailed off. He lifted his eyes to look over her head and that's when she heard Gabby shouting at the top of her voice as she walked towards them.

"Mark, can you take me home please?" Mark stepped around her and asked Gabby what was wrong. She would not say, she just insisted that he takes her home; she was hysterical. David stood behind her trying to calm her down but she pushed him, almost knocking him off his feet. Mark led Gabby outside hoping to disperse the gathering crowd. Nyah followed them from a distance and watched as Mark opened the door for her and she slid into the passenger seat of his truck. He walked around to the driver's side and within a few seconds, they drove off.

"What happened?" Nyah asked David but he did not respond.

He rubbed his head frantically, "it's nothing, just another one of her jealous fits," he said and went back inside the building.

"What was that all about?" Sheila stood beside her.

"I'm not sure," Nyah shrugged her shoulders.

"Wasn't that your man leaving with the crabcake?"

"You know Mark and I aren't together anymore, he can leave with whomever he wants."

"Bullshit, that's your man; nothing is going to change that." Nyah lost interest in the party and after getting a bite to eat, they drove back to her house.

She noticed his truck before Sheila turned into the driveway. He got out as they pulled in, waved to Sheila and waited for her on the porch.

"Are you gonna be okay?" Sheila asked before she left the car. Nyah smiled and leaned across the seat and hugged her friend.

"He's harmless, drive safe."

She walked past him, opened the front door and he stood outside waiting for her to invite him in which she did.

"I wanted to make sure you got home okay."

"Is Gabby all right?" Nyah asked.

"She'll be fine," he brushed against her arm as he walked past her into the foyer and she felt an electrical charge throughout her whole body. "I'm sorry about what happened at the hall."

"Gabby needed you; I understand that friends come first. Can I get you something to drink?" She could not control the hammering in her heart, as he held her gaze, all the air was sucked out of the room and she couldn't breathe.

She left him standing in the foyer and walked through the living room into the kitchen. She was facing the counter when he stood behind her, pressed his body against her back and she tilted her head slightly, welcoming his lips as they forged a warm path down the side of her neck. He turned her around, cupped her faced in his hand and kissed her tenderly. She raised her arms impulsively and wrapped them around his neck, pulling him closer to deepen the kiss. They stood unmoving for a long time, tasting, prodding, and teasing each other's lips, making up for lost time. She moaned as he lifted her onto the counter, unbuttoned her shirt and let it fall from her shoulders. He lowered his head and kissed the top of her breasts before traveling back up to her lips.

She parted her legs and he nestled between them, kissing her with the intensity of a hungry man.

Her whole body yearned for his familiar taste and she could not restrain the fire that burned inside her soul for his touch. She unbuttoned his shirt, planted soft kisses all over his chest, and ran her tongue across his bare nipple. He moaned deep in his throat and she let out a soft whimper when he picked her up in one swoop and carried her up the stairs to her bedroom. He put her down gently on the bed and she felt a chill when he tore himself away to take off the rest of his clothes.

He began at her toes and leisurely and deliberately used his hands, lips, and his mouth to devour every inch of her body. He took her nipple between his teeth and closed his mouth around it. First one, then the other, moving back and forth between them pulling, biting and sucking until they were tender; he could not get enough. When he finally reached her lips, his kiss was raw and deep, the longing he ignited within her transcended every sensation they had shared up to that moment.

She opened her whole being to receive everything he gave her, wrapped her arms and legs around him, and met him all the way. It was not long before her body took on a life of its own and moments later, he too reached his peak, they lingered on the mountaintop and began their unhurried descent back to reality.

He was lying on his back and she was on her stomach with the side of her face resting on his outstretched arm, both completely exhausted.

"Now that's what I'm talking about." He smiled peacefully.

"That was wonderful," she said gently raking her fingernails across his stomach, "but what do we have besides this?" she asked and felt his body stiffen. She regretted saying the words, but it was too late to take them back.

"This? You mean sex. What is it with you? Is that how little you value yourself?" He sighed heavily, stood up and began putting on his boxers.

"What do you mean by that?" she asked indignantly; watching as he pulled on his pants.

"You're the one who's always talking about sex. Maybe that's all you need me for." He stopped buttoning his shirt, "believe me, getting sex is not a problem for me." He sat down on the bed and looked at her, "why are you so mad at me?"

"What makes you think I'm angry with you?" she asked hotly.

"I had nothing to do with your niece's suicide attempt, it's not my fault that you decided to abort our baby or that your grandmother died. Or maybe you're angry because I had a front row seat when all your bullshit came crashing down around you." The tone in his voice revealed that he was more frustrated than angry.

"You don't have to be so nasty," his words tore through her and she could not hold back the tears.

"Nyah, I have spent the last few months trying to be there for you, but you pushed me away at every turn."

"I guess you believe it's all on me," she said angrily, "You said I could trust you and then you left me for someone else."

"I didn't leave you, you walked away. When Meaghan showed up at my door with Jason, I handled the situation badly, but I could not just ignore them. All I saw was a young boy who needed a father, like I did when I was a boy and I thought you, of all people would understand that. I did not question whether he was my son or not, maybe I should have but I didn't. When the paternity test came back and I found out he wasn't my son, I was disappointed but I still couldn't just turn him away." Nyah stared at him blankly, it was the first time she'd heard about the paternity test. "By the time I found out you were pregnant, it was too late; the baby was already gone and I couldn't find you for weeks." He paused and inhaled sharply. "I've tried, but there's nothing I can do to get you to see beyond yourself, I got nothing left." He looked at her squarely, and then shook his head in frustration before heading towards the bedroom door. "Oh, and thanks for the sex." He left the room and closed the door behind him. Nyah watched the door, hoping he would come back, and when he did not, she knew that she might have pushed him away for good.

Thirty-one

Nyah used the small broom to sweep the dirt off her grandmother's headstone, cleaned the marble with a damp cloth and adjusted the fresh lilies on top of the grave.

"Gran, I know you can't hear me; how I wish you could," Nyah sighed. "I couldn't see the edge of the cliff, when I fell, my body hit the landing hard; it was so painful. I'm starting to find my way through the darkness of losing my baby and losing you; if only I could change the past. The truth has come out and you were right about being free. On one hand, it feels good that I don't have to pretend anymore but on the other hand, I feel so unprotected. You'd be happy to know that I'm here in Wisconsin because I called a family meeting at the Big House. I don't know if anyone will show up, I can only hope they do. I love you Gran, and thanks for listening. I'll see you next year, same time, same place." Nyah could only imagine hearing her Gran say 'I'll be here baby; I ain't going nowhere'.

Uncle Floyd, Aunt Patsy, Uncle Richard and Aunt Gail, Pamela and the three boys, Graydon and his girlfriend Cecelia were all at the Big House when Nyah got there. Everything was back to normal, well as normal as it could be without Gran. The women, except for Cecelia who sat with the men playing dominoes, were in the kitchen cooking and marinating the steaks for the barbecue. No one cared that it was minus 10 degrees outside. When she entered the kitchen, Aunt Gail asked her to peel some potatoes for the potato salad; Nyah heard the tail end of the conversation.

"Listen, that man is so fine, if I weren't a woman of God, he'd be in big trouble." Aunt Gail held her belly and laughed.

"Gail, you're all talk. That man wouldn't want you; the old men these days are looking for fine young things like Miss Nyah over there."

"I'm even too old for some of them," Nyah said smiling.

"You got that right," Aunt Patsy said. "Well, they don't know what they're missing. These little girls may have one or two tricks up their sleeves but a real woman, like me can wrap him up, tie him in a bow and set him under the Christmas tree." There was resounding laughter in the kitchen and the two women went outside to put meat on the barbecue. Nyah and Pamela were left alone in the kitchen.

"Thanks for coming," Nyah said.

"I took a month off work to spend with the kids, so I had the time." Pamela fidgeted with a piece of string. "Your friend Sheila called me a few months ago and blasted me for allowing Sean to hurt you; I thought you put her up to it." Pamela began to cry so hard she began to wheeze. "Nyah, I'm so sorry. I know that can't possibly be enough; oh God…" She covered her face and sobbed.

Nyah moved Pamela's hand to look directly in her face.

"What happened with Sean wasn't your fault; I should have said something."

After a few minutes passed, Pamela tried to regain her composure.

"Anyway, thanks for not giving up on me, or Nikki. It gave me the courage to save her and to finally do the right thing." She handed Nyah a manila envelope. "Here is ten thousand, I'll get the rest to you as soon as I can."

Nyah did not take it.

"That was a gift Pam."

"So you said, but I don't feel right keeping it," she put the envelope on the table.

"If you don't want it, give it to the kids, my college fund contribution." Nyah smiled and walked to the deck to join the two older women. She shivered and hugged her body as the cold air flowed through her.

Aunt Patsy had invited a few people from the church to the house. After they ate and cleaned up, the church folks left and Nyah was ready to tell everyone why she called the meeting.

"Thank you all for coming," she said timidly; it was her first time calling a family meeting and she wasn't sure about the kind of reception she would receive. "When Gran died, I felt like a part of me died with her and I was mad at the world. Instead of turning to my family, I pushed you all away and I am so sorry. The week before she died she said, 'no one is an island' I truly understand now what she meant when she said that. The reason I called this meeting is to share with you all, some ideas I have for the house and the restaurant. Gran was very generous to me in her will." Nyah paused and waited for everyone to stop grumbling. "I would like to convert the Big House into a home for troubled youth and I was wondering if anyone here would like to run it?" Nyah looked at her sister.

"That could work," Gail said.

"It would need someone to oversee the business itself and another person to manage the day-to-day operations. The second reason I'm here is, Graydon, I would like to give you my portion of the restaurant."

He stared at her in disbelief.

"Are you serious?" He jumped up and hugged her. "Are you sure?" he asked again.

"Of course I'm sure, I think you would make a great restaurateur and you'll do a better job of running it than I ever could."

"Yeah, now you can have a real job," Floyd teased.

"I will call the lawyer and ask him to make the changes. It would be nice if we could all work together as a family, I'm sure Gran would have liked that." "Finally, since none of you have been to my home in Riverdale, I would like to invite everyone for Christmas dinner this year. I know it's only one month away but I hope you all can make it."

"And I'll cook," Graydon volunteered.

Nyah stayed an extra week in Wisconsin to finalize the transfer of the restaurant to Graydon and to get estimates on how much it would cost to convert the Big House into a youth home. The company that she hired to manage her finances took care of all the details.

Nyah felt a little sad leaving the Big House, knowing it was the last time the whole family would gather there. However, she believed that her grandmother's energy would continue to touch the lives of everyone who lived there.

Thirty-two

Nyah's heart was pounding in her chest as she watched the entrance, waiting, hoping that he would show up. She had not seen Mark since the night he walked out of her bedroom, and she was not sure he wanted to have anything more to do with her. She had found his watch on the night table the next morning, and hoped he would have returned to pick it up, but he did not. She kept it as her only reminder of him, and the only excuse she could find to get him to meet her.

When she saw him walking towards her in the coffee shop, dressed in a blue t-shirt and jeans with a light tan hooded coat, she nervously fiddled with the brown scarf that she wore around her neck. Seven weeks was a long time, and she was certain he had moved on, but she could not resist the urge to see him one last time. As he got closer to the table, she searched his face, but could not determine how he felt about her request to see him.

"Thanks for coming," she said.

"You said it was urgent," he said and pulled out the chair to sit on.

"I lied," she said apologetically. "Are you still mad at me?"

"No," he said.

"Oh, I've got something for you," she reached into her handbag, "here's your watch." She felt awkward and was sure he knew it.

"You called me here to give me a watch?" He took it and lay it down on the table. "Tracie, why am I here? What do you want?"

"I don't know," she said truthfully."

His eyes penetrated her mask and she expected him to get up and walk away but he did not so she started talking.

"When I was nineteen, in my second year at university, I was raped by a man who had just married my sister *and* by his friend." She paused and waited for a reaction from him, when none came, she continued. "For years I kept it a secret, I didn't tell anyone. I figured I had two choices. I could either crawl under a rock and feel like a victim or I could steel myself against ever being violated like that again. I chose the latter." She looked directly into his eyes and continued.

"Sean used sex as a weapon to hurt me and it became very hard for me to attach love to it. Gran loved me. She loved me without any conditions. Until now, I thought her love was the only love that was real. The only love that I needed and wanted to accept. I don't know how it happened but I reached a place in my mind where I could only accept sex or love, but not both, then I met you and things got very complicated for me. You offered me both, at the same time and I didn't know what to do. It was easier for me when I thought it was just physical because I could simply walk away. I called you because I wanted to see you and I wanted to tell you that I never meant to hurt you or push you away."

He stared at her for a long time without saying a word; she thought she was going to dissolve under his gaze. The waiter came to ask if they wanted to order but Mark waved her away.

"Trace, if I could change the past for you, I would, in a heartbeat and I'm sorry that you had to go through that. What that asshole did to you was fucked up, he deserves to be shot, but I'm not that guy; I don't see women that way. I'm not perfect, I've done some things; made some choices that might have worked better another way but I don't second-guess myself. People go through shit every day, that's life. A part of what makes it all bearable and worthwhile is knowing there is someone in your corner; someone who's got your back. I don't feel that with you, you're a runner. When things get too real for you, you run away. Frankly, I can't trust that. I need someone who wants to be with me when things are good and when things are not so good."

Nyah acknowledged what he said by nodding but she did not say a word. The more he spoke the deeper her heart sank. She knew he was right. She moved to Riverdale because she was running away from her pain. She didn't tell him about the baby because she was running away from rejection. Sitting at the table across from him she felt exposed and soiled, and that was something she could not run away from.

"Yeah, I know what you mean," she said and stood up. "I'm glad you came and I'm sorry." As she walked away, she felt a lump growing in the back of her throat. Her heart was broken and she struggled to open the car door through her tears.

"That's exactly my point; you are getting ready to run." Mark startled her and she dropped the keys. He bent to pick them up and held them between his fingers. "Trace, sometimes you have to stand and fight for what you want."

"I'm not running," she said, "and I do fight for what I want."

"You didn't fight for me," he said.

She turned to face him.

"I know it may not look like it, but I did fight for you." She couldn't stop the tears. "How can you fight for what you've already lost?"

"Hey," he raised her chin to look into his eyes." I'm here aren't I?"

She nodded and smiled through her tears.

"This is exactly where I want to be," he pulled her into his arms, kissed her tear-stained face and held her right there in the parking lot until she stopped crying.

"Come on, let's get some real food," he said.

They dropped off her car at her house and half-hour later; they pulled into his parents' driveway.

"Mom makes the best macaroni pie of anyone I know, and dad's been asking for you."

* * * * * * * **

They got back to her house around 9:30 to find Sheila sitting in the living room watching television.

"Well it's about time you showed up," she said.

"You really need to stop 'mother henning' me," Nyah said and Mark chuckled. Sheila had not left her alone for more than a week since she came home from the hospital.

"So you interpret my loving concern for you as mother henning?" Sheila acted hurt, "thanks a lot."

"I don't," Nyah hugged her, "you are the best back watcher ever."

"Now that's more like it." Sheila hugged her tight.

"Thank you." Nyah whispered in her ear, Sheila released her and stood beside Mark.

"Girl, you are *extremely* lucky I was not on that boat with you. This lovely specimen would have been mine."

"In your dreams," Nyah said.
Mark chuckled. Shaking his head, he walked over to the piano and began to play softly.

"Cute and talented, nice. Well, I would love to stay here and watch you guys make out, but I've got to get home; my sister could have her baby at any minute."

"I didn't know Diane was pregnant." Nyah was surprised.

"Neither did anyone else. I'll call you later, bye Mark." Sheila was on the porch when she yelled over her shoulder. "Oh, Pearline called, she says you need to call her ASAP."

Nyah sat beside Mark on the piano bench, he continued playing and she closed her eyes totally engrossed in the song.

"Marry me," his voice was barely more than a whisper. She opened her eyes and looked at him, not sure if she'd heard him correctly.

"What did you say?" he stopped playing and reached into his pocket, pulling out a tiny blue box.

"I want to spend the rest of my life with you."

"Mark," her eyes filled with tears and she stood up. "I'm so open right now; everything about me is so raw and transparent. Are you sure this is what you want?"

"You're beautiful, smart, sexy, giving; what I see, is what I want," he said. "You're my heartbeat."

"But marriage; it's so binding, you'd be stuck with me forever."

"Don't tease me like that." He reached out and drew her between his legs.

"Did you really believe I aborted our baby?"

He sighed and buried his face between her breasts.

"I'm sorry," his voice was muffled. "Forgive me."

"I didn't, I would never do that," she whispered. "I lost the baby at almost twelve weeks."

"I know," he said and penetrated her soul with his gaze. "And not being there for you…" she touched his lips with her fingers.

"You didn't know; I should have told you."

He raised her blouse and kissed her belly.

"No more secrets?"

"No more secrets. And yes, I'll marry you." Nyah's heart began to race as he opened the box and revealed a princess cut diamond ring.

"It's beautiful," she whispered as he slipped it on her finger.

"I love you so much." The words rolled sweetly off her tongue.

"Mmmm, music to my ears; I love you too."

"And just so I'm clear; not that it matters, will I have to take your last name?"

"I'll take yours," he smiled.

When their lips met, she felt like she was being kissed for the first time and an hour later, laying side by side on the rug; exhausted but thoroughly satisfied, they talked about their next Christmas vacation and setting a date for the wedding.

Thirty- three

"I'm glad you decided to come, I wasn't sure you would." Nyah stepped inside her mother's home for the first time in twenty-one years. When Pearline invited her, Nyah debated for a long time whether she really wanted to go. Although Pearline had given birth to her, she did not regard her as her mother.

The condominium she shared with Spencer was tastefully decorated; the walls were painted in bold shades of red.

"Spencer and I have been traveling, right now we're between stops," she motioned for Nyah to sit down at a small square table.

"Can I get you anything?" Nyah could tell her mother was nervous.

"No, thank you," she just wanted her mother to get to the point.

"Nyah, I'm sure you must hate me for not being there, when you were growing up."

"I don't hate you mom," she said.

"Well, whatever you feel, I'm sure your grandmother filled your head with venomous lies about me," Pearline's voice was shaky and Nyah had never seen her less than controlled. She never pictured her mother as the sort of woman to care about what others thought of her.

"I married Charles when I was 15 years old because I was pregnant with Pamela. He was 25 and mom told him that if he did not marry me, she would tell everyone he raped me and get him thrown in jail. A little over a year later, I had Graydon. We were both very young I guess the strain of having a wife and 2 babies to care for was too much for him so he started to drink. He would stay out late and even though I could not prove it I knew he was sleeping with other girls, the only way I was able to cope was because my best friend Karen was there for me.

I met your father, Keith at a college party I attended with Karen when I was 18, he was 13 years older than I was and I guess that was the attraction at first. He was kind, warm and loving, he promised me the moon and I believed him. I did not tell him that I was married or that I had two kids, I did not want to lose what we had. We were together for about a year and then he began to act strange; he hardly had time for me anymore. When I got pregnant with you a few months later, I knew you were Keith's but I didn't say anything to anyone." Pearline paused and went to the bar to pour a glass of vodka. Then she returned to the table, sat down, and picked up her story where she left off. Nyah just listened.

"After you were born, questions were raised about Charles being your father because you were very fair, you had light brown hair and Charles had dark skin. I denied accusations because no one could prove anything. The day you turned six I'd had my fill of Charles' whoring and his drinking. I was going to tell him everything, about Keith, you, everything. I wanted to tell Keith the whole truth about my kids, my marriage so I went to his house; I knew he was at home because his car was in the driveway. When I went inside, I was not prepared for what I saw. There he was on the sofa humping my best friend Karen. Well, needless to say, I lost it; I ended up breaking her nose. They got married and as far as I know, they are still together. For a long time I was angry at the world, I hated everyone, especially him and from that day, every time I looked at you I saw him and I became extremely depressed. I endured the torture for the next year and then I decided to get rid of my pain." She paused and looked at Nyah, "well, the rest is history."

"So, that's your story," Nyah said.

"I know you may not approve of me or my decision to leave you with mom but I did what I had to do to preserve my sanity. I figured you were a child and children always bounce back."

"Why didn't you come get me?"

"It took me a few years to get past the betrayal to even look at you. I did come back when you were twelve but you seemed so happy with mom, I didn't want to interrupt your life," she said candidly.

"At least now I know why you can't stand me, but it's been twenty-one years mom, Gran was right, you need to get over it." Nyah stood up and walked to the door.

"Where are you going? We need to talk about this."

"What's done is done, let's just leave it alone," she said and left her mother's apartment.

Nyah felt numb. She heard every word her mother said and deep down, she sympathized with her pain, but that was not enough to forget feeling abandoned and unloved for so many years. It did not make it any easier to find out it was because of a man.

Thirty-four

Nyah woke with the dawn, removed the stick from under her pillow and looked at it again, making sure the plus sign had not changed. Sheila was with her when she did the test the night before, and almost flew through the roof with excitement at being a godmother. She wanted to share the news with Mark right away but Sheila stopped her and told her it was bad karma for the groom to see the bride the night before the wedding, and then she slept in the room to prevent Nyah from sneaking out and Mark from sneaking in.

Nyah gently rubbed her belly and a rush of joy swept over her when she thought about being Mark's wife and the mother of his child. She hired a wedding consultant, they spent the last six months planning for this day, and now, it was finally here, she could not believe it was her wedding day. Glancing out the hotel room window Nyah realized it was going to rain, a sunny July day was not in the forecast but that fact could not change her mood. She closed her eyes in an attempt to relish the feeling but opened them when she heard a soft tap on the door.

"Auntie, can I come?" Nikki's voice was very soft. She sat up in the bed and pulled the sheet up to her waist.

"Sure honey," Nikki came in and sat down on the bed. "Why are you awake? It's so early."

"I couldn't sleep; I'm too excited. You're getting married today." They held hands and grinned like a bunch of schoolgirls. "Are you scared?"

"Not scared, anxious maybe, to get it over with." Nyah looked at her niece and smiled. It was almost nineteen months since she tried to commit suicide and the road to recovery proved to be an uphill battle for her, but Nyah and the rest of the family made sure she knew that she was not alone. Children's services finally allowed her to live with Pamela again after her divorce from Sean became final; last she heard, he was serving time for statutory rape. Nyah did not attend the trial but Graydon said he pleaded 'innocent' to the charges that the family of the fourteen-year-old girl brought against him. She felt that although justice was served on some level, the innocence he stole from Nikki and from her, nine years, six months earlier was lost forever, and could never be replaced.

"Thanks for making me a part of your big day," she said.

Nyah hugged her. "I wouldn't have it any other way."

"Knock, knock," Pamela announced her entrance into the room with big rollers in her hair and a wide grin on her face, "I hope I'm not interrupting."

"You're not," Nyah said. She came into the room and kissed Nikki on the top of her head; Nikki smiled gingerly but did not touch her mother.

"We have hair and makeup at ten and I have to take a trip to the florist to see if they've finally got the flower order correct." Nyah smiled, she was happy that her sister was around to share her wedding day. Nyah paid for rooms at the hotel for everyone who was involved in the wedding ceremony and before long Sheila and her four bridesmaids Pamela, Cindy, Nikki and Sage were in her room, eating breakfast; caught up in the excitement.

After about an hour, everyone left to get ready for the pre-ceremony bridesmaid photos; Sage lingered.

"So, the best woman won."

"I don't know about that," Nyah tried to make light of Sage's remark.

"Don't kid yourself, I personally know some women who are in tears today."

"Why? Marriage won't stop him if he wants to cheat on me."

"You weren't around him when you guys broke up, he's hooked." Nyah turned away from her and stared at her reflection in the mirror; she was not going to make the mistake of talking about Mark to any of her friends again.

"You haven't asked me about my date," Sage said bursting with excitement.

"I figured you'd tell me when you were ready," she said not keen on hearing the details of a night of passion Sage shared with her brother.

"It was amazing, he was amazing," she said with a dreamy look on her face, Nyah stopped her.

"That's enough, I get it."

"This isn't weird for you is it?" Sage asked.

"No, it's not," Nyah hugged her, "there are just certain images of my brother that I would like to keep out of my head."

"I've got to go get ready," she said. "I still can't believe it; Mark Allen is getting married today."

"I hope you have your razor sharpened," both women laughed remembering a conversation they shared over lunch almost two years ago.

Sheila came in the room, set a relaxing bubble bath for Nyah, hung the 'do not disturb' sign on the door and left to make sure the bridesmaids were on track. When she emerged from the bathroom refreshed and relaxed, her mother was standing by the window.

"I'm sorry for coming here unannounced, I knocked but there was no answer," she said apologetically. Nyah did not respond, she secured the towel around her body, walked over to the table and began saturating her legs with lotion.

"You didn't tell me you were getting married," she said.

"How did you find out?"

"Graydon told me." Pearline inhaled deeply and held her head down before she spoke. "I have no idea how to repair the damage I've caused. Nyah, I was just a child, I felt my mother was not there for me, I was alone and I made horrible mistakes. I can't go back and undo what has been done."

"Mom, this is a very special day for me and I don't want to..." Nyah interrupted her.

"I'm not here to upset you, I promise." She walked over to where Nyah was and looked directly at her. "I was too ashamed to ask before today, and I know it may be a lot to hope for but I would like to come to your wedding. I'll just sit in the back; you won't even know I'm there." Nyah saw the tears gathering at the corner of her mother's eyes. They stood facing each other, neither one reaching out to the other.

"That's your choice, you can come to my wedding if you want to, and you don't have to sit at the back."

"Thank you," she said and left the room.

Nyah walked over to the treasure chest she took from her grandmother's room at the Big House right after the funeral. She had opened it only once before, to put in the wooden butterfly necklace that her grandmother gave her so many years ago. She opened the chest slowly and ran her fingers over all of the trinkets inside the box. She picked up the paper, sat on the edge of the bed before unfolding it, and after the first two lines, felt the tears rolling down her cheeks as she read it.

Touched By an Angel
We, unaccustomed to courage
exiles from delight
live coiled in shells of loneliness
until love leaves its high holy temple
and comes into our sight
to liberate us into life.
Love arrives
and in its train come ecstasies
old memories of pleasure
ancient histories of pain.
Yet if we are bold,
love strikes away the chains of fear
from our souls.
We are weaned from our timidity
In the flush of love's light
we dare be brave
And suddenly we see
that love costs all we are
and will ever be.
Yet it is only love
which sets us free.
-Maya Angelou

"Girl, you'd better stop that crying or your eyes are going to look puffy and red for your husband." Sheila walked into the room and sat down beside her. "You need to put that shit away right now and get ready."

"Did you let my mother in here?" Nyah asked wiping her eyes with the back of her hand. She refolded the poem, walked over to the chest and put it back inside and at the same time, she removed the butterfly necklace, placed it around her neck and asked Sheila to fasten it for her.

"I had no choice; she looked like a puppy dog." Sheila made a weepy face and Nyah smiled. "This is pretty," Sheila said holding the butterfly pendant in her hand, "I guess it's your something old?"

"Actually no, it my something new, you're my something old," Nyah teased. "You're lucky to be my maid of honor."

"No, you are lucky I am your maid of honor or there would have been some serious problems up in that church today, we've been girls for a long time, I've earned the right to stand beside you on your wedding day *and* my free plate of food," she said playfully. "And you have no idea how hard it was trying to keep stud muffin away from you last night."

"That's okay, your work here is done, I'm sure we won't need your services tonight." The thought made Nyah warm and tingly.

"So how does your stomach feel?"

"Sheila, I hope you haven't told anyone about the baby, I want Mark to be the first to know, well first after you."

"Mum's the word," she pressed her lips together.

"I haven't eaten anything yet, so I'm okay for now." Sheila touched Nyah's belly.

"Listen, you little person, you need to chill and allow your mommy to get through this day. Don't let me come in there."

"Sheila, you're a mess," Nyah smiled. "Help me get my dress on."

* * * * * * * **

It had started to drizzle by the time the limousines picked up the bride and the bridal party at the front of the hotel to drive them to the church.

She sat in the limousine, alone with her thoughts when Graydon opened the door and slipped in beside her.

"Look at you," he whistled, "you look incredible!"

"You don't look half bad yourself. Is Mark inside the church?"

"You can relax, he's in there. I can't believe you're getting married before me."

"Please," she said sarcastically, "you don't want to get married."

"Not now, but someday I might, your friend Sage is pretty hot." Graydon laughed.

"Gray, she's a nice girl, don't hurt her," Nyah scolded her older brother.

"I'm a lover, not a fighter," he said grinning.

"You are so corny," she shook her head. "Sheila was right; you just may be her future husband."

"Yeah, when I'm dead."

They laughed.

"So Atlanta huh," Graydon's tone became serious.

"Mark's studio will be done in about a month, and we close on the house in a couple of weeks."

"I'll miss you."

"It's only Atlanta, you can come visit."

He reached across the seat and kissed her lightly on the forehead before lowering her veil.

"They're ready for you." He got out of the limousine and held the umbrella open for her.

Inside the church, Nyah stepped into purple heaven. She knew purple was her grandmother's favorite color so she had everything in the church and at the reception hall decorated using different shades of purple to honor Gran. The bridesmaids' dresses were lilac and Sheila's dress was a rich purple, the pews, even the flowers were purple and white. The music started and Nyah watched as the bridesmaids and the groomsmen marched down the aisle together, followed by her nephew Byron, the ring bearer and the flower girls.

Graydon gave her one last reassuring look then took her hand, pushed it through his arm and squeezed it.

Everyone stood up when Leah Blaque began singing a love song that Mark wrote for their ceremony; the words made her teary. She looked at him, standing in the center of the aisle in a gray tuxedo, his hands by his side, smiling at her, waiting for her. He had seen her at her worst and wanted her before he saw her at her best. She was tempted to run the short distance down the aisle and into his arms but resisted the urge and walked unhurriedly towards him, not once taking her eyes off him. He hugged Graydon and took her hand pressing it gently against his soft lips before pushing it through his arm.

"You're stunning," he smiled and there was no doubt in her mind or in her heart that he loved her.

"I hope you can say that seven months from now," she whispered, it took a second but he finally realized what she meant and his face lit up like a child's on Christmas morning.

They stood side by side at the altar, facing the future, at the beginning of their journey, surrounded by all their family, friends and the memory of Nyah's beloved Gran.

Uncle Richard cleared his throat and began the ceremony.

"Dearly beloved."